Mystery
at
Saltwater
Cottages

BOOKS BY CLARE CHASE

Mystery at Saltwater Cottages

CLARE CHASE

bookouture

Published by Bookouture in 2023

An imprint of Storyfire Ltd.
Carmelite House
50 Victoria Embankment
London EC4Y 0DZ

www.bookouture.com

ISBN: 978-1-83790-407-5
eBook ISBN: 978-1-83790-406-8

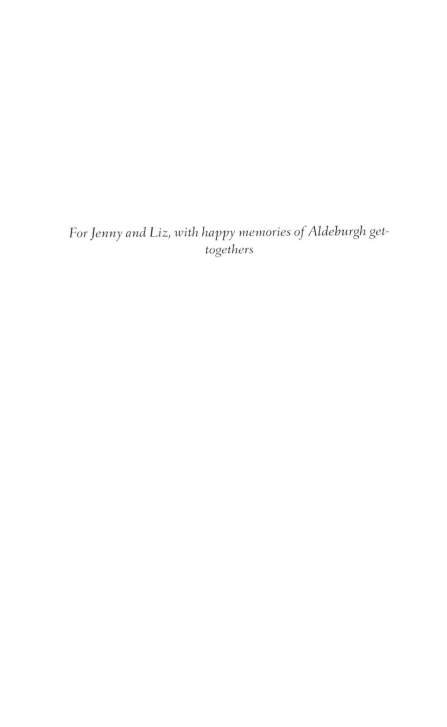

For Jenny and Liz, with happy memories of Aldeburgh get-togethers

PROLOGUE
SUNDAY EVENING

Nena Field smiled to herself as she walked away from the comforting glow of Saltwater Cottages.

The place was such a quaint rural venue. Who'd have thought she'd get a kick out of being here, running residential art courses? She was the centre's most famous tutor by far. A household name. An enfant terrible of contemporary art.

Everyone was wondering how some two-bit venture in the Suffolk countryside had secured her services. The clamour for information was a hoot. In truth, it was down to a dark point in her past. Nena gritted her teeth. It hadn't been her fault. Others could have acted differently. Should have. She was on a mission to rub that in.

Mind games were a satisfying form of revenge. And they cost her nothing. Although she had enough money to do as she liked.

She pushed the thoughts away. Replaced them with ones that warmed her. It was serendipity. She'd come here for one kind of sport and been offered another: a new lover. He was married, which was a bonus. She'd never really gone for single men. There was no challenge involved. If he left his wife, she'd lose interest, but right now, she was obsessed. Keener than she'd been on anyone for ages.

She didn't pay her surroundings much attention as she entered the trees between Saxford St Peter and the sea. Blind Eye Wood. An eerie name. She shivered, then spun round at a rustle behind her, but there was no sign of movement. She shook her head. She'd been brought up close by. She knew the woods were full of creatures late at night.

She was focused on the surprise she'd cooked up: flattering but dangerous, yet oh-so-hard to turn down. Uneasy delight was the effect she was aiming for. It was all sorted. She just needed to check a couple of details.

She reached the heart of the wood. The moon was full but she was struggling to see her way, the trees were so densely packed. As she took her phone from her pocket, ready to use its torch, she heard a crack behind her.

Someone stepping on a branch?

Her rendezvous? But if so, why hadn't they called out?

She was just turning to see when the blow came.

The darkness of the woods faded to black.

1

TWO DAYS EARLIER

Eve Mallow was sitting with her best friend Viv at the scrubbed oak table in Honeysuckle Cottage, a lamp glowing in the dark autumn evening. The house belonged to Viv's brother Simon, and Eve associated it with cheerful, relaxing get-togethers. Simon, with his passion for business, was level-headed. But he was also warm, friendly and fiercely loyal, just like his more chaotic sister.

Both Eve and Viv found his wife Polly hard to take – prissy and far too young and perfect – but she loved Simon just like they did, so they had to make allowances. They'd spent countless evenings around the couple's table with close friends and neighbours, laughing and sharing news.

But tonight was different. Eve's stomach was in knots. Even Gus, her dachshund, looked concerned, his soulful brown eyes on their host.

Simon had a tumbler of untouched whisky in front of him, his head in his hands.

'First it was the news that big investment I'd made had gone south. It looked like a dead cert. But, of course, I'd allowed for it to fail. It's my rule.'

'You always were the sensible one.' Viv gave his arm a fond squeeze, her hair, currently a rather startling purple, falling over one eye.

'But now I've had a report saying the house needs underpinning – urgently. The insurers won't extend our cover unless we get it sorted.'

Viv leaned forward. 'Blimey, Simon, I'm so sorry. Right after losing the two horses as well.'

Simon ran the riding stables adjacent to his house. He nodded. 'It's been the worst possible timing. I used the contingency I had to replace them and cover the investment losses. I've sunk the rest of my savings into Saltwater Cottages.'

Eve shifted in her seat, wondering if Simon really wanted her there as he poured out his woes. It was so personal, and he was used to swimming, not sinking.

She half rose. 'Would you like some time in private?' Most of the village was in the next room. She could go and join them.

But Simon shook his head quickly. 'No, no. You're family. As good as. I'd like your take on this too.'

The comment made Eve's eyes prickle. He and Viv were precious to her.

Viv's smile betrayed a mixture of hope and anxiety. 'It'll be all right. You're great at business. You'll turn this around. You know you will.'

Eve wanted to agree but the knots in her stomach were getting worse. In the silence, she heard a crash from the cottage's garden, followed by furious barking. Gus barked back like a dog six times his size.

Eve shushed him, with a pat to show she sympathised, and leaped up to pull back one of the curtains. It was no good. It was too dark to see anything and the barking had stopped.

'It's probably just the stables falling down,' Simon said with a humourless laugh. 'And it sounds as though Pete Blenkinsop's dog's got out again. I've told him he needs to mend the hole in his fence. The animal's a brute. It's just as well it's round the back, otherwise I'd fear for the villagers when they leave. Can you imagine if I sent one of them home with a dog bite? Talk about the final straw.'

Eve returned to her seat. 'What does the bank say?'

'They're being as accommodating as they can.' He blinked. 'I-I haven't told Polly how bad things are yet. I didn't want to worry her. And it's so hard with her not being here. It feels impossible to talk properly over the phone.'

Polly was in the States for work. Eve felt more uncomfortable still. She shouldn't be hearing this before Simon's wife.

'You should tell her,' Viv said. 'One of her redeeming features is that she loves you to bits. You need the support, and the longer you leave it, the worse it will feel.'

Eve wouldn't have felt she could say it, but she agreed wholeheartedly. She watched one of Simon's neighbours cross the hall, carrying a glass of Prosecco. The villagers had come to celebrate the launch of day courses at Saltwater Cottages in addition to the residential ones. They were last minute. Simon was pulling out all the stops to make a profit as quickly as possible.

Eve had the urge to mingle. The villagers would know something was up if the three of them carried on hiding away in the kitchen.

She was about to excuse herself when Simon turned to her.

'Your article's a blessing. Thank you for agreeing to do it.'

She and Viv were due to begin a week's stay at the cottages the following day and she'd managed to get a commission to write about the centre. The article would go into *Icon* magazine. Eve had written for them many times. Mostly obituaries, which was her speciality. It was a prestigious publication, but there was no way the piece would appear in time to help Simon through his current difficulties. She couldn't bear to say so, though. The hope in his eyes was too important. He needed to fight.

'I'm looking forward to it,' she said instead. The visit was meant to be a treat for her and Viv while Eve's partner Robin was away for work. 'At least you've got Nena Field. She's a huge draw.'

Simon nodded, though he still looked depressed. 'I was amazed she agreed to come. She was brought up in the village, of course, but Paris and New York are more her bag these days. When she's not at home on the French Riviera, that is.'

'How did you persuade her?' Eve had been curious from the moment she'd arrived.

Simon frowned. 'She claims to remember me from when she took riding lessons as a teenager.' He blushed. 'She says she had a massive crush on me back then, though I'd have been a good ten years older than her.'

'You don't remember her?'

His frown deepened. 'I can't say I do.'

That was odd. Nena was striking and made it her business to stick in people's minds. Eve was sure she'd have done that if she'd really had a crush on Simon. Maybe she'd exaggerated their connection, but if so, why had she really come?

'Either way, you're right,' he went on. 'Bookings have been excellent, thanks to her. It's the one saving grace.' He looked from Eve to Viv with troubled eyes. 'I'm terrified of the whole venture folding. It would be terrible to have to let people go. Nena wouldn't suffer, of course. She could earn more elsewhere. I suppose she's here for a taste of home.'

Could that really be it? A bout of nostalgia? Eve had seen Nena interviewed and she didn't seem the type.

'The full-time staff are another matter,' Simon went on. 'Some of them are hard up. The woman who's teaching print-making and her brother, the night manager, have a mother who's in a home and a dad who's a dysfunctional drunk. He runs up debt with abandon. They'd been freelancing until I took them on. I could see how relieved they were to get something regular. I scheduled extra print classes to increase the hours I could offer.'

That was like Simon. He'd been canny enough to succeed until now, but he was thoughtful as well. Eve knew the print tutor a little through an event committee: a sweet-natured woman with worried eyes.

'What if they've lost their other work and Saltwater goes south too?' He closed his eyes as peals of laughter came from an adjoining room.

'We'll be walking adverts for Saltwater,' Viv said. 'We'll tell everyone how great it is, and even if—'

Eve never discovered what she would have said next. There was an almighty crash and glass rained down on her and Viv. Eve leaped up and checked for Gus, but he was safe under the table, thank goodness. He joined in with the tremendous volley of barking from outside, interspersed with growls from the other dog, and plaintive whines from him.

A gust of chill air reached them at the same time as shocked exclamations from neighbouring rooms. Villagers appeared at the door, pale and anxious.

There was a brick in the middle of the kitchen floor; the clay tiles underneath had cracked.

Around the brick was tied a piece of paper. Eve was closest and approached the object mechanically.

Viv got up too, in slow motion, looking towards the window, eyes wide with shock. A shard of glass fell from a fold in her jeans.

Eve's hands shook as she pulled the string that held the paper in place around the brick.

Look to your employees. There's a secret to uncover and it's your responsibility. Work fast, or I'll make sure everyone knows. The clock is ticking...

2

Eve found glass in her boot when she and Viv walked home from Simon's. Her foot was cut but she hadn't noticed the pain until then. She'd been too bound up with what had happened.

Simon hadn't wanted to call the police. 'What will people say if word gets out that I've been targeted? And because of an employee? It's probably some meaningless grudge, but bad publicity now would be disastrous.'

Eve couldn't help seeing his point. She told Robin, though. That was almost like telling the police. He was a former detective inspector who'd been forced to adopt a new identity after informing on corrupt colleagues. She'd first met him in his new guise, as Saxford St Peter's jobbing gardener.

Just over a year earlier, the criminal network he'd uncovered had finally been brought down. Robin could be open about his past and Eve could breathe easily. In theory. They now lived together, which was bliss, but Robin was currently in London, doing consultancy work for the police. The thought of it made her shiver. He was working on a massive drugs operation involving the most ruthless criminals.

She hadn't intended to tell him about Simon's brick. It was

the last thing he needed when he was so preoccupied. But he knew her too well and sensed something was up.

'*Just promise me you'll take care,*' he'd said, when she'd spilled the beans at last. '*It's not just the possibility of bad publicity. This person is full of hatred for one of Simon's staff, and unless they're bluffing, they have damaging information on them too. That's a very volatile situation.*'

The following morning, Eve and Viv were in Monty's Teashop, baking sloe-gin spice cakes. Monty's was Viv's baby but she'd brought Eve in part-time. For Eve, it was the perfect way to ensure a regular income alongside her freelance journalism. She enjoyed the company and relished organising Viv, who 'planned' life with seconds to spare.

Baking provided solace too, which they needed that morning. Eve had slept uneasily, jumping at the tiny creaks that always featured in her seventeenth-century cottage. Even the reassuring presence of Gus hadn't been enough to calm her.

'Poor Simon looked shattered by the time we left,' Viv said. They'd been talking about it all morning.

'It was lucky that the glazier was at the drinks party.' He'd gone to fetch his kit immediately.

'Luck's got nothing to do with it,' Viv said darkly. 'He goes to every event where there's free booze and he's not the sort to attend art classes. Simon really is too kind sometimes.'

'I suppose the glazier might big up Saltwater Cottages to his friends,' Eve said doubtfully. She was sifting flour as Viv drained some fruit after its overnight soak in sloe gin.

'I hope you're right. Simon needs all the help he can get. To get that brick through his window on top of everything else...'

There was a catch in her voice and Eve turned to see she was in tears. She downed tools and gave her a hug. All the protective instincts she had towards her now-adult twins kicked in. It gave her the fire she needed to sound strong. 'It's a horrible situation but he won't face it alone. We'll strain every sinew to help.' It was disturbing that Simon had troubles on more than one front. 'We should focus on the brick. Identify the thrower, figure out what the scandal is and shut it down. We'll be well placed to investigate the Saltwater Cottages staff.'

Viv nodded. 'Assuming the note referred to one of them. There are the stable hands too.'

'True.' Eve stirred the fruit, plump with sloe gin, into her cake batter. 'But they've been with him for years, haven't they?'

Viv nodded, her eyes still red. Eve steered her gently to a stool and fetched her a cup of tea.

'I'd guess the note refers to one of the Saltwater lot then. And whoever threw the brick is either a close connection from the village, or another member of staff.'

Viv sipped her tea. 'Makes sense.'

Eve had made up her mind to investigate the moment she'd read the anonymous note. She'd asked Simon for a staff list as they'd waited for the window to be fixed. Many of the employees lived on the Saltwater site. She knew the location of their suites thanks to a map Simon had sketched.

Eve and Viv's stint at the cottages was due to begin that afternoon. This would be their last session at Monty's for a week. Normally, the prospect would have sent Eve into organisational overdrive, but Viv's eldest son was holding the fort. Jonah owned his own café down in Kent and was taking time out while it was refurbished. Eve watched him through the kitchen doorway, checking Monty's appointment book. On the whole, she felt a lot more relaxed leaving him in charge than she did Viv. His baking had the same stand-out flair, and he was far less likely to run out of ingredients or triple-book the window tables.

Back at her home, Elizabeth's Cottage, Eve considered the puzzle of the anonymous note as she ate lunch. It could refer to multiple people, but it was Nena that she googled. She got publicity by ruffling feathers. Eve could easily imagine her being the subject of the brick-thrower's ire. But if they knew something damning about her, why not come out and say it, instead of pressuring Simon to investigate?

There was plenty of information about Nena online. She'd been born and brought up in Saxford, but it hadn't been a settled childhood. Her parents had separated and fought over her in court. Eve sensed she'd been pulled this way and that. She was an only child and every account implied she'd been loved and wanted by both parents, though at some stage, a friend of her mother's, Celia, had looked after her for six months, carting her off to somewhere called Porthruan. Maybe her mother had been ill.

There were articles aplenty – Nena got herself talked about – but though the media bigged up her bad-girl reputation, they revelled in it too. She courted them and they loved her for it.

Eve didn't share their feelings. She felt especially sour when faced with a photo of Nena kissing the husband of a Hollywood actress. She had personal experience of being cheated on. She knew there were two sides to every tale, but Nena's expression set Eve's teeth on edge. She looked glad to have been caught.

Still, Eve wouldn't make up her mind until she'd talked to Nena. It was time to leave for Saltwater Cottages and begin her research in person.

3

Simon's venue was a row of cottages on a track called Saltwater End overlooking heathland, the sea and the start of Blind Eye Wood to the north-east. The cottages had been a bargain. Simon's money had turned the out-of-the-way, down-at-heel dwellings into an idyllic hideaway. If only his work didn't go to waste.

Eve matched the sketch map he'd given her with reality. There was the extended building in the centre of the row, Curlew Cottage. It housed most of the staff as well as the bar, restaurant, reception area and offices.

'If appearances count for anything, this place ought to be a raging success,' Eve said to Viv as they approached. Even on this gloomy autumn day, the buildings looked fresh and appealing. They were painted a mix of muted blues and creams, the colours fitting with the turbulent grey sea, their red-tiled roofs and sash windows adding character.

They were greeted by an elegant, silver-haired woman of around sixty in a well-cut black dress. Eve saw from her name badge that she was Sadie Thornton, the general manager Simon had told her about. She was an outsider who'd moved to Saxford to take up the job.

Eve could see why Simon had picked her. She was as classy as the venue: flawlessly turned out and seamlessly welcoming, yet with a professional distance. As someone who liked her own space, Eve appreciated that. People often asked for her life story when they heard her accent. She was fine with telling them about her American mom and British dad in Seattle and her move to London to study. Mentioning the twins was a source of pleasure too. She was less keen on detailing her divorce, which had preceded her move to Suffolk. People tended to find that the most interesting part.

Sadie showed Eve, Gus and Viv to their rooms, which were next door in Avocet Cottage, then left them to get settled. Eve arranged to meet Viv for drinks later and began to unpack. Her suite was smart with pale wooden floors and rugs, and a four-poster bed with cream linen and taupe cushions. Everywhere smelled of cleanliness and faintly of new paint. Pets were welcomed but she still feared the effect of Gus's muddy paws.

As soon as she'd hung up her clothes and unloaded his travel bed, she went to explore, leaving Gus to examine his new surroundings. He seemed fascinated with the bed's valance and kept worming his way underneath, then reappearing, nose first. Eve felt a pang of envy. The saying it's a dog's life made no sense. It looked blissfully simple.

As she walked up Saltwater End, she passed a good-looking man of around forty in a well-cut dark suit and crisp white shirt. She glimpsed his name badge. Iggy Norland, Concierge. He hadn't noticed her. He was talking on a mobile, a smile playing on his lips.

'How many spillages is that now?' He laughed. 'Don't worry. Liam will sort it.' He listened some more then added. 'Joking apart, what's some ink between friends? And at least you've got a patterned rug. Maybe we can get the stain out.

Besides, you're bound to bring in more money than you cost us. I get around fifty calls a day asking to book onto your course.'

She guessed he was talking to Nena.

'No worries,' he added a moment later. 'Liam'll be with you soon.'

Eve paused to check her notes. Liam Norland was the custodian, in charge of maintenance and security, and Iggy's brother. They were both Saxford locals.

As Iggy finished his conversation, Eve heard a voice behind her.

'Was that Nena?'

She peeked over her shoulder and saw it was the striking silver-haired manager.

'You guessed it,' Iggy replied.

'She's certainly keeping Liam busy.' Sadie said it with tired resignation. 'Thanks for sorting it out, Iggy.'

A moment later she heard Iggy's voice again, fainter this time. He was on another call. 'You're in demand, Liam. Nena's spilled ink over the rug in her room. Bring it to me and I'll try to get the stain out. If it's too far gone I'll see if Simon's happy for me to pass it on. Someone in the village might make use of it.' There was a long pause. 'You might have forgotten, but it's your job. Playtime's over, little brother. Grow up.'

His tone dripped with disdain and jarred after his easy-going, light-hearted chat with Nena.

So Liam wasn't amused by the spilled ink. Perhaps he'd written the anonymous note. He might know something about Nena and be making waves. She wondered again about the cryptic nature of the message. If Nena was crucial to Saltwater's success, perhaps the writer wanted someone else to take responsibility for bringing her down.

But there were other possibilities for the note's subject. The Norland brothers' relationship sounded strained. One of them could be out to discredit the other. Seeing the dynamics was useful, but it was information on damaging secrets which would really count.

Iggy had referred to 'her room' in his call to his brother. It sounded as though Nena's damaged rug was in her suite, not one of the studios.

Eve strode back towards Curlew Cottage, the salt wind whipping her hair. According to Simon's map, Nena's quarters were opposite the reception desk. She might get a look at her in person, and Iggy's brother too. She wanted to watch them interact.

The foyer was empty, which was a blessing, and just beyond was a corridor. Eve found it led to a bar which was currently deserted. There was a place to pause next to a ladies' cloakroom. She tucked herself amongst some coats and hoped no one disturbed her. If she could crack this mystery, she might help Simon on one battlefront at least.

A minute later, a man who could only be Iggy's brother entered the foyer. He had the same dark hair and chiselled features, though his sleepy eyes looked more dangerous.

He knocked on Nena's door. Eve could feel his tension as he waited, his shoulders hunched. Why didn't she open up? Thanks to Iggy's phone call, she knew Liam was on his way, yet it took her a full minute to appear.

'Seriously?' Liam stood back, his head on one side.

Nena gave a light laugh. 'I have to be able to see you some-how.' Her voice was low, seductive. 'I can't wait for our liaisons. I want you too much.'

'For pity's sake, Nena!' Liam looked over his shoulder and Eve shrank back in her hiding place.

The artist produced a cat-like smile. 'Relax. There's no one here.'

'Do you really have to pour ink over our property? Give me extra work?'

She pouted. 'It was a genuine accident. Why? Don't you

think I'm worth it?' She approached him, her face tilted towards his.

Eve heard him sigh as he moved closer. 'Let me in, then.'

Nena gave another laugh. 'You worry too much. Out here's more exciting.'

She tipped her head towards his and their lips met. He was kissing her back now, with a passion, though he pulled away a moment later. 'This is madness.'

Eve was sure there was some kind of internal battle going on, but Liam was too weak to put up a proper fight. All she could think of was his wife, the printmaking tutor, sweet-natured and sad. If she knew about her husband's affair, she could have thrown the brick. But whoever was responsible, it seemed unproductive; the message was so vague.

Eve carried on watching. In Nena's room, there was an empty pot of ink on its side as well as a rolled-up rug. It was large, with a woven backing, and had probably cost Simon hundreds if not thousands. The black stain was sizeable.

'You haven't even bothered to pick the pot up.' Liam sighed.

'But I got the rug ready for you.' Nena raised a finger and ran it down Liam's cheek. 'You see, I can be considerate. The ink's pretty dry now; you needn't worry about staining your clothes.'

Like his brother, Liam was wearing a white shirt, but it was less crisp, and he was in dark jeans, not a suit. The shirt showed off his tan. It figured. Liam was the custodian. He'd work outdoors as well as in.

He sighed heavily. 'Iggy thought he might get the stain out, pathetic little do-gooder that he is. But he's right. He can pass it on to someone in the village who isn't as rich and entitled as you are.'

She approached him again, looking into his eyes. 'I've offended you. I'm sorry. But I've a wonderful surprise for you. Just you wait and see.'

And once again he weakened and walked into her room, leaning forward to kiss her passionately.

'Do you forgive me?' she asked in a husky whisper.

If ever anyone deserved a kick in the pants...

There was a pause but then Liam replied, his voice gravelly. 'It doesn't matter whether I do or not. I can't resist you. But you're not good for me.'

'Liam?' a female voice called from an upper floor.

There were footsteps on the staircase. *Heck.*

Nena's mouth twitched in amusement. 'For better or worse,' she said loudly. Unapologetically. Though she'd stepped back from Liam.

Liam lifted the rolled carpet onto his shoulder as though it weighed nothing. 'That you, Tess?'

As Tess Norland appeared, Eve was reminded how pretty she was, with her blonde wavy hair and huge eyes. 'Yes. I'm just going to do some prep.'

'Sure.' Liam kissed her, then she held the door open for him to exit with the rug.

As she turned, Eve saw her face was etched with worry. How much had she heard before she'd reached the foyer?

Nena and Liam were playing a dangerous game.

4

Eve returned to her room and texted Simon to tell him what she'd seen. Spreading gossip felt awkward but he needed to know. At least she'd discovered something concrete.

He messaged back to say he'd ask the manager to monitor the situation and have a quiet word if necessary.

A short while later it was time to meet Viv for pre-supper drinks. Eve and Gus made for the bar. She was delighted that well-behaved dogs were allowed in all areas of the venue. Simon had said he'd thought of her when he made that rule, which was touching.

The place was all polished wood and whitewashed walls with sophisticated slate-grey accents. The low pendant lights over the tables created a warm atmosphere. It hit the right note – smart Londoners would love it – but it must have been expensive.

Eve spotted her beloved neighbours, Sylvia, a photographer, and Daphne, a potter, sitting with Viv. They'd agreed to teach courses at Saltwater.

Sylvia got up, her long grey plait swinging. 'Let me get you a drink. What's it to be? And then we need to talk tactics. Viv told me you're looking into Simon's brick.'

Eve asked for a glass of Shiraz and sat between Viv and Daphne, who bent to fuss Gus.

'Discovered anything yet, Sherlock?' Viv asked, raising her glass to her lips.

'Yes, but if we're going to talk about it here, can you please keep your voice down?'

Viv rolled her eyes.

As Sylvia re-joined them, Eve reported back.

Viv frowned as she finished. 'So Iggy and Liam's relationship is tetchy, and Liam's having an affair with Nena. I can't say I'm surprised. He's always struck me as wild and unreliable. I was worried when Simon took him on, but it was too late to say anything.'

Eve nodded. 'We should consider Tess too. She has every reason to hate Nena.'

Daphne's eyes clouded. 'Such a gentle person. And very beautiful.'

Sylvia nodded. 'I'd love to photograph her. All that golden hair and those huge troubled eyes. I wondered what was bothering her. Perhaps she already knows about the affair.'

Eve remembered what Simon had said about her family situation. 'I gather she has financial worries too.'

'Yes, that's right,' Daphne said.

'Her dad's a waster and her mother's in a home,' Sylvia put in. 'She and her brother have been struggling to pay the fees from what I hear.'

'I wonder if Tess threw the brick with Nena in mind,' Eve said. 'Or Tess's brother could have. He works here too.'

'A proper family business,' Daphne said.

'Which, frankly, is a recipe for disaster,' Sylvia added.

Daphne shook her head. 'You're such a cynic.'

'Just a realist.' Sylvia sipped her whisky.

'Tess and her brother probably want Nena gone if they know about the affair,' Eve said. 'Though I'm sure Liam's feelings are complicated too.'

'You think he could be the thrower?' Daphne's kind eyes were on Eve's.

'Only if he doesn't mind Simon finding out about the affair. He seems less likely to me for that reason. A lot of bosses would let him go.'

'Either way, Nena seems like a strong candidate for the subject of the note.' Sylvia smiled grimly.

'I'll be spitting blood if she's at the root of all this,' Viv said. 'Simon's treating her like royalty. I peered through her suite's window. It's gorgeous. Floor-to-ceiling bookcases and a huge antique mirror. I had to get really close even to see the frame.' Eve imagined her with her nose against the glass. It wouldn't be the first time. 'It's all gilt and scrolls,' Viv went on. 'Very much more than she deserves, I'd say.'

'I'm sure you're right.' Sylvia's eyes were thoughtful. 'We heard her kicking off yesterday. She blamed one of the cleaners for breaking a beautiful bowl of Simon's when it was she who'd left it teetering on a stool, just inside her studio door, where it was bound to get knocked.'

Daphne sighed and nodded. 'She'd set it up as part of a still life, then left it there and made everyone leave via another exit.'

Sylvia's jaw was rigid. 'It's unforgivable to abdicate responsibility and blame someone junior to yourself. The brick thrower must be badly upset to bring Simon into it; Nena's just the type to rouse that sort of feeling.'

Eve agreed and Robin was right: the situation was volatile. She turned to Sylvia and Daphne. 'Do you think the cleaner could have thrown the brick?'

But Sylvia shook her head. 'I highly doubt it. She's a temp. She only came on Thursday. Very young and timid.'

'So what's the plan?' Viv said.

Eve turned to her. 'Investigate the suspects we have and look out for others. Keep an especially close eye on Tess and her brother. Ask questions. See who twitches. Let's set up a WhatsApp group for updates.' She got busy on her phone. She felt strongest when she had control over details. For once, Viv didn't tell her to relax.

Tess entered the bar. It was time to make their conversation more general.

'How's the tutoring going?' Eve asked Daphne. The residential courses had begun four weeks earlier.

'Very interesting. I'm sure it's good for me to have a new challenge.'

Sylvia cackled. 'Daphne now remembers why she gave up teaching, but is too polite to say so.'

Her partner went pink. 'Not at all. Though some of the guests are more testing than others.'

'Speaking of which...' Sylvia nodded at a man who'd just entered the bar. He was expensively dressed with greying hair and frown lines around his mouth. She lowered her voice. 'I saw him in action earlier. He's not one of ours, thank goodness. Nena will have the pleasure of his company. They deserve each other.'

The man's moustache twitched angrily as he bought the glamorous woman on his arm a gin and tonic. 'Surely there must be someone here from the management,' he said haughtily, casting his eyes left and right.

But other than the bartenders, Sylvia, Daphne and Tess were the only staff Eve could see.

Sylvia smiled and sat back in her chair, as though watching a play.

Daphne looked uncomfortable. 'I feel we should help.' But her partner put her hand on her arm.

'We sorted him out earlier. It's someone else's turn!'

It was Tess who approached the grumpy-looking man. She

kept her voice low, but Eve was close enough to hear. 'How can I help? Is there a problem?'

'I'll say there's a problem!' The man's voice was wobbly with rage. 'I paid extra for your taster session this afternoon and now I've got ink on my jacket. It's Savile Row. I'll be sending you the cleaning bill. And what about my watch? It's a vintage Rolex Submariner Comex. I'm starting the painting course tomorrow. I can't have acrylics gumming up the works.'

Sylvia raised her eyes to heaven as Eve's adrenaline went into orbit. What an utter jerk. She was tempted to leap up to say all the things Liam's wife couldn't.

She was handling the man with admirable restraint: quietly sympathising, then suggesting casual clothes and leaving his watch in his bedroom.

'Leave a valuable like this in my room? Can you possibly be serious?'

Eve counted to ten. Making a scene wouldn't help Simon's business but it took all her willpower to keep quiet.

The elegant manager must have heard the rumpus. She entered and glided calmly towards the man. 'Perhaps you'd like to put it in our safe?'

'I shan't want to go to and fro with it. This is ridiculously inconvenient!'

'Please feel free to leave it there for the duration of your stay,' Sadie said. 'It will be quite secure and all the rooms have clocks. Come this way and I'll show you. Then you and your wife must have a glass of champagne on us.'

The man followed her, still grumbling, though the volume had decreased. It was good customer management, but deeply frustrating to see bad behaviour rewarded.

Dinner was held in the next-door room, which was just as elegant as the bar. There were double doors onto a landscaped garden and terrace, which would be lovely in summer. Eve kept a close eye on the staff and guests as planned.

Iggy, the concierge, dark and handsome, was in evidence, flitting in and out of the kitchen. He needn't worry; the food was excellent.

She was interested to watch Liam too. As the evening wore on, he'd migrated to the bar. He was making a conscious fuss of his wife. Perhaps guilt was kicking in. Nena watched the pair of them but there was no jealousy in her eyes. She was smiling, as though at a private joke. Eve wondered if she was supremely confident or didn't really care about Liam. Perhaps it was both.

Eve turned to the others. 'I think it's time I spoke to Nena. She's probably the answer to half of this puzzle.' The article for *Icon* was the perfect excuse. The magazine was prestigious; even big names tended to enjoy being quoted there.

Nena looked Eve up and down as she approached, her assessing glance laced with amusement. 'Hello.' She raised an eyebrow. 'And what can I do for you?'

Eve strove to ignore her expression and explained the piece she was writing. 'It would be a huge help if you could spare me five minutes. *Icon*'s readers will want to know more about your involvement. Can I get you a drink?'

But Nena shook her head. 'I'm happy to talk, but I'll get you one. What'll you have?'

It put Eve further off balance. She was used to her intervie-wees subtly acknowledging they were doing her a favour and accepting a drink and careful treatment in return. It shouldn't matter of course, but as Eve analysed it, she realised it altered the balance of power.

'I'm all right for the moment, thanks. What made you decide to come and teach here?'

Nena repeated the story about having a crush on Simon, which wasn't something Eve could use to big up his arts venue. Or not in an acceptable way, anyway. Come and take a course and feast your eyes on Saltwater's owner... No. Imagine Polly's reaction.

'But there must have been other reasons too.'

'Oh yes, there were. But I don't really want to talk about them.' She smiled. 'You can quote me on that. People love intrigue, don't they?'

Eve knew she was being used, and it wasn't a nice feeling. 'What are your impressions now you're here?'

'I'm having the time of my life!' She glanced around the room, her eyes skirting over Liam. 'The scenery's wonderful, of course.' That smile again. 'I'm finding it very... stimulating.'

Eve was going to have to rely on comments from Nena's students for the article. She was right, though; readers would love the intrigue around why she'd come. Eve was tempted to leave that bit out and make her sound as dull as possible.

'Now, tell me about you,' Nena said, her eyes never leaving Eve's. 'I want to hear it all. I'm fascinated by people. Where were you born?'

'Seattle.' Eve said it before she'd had time to work out her strategy.

'And you moved to the UK. You hated your family, I suppose.'

That was so far from the truth that Eve was almost goaded into replying. Almost. But she could tell Nena was playing her. Making a blunt statement so it was nigh on impossible not to respond.

Eve glanced at her watch. 'I'm afraid I can't give you my life story. I need to get back to my friends.'

Nena smiled. 'Touché.'

Eve crossed the room feeling oddly shaky. Nena's tactics were so blatant. Everything she did seemed geared towards giving her the upper hand. Iggy smiled as she passed. He was chatting with the guests now, making sure no one was left out.

'Are you all right?' Viv gathered her back into their fold, her eyes concerned.

'Not entirely. That was unsettling.' She explained. 'I'd say she's very clever, very manipulative and supremely confident.'

Sylvia shook her head. 'I rather wish she wasn't here.'

The conversation continued to bother Eve, but she needed to switch focus because Tess's brother, Jamie Caister, had arrived. He was the night manager and like Tess, Eve knew him a little as a Saxford local. He had a warm smile and an open friendly face. But that night he seemed watchful. Almost shifty. More than once, she saw him huddled with Tess, deep in what appeared to be a tense conversation. They looked close. Either of them could have thrown the brick, the note referring to Nena and the affair. Eve doubted Nena would care if she was found out, but Tess or Jamie might hope Simon would put a stop to it. If so, their threat to publicise it was probably a bluff. She doubted Tess wanted her dirty linen aired in public, but the note could be a cry for help. Tess might want to avoid giving Liam an ultimatum which could end the marriage.

Either way, she needed to know if Tess or Jamie were aware of the affair. Without that knowledge, they were less likely candidates.

When Jamie left the bar, Eve told the others she wanted to fetch a jumper and followed him. He reached reception ahead of her, nearing Iggy, who was on the front desk, talking on the phone.

'No, I'm very sorry, but there isn't anything I can do,' Iggy was saying. 'Nena's courses are fully booked for the entire season. But we have other excellent options on offer. Our print-making classes have spaces, and the tutor Tess Norland is highly—'

He was cut off mid-sentence.

'But she—'

And again. At last, he sighed. 'I can put you on a waiting list if you'd like?' He scribbled on his pad, finished the conversation and hung up.

Jamie's fists were bunched and it shocked Eve. The conversation had been run-of-the-mill. Not everyone would want to swap a fine art course for a print one. It didn't have to be personal.

'Ah, sorry, Jamie.' Iggy flushed. 'I was hoping—'

Jamie cut across him. 'People just don't see through Nena, do they?' He ground the words out. 'They don't realise what a self-centred abomination she is. If there was any justice in this world, she'd get what's coming to her.'

His tone was as passionate as his words. Whatever he knew or didn't know, his hatred was clear.

Iggy caught sight of Eve behind Jamie and flashed her an apologetic glance.

Jamie saw her then and flushed deeply before dashing outside.

Back in Curlew Cottage with her extra sweater, Eve stood by the front window in the guest sitting room, watching the crowds disperse as the bar closed. Most disappeared into the cottages, but Nena walked beyond, glancing over her shoulder.

Iggy had left reception and was out in the lane too. He paused outside the final cottage as though he was about to go in but after checking behind him, he followed Nena. What was that about? She needed to know.

'I have to follow them,' she said to Viv, as she moved to the door. 'The more information we get, the more likely we are to identify the brick thrower and shut down the scandal.'

'I'm coming with you,' Viv said. 'You can't go sleuthing on your own.'

'All right, but we have to be quiet.' Viv didn't know the meaning of the word. Gus, who would have to come too, was far more reliable.

They found a path along the back of the houses and

followed Nena and Iggy that way, creeping along in near darkness. The night was cloudy but Eve didn't dare use her torch.
Gus's eyes glinted in the moonlight. He was almost silent,
though she could hear his name tag chinking.

At the end of the path they found themselves in the staff car
park. Eve emerged to see a shadowy figure to her right, crossing
the perimeter of the parking area like a ghost. Not Nena or Iggy.
She stared into the night. At last, the outside light from the end
house caught the figure side on.

It was Jamie.

There was no reason he shouldn't be there. He could be
fetching something from his car, or simply walking off his fury.

Eve navigated through the vehicles and caught her breath.

In the middle of the car park was a Porsche 911, its tyres
slashed. She and Viv exchanged a glance. The guy with the
Rolex was probably rich enough to own a car like that, but this
was the staff car park. Eve would lay bets that the vehicle
belonged to Nena Field.

5

Eve and Viv didn't follow Nena any further. Reporting the slashed tyres was the new priority. Eve wanted to see Jamie's reaction if he made it to the front desk before they did. He went on duty at 10 p.m., according to Simon's notes, so he'd been cutting it fine.

After his outburst in reception, she could imagine him vandalising Nena's car. 'I'd like to talk to him,' she said to Viv as they cut back to Curlew Cottage. 'Any chance you could hang back a bit and pretend you're not listening, so he doesn't feel persecuted?'

Viv sighed. 'One day, I want to be Sherlock. But I suppose you do have more interviewing experience.'

Jamie had beaten them back. She watched him closely as she told him what she'd seen.

He flushed deeply. Guilt? Or embarrassment at the furious words she'd overheard? 'You're right. That is Nena's car.'

'I saw you close by.' She didn't take her eyes off him. 'It was immediately after I noticed the tyres.'

His blush deepened. 'I can imagine what you're thinking. But my outburst earlier was a spur-of-the-moment thing. I'm not unprofessional, honestly. Simon's told us about the article you're writing. I'd hate you to think...' He leaned on the front desk for a moment, head in his hands. 'I really need this job. It's just that Nena...' She sensed he was holding back tears.

She felt so sorry for him that she met him halfway. 'She's not an easy person.' She'd lowered her voice to a whisper. 'I've worked that out and I only arrived today.'

He let out a breath. 'Thank you.'

'I won't mention it in my article.'

'And to Simon?'

'Not if I don't have to. But you seemed out of control when you sounded-off to Iggy.' She let the sentence hang.

'I know.'

'You really hate her, don't you? What is it about her? Is there something you know?'

Jamie flinched. The brick thrower, or not?

'I'm not sure what you mean,' he said at last.

But her question had been clear and he'd paused before he replied. She was sure he knew something. It could be about Liam and Nena's affair, or possibly something else.

When Eve stayed silent, Jamie burst out, 'I didn't slash the tyres! I don't even drive in; I only skirted the car park. I was taking a walk before my shift started. I'm still adjusting to working nights. The fresh air helps.' His youthful face looked drawn, with dark shadows under the eyes. She thought again of the worries he was facing: his spendthrift father and the challenge to pay his mum's care-home fees. 'Please believe me.'

At last, Eve nodded, but his excuse for being outside seemed odd. Surely the walk from Saxford would wake him up? He'd arrived early for work. Perhaps he'd wanted time to vandalise the car. If he knew about the affair she could definitely see it. He and Tess had looked conspiratorial that evening.

Jamie must have taken her silence for acceptance. He picked up the phone. 'I'll let Nena know and call the police.'

Nena appeared while Jamie was on the line to Blyworth police station.

'I'm sorry,' Eve said. 'It's a horrible thing to happen.' But deep down she didn't feel as sympathetic as she should.

Nena raised an eyebrow. 'The day I'm not causing a stir I'll be worried. It'll make the papers and you know what they say about publicity. You can put it in your article! Besides, life's like an omelette. If you live it to the full, you break eggs.' She smiled.

'The publicity won't be so good for Simon.' There was an edge to Viv's voice as she stepped into the fray again.

Nena waved a hand. 'People will know it was personal. They won't blame the venue.'

'Doesn't it frighten you?' Eve asked. 'I'd be scared, if it were me.' She had the unkind desire to drive the point home.

Nena raised her eyebrows. 'It'll blow over. You'll see. Only the most inconsequential people exist without upsetting anyone.'

Eve couldn't understand her nonchalance. The tyre slashing was a violent act and Nena was having an affair with a married man. What made her so impervious to other people's feelings?

Sadie appeared. 'I've just heard. How awful for you, Nena. We'll sort out the insurance, of course, and hopefully the police can do something.'

'I wouldn't worry about it.' Nena put a hand on Sadie's shoulder and Sadie leaped back as though she'd been given an electric shock.

The reaction seemed so strange. Eve knew some people didn't like being touched, so perhaps it was that. Sadie looked embarrassed and started talking busily to Jamie about the police.

Eve caught Nena's smirk as she turned away.

.   .   .

At last, Eve got ready to return to her room for the night. Gus looked as though he'd have liked to be in his travel bed hours ago. But as she and Viv walked up Saltwater End, she saw Tess Norland through a window in a neighbouring cottage. It must be her classroom – part of a large extension at the rear with huge glass windows. She was at work still, leaning over a table.

'She's up late.'

Viv nodded.

'I think I might nip in before I go to bed. Have a quick word.' She turned to Gus, who was shooting her accusatory looks. 'Don't worry. I'll get you settled first.'

Once he was sorted and she'd said goodnight to Viv, Eve retraced her steps.

She wasn't sure Tess would welcome the late-night interruption, but her lonely figure drew her in. It would be far easier to talk to her privately at this hour. She watched through the window, protected by darkness, as Tess inked up some lino, then took a print from it. The image was large and bold, but she couldn't see what it represented at that angle.

Then suddenly, Tess thrust the print down on a table, took a lino-cutting tool and scored it across the picture. Hard and fast. And again and again.

It was extraordinary to see gentle, softly spoken Tess attack her work so viciously. Perhaps it was she who'd slashed Nena's tyres. It looked as though the violence was providing relief.

Eve watched and waited for her fury to die down. And then she went in. If she wanted to solve Simon's problem, holding back wasn't an option.

Tess gasped when Eve appeared in the doorway.

'Sorry. I saw you through the window and the front door was unlocked.' Eve looked at the lacerated print. 'You looked upset.'

Tess put her hands to her cheeks and stumbled over her words. 'I hate it when something I've spent so much time on goes wrong.'

Eve instantly thought of her marriage.

'The print's terrible,' Tess added quickly. 'I don't want my students to see it. What few there are of them.' She was standing in front of the work, shifting as Eve moved so her view was blocked.

'I'm sure numbers will grow.' Eve walked over to a display wall. It was covered with the most beautiful etchings, silkscreen prints, wood and lino cuts. Landscapes full of emotion, lonely, with wide skies. 'These are yours? They're amazing.'

She meant it. She felt her eyes prick when she looked at them.

Tess looked tearful then too. She must have realised Eve was being genuine. 'Thank you. I'm a bit of a poor relation here, though, compared with Nena.'

'You should be as famous as she is.'

'I hope that happens.' Tess looked exhausted.

'Do you always work this late?' Eve wondered if she was distracting herself from her worries.

'Often. I wasn't sleepy.'

Now was Eve's chance. 'Are you worried about anything? More than the success of the courses, I mean? Another member of staff?'

Tess looked at her sharply. 'No. Not at all.'

But Eve didn't believe her. As she crossed the room she caught a glimpse of the lacerated print at last. The picture was of Liam and Nena.

A barrage of thoughts filled Eve's head as she prepared for bed that night. Jamie and Tess both hated Nena. Tess knew about the affair, judging by the print, so Jamie probably did too. Either of them could have thrown the brick and slashed the tyres. It didn't follow that the two incidents were related, but it seemed likely.

Tess and Jamie weren't the only suspects, though. Nena could have thrown the brick and vandalised her car herself, for publicity. She'd passed the car park minutes before Jamie had. It would explain her breezy response.

Or, based on opportunity, perhaps Iggy had slashed the tyres, though Eve didn't know why he would.

She glanced down at Saltwater End before getting into bed. The expensively modernised sash windows were double-glazed. She was warm. Cocooned. But outside the wind thrashed the trees and the sea was stormy. The turbulent world pressed in close as she snuggled under the duvet and switched off the light.

6

The next morning, as Eve walked towards Curlew Cottage, she saw the police had arrived. Close to them stood a worried-looking Simon and some reporters. How had *they* heard? Again, Eve wondered if Nena could be drumming up publicity. If so, it was at Simon's expense. Viv was with him, her arm around his shoulders. The sight of them looking so vulnerable made her heart contract.

Eve watched Nena flatter the male officers who'd attended.

'She'll have them eating out of her hand.' The voice made her jump. It was Liam, watching Eve watch the spectacle, hands shoved in his pockets. His tone was bitter.

'You'd think she'd be nervous.'

He nodded. 'People don't slash tyres for nothing.'

She glanced at him. 'Maybe she's got secrets. What do you think?'

He didn't flinch under scrutiny. 'I wouldn't know.'

'She used to live in the village, didn't she?' Eve guessed she, Liam and Iggy must be around the same age. 'Did you know each other, back then?'

'Oh yes.' Liam's expression was unreadable. 'Old, old friends. She christened Iggy.'

'Excuse me?'

'It's not his real name. He was born Jack, but he fell overboard on a boat trip and after that she called him Iggy. Short for ignoramus.'

Charming. Eve wondered if the nickname had been a gentle tease or a put-down. From what she'd seen of Nena, the latter seemed likely.

'Why did he adopt it?' Though it was one way of fighting back. Making out you didn't care.

'He didn't have much choice. I kept calling him Iggy without thinking, it felt so right.' He was grinning now. 'He needed taking down a peg or two. He was holier than thou then, just like he is now. You must have noticed.

'By the time he went to uni, the name Jack had been forgotten. Dad called him Iggy when he dropped him on campus and one of his coursemates heard and asked him about it. By the time I started studying at the same place, he was a huge hit and I'd swear it was down to the name. Can't think of any other reason. Dad couldn't believe it when I told him. The stupid posh girls loved the idea that it was short for Ignatius and the musos thought it was cool that he was named after Iggy Pop.' Liam's expression had turned sour, but a moment later his lips twitched. 'I made Iggy pay me in beer not to tell the truth. He was very keen to keep it quiet.'

As an only child, Eve had missed out on the joys of siblings. She'd never felt quite so glad of it before. 'Who do you think slashed Nena's tyres?'

Liam shrugged. 'Someone with a serious grudge.'

The police interviewed Eve and Viv straight after Nena. Naturally, they wanted to know why they'd been walking behind the cottages, not along the road with its view of the sea.

'It was dark and windy.' Eve looked the constable in the eye. 'The back path was more sheltered.'

She could imagine what Detective Inspector Palmer, her arch-nemesis on the local force, would say. That Eve was up to something. Had somehow known there was trouble afoot and had been investigating. He'd be right, of course.

Eve and DI Palmer had come into contact before, when Eve had written the obituaries of various murder victims. It was inevitable that she'd stumble across evidence as she interviewed the deceased's friends and relatives. She always passed it on and dug deeper when she could. She'd helped solve multiple cases, yet Palmer was anything but grateful.

Once again, Eve wondered why Iggy had been following Nena, unless Nena was having affairs with both brothers. It seemed like her style. She'd probably find it amusing to play them off against each other, given their antagonistic relationship.

Eve thought back to her and Viv's arrival in the car park. To seeing Jamie. She'd have to mention it, though she hoped he was innocent.

The constable frowned as she passed it on. 'But I gather Jamie had just slipped out for a walk. I didn't see him near Nena's car.' She told him about seeing Nena and Iggy too.

Assuming the brick thrower and the tyre slasher were one and the same, Nena was their focus. It was a shame Simon hadn't reported the brick. The police were working with partial information. But Greg Boles, the detective sergeant on Palmer's team, might help. He was married to Robin's cousin. Greg found Palmer as obnoxious as Eve did and was prone to discussing cases with Robin as a like-minded outsider. With Simon's permission, she could tell Greg about the brick in confidence.

Over lunch, Eve carried on her enquiries. She managed to chat to Saltwater Cottages' general manager, the elegant silver-haired Sadie Thornton. Eve guessed she'd be the toughest nut to crack when it came to extracting information. She was far too polished and reserved. Watching her surreptitiously might work better.

'Have you worked in an arts centre before?' Eve hoped a non-controversial opener would relax her.

Sadie shook her head. 'No, but I had the right skills. I worked at a conference centre in London and at a hotel down there too.'

'Ah, you're a Londoner born and bred, are you?'

Sadie smiled, but Eve could tell she was tense. 'As good as.'

That seemed slightly evasive. 'You started out elsewhere? I did, as you can tell. Seattle, to be precise.'

She'd wanted to give some information to get Sadie to open up, but it backfired.

'Oh, Seattle! I've always wanted to go there. Tell me, what's it like?'

Eve would have to respond, then push again afterwards. She told her about Pike Place Market and Discovery Park and felt a twinge of homesickness.

Sadie looked at her intently. 'I know that feeling.' Her eyes were kind and sad.

'What's the place you miss most?'

'Oh,' Sadie sighed, 'London.' But she didn't meet Eve's eye.

Eve opened her mouth to ask more, but at that moment Sadie introduced her to their resident chef, Gemma Redpath, who was passing.

Eve could tell there was a slight tension between them. They were different types. They were both dressed smartly, but Gemma came across as rough and ready. Uncompromising, with none of Sadie's smooth veneer. The smile she gave Eve was rather wintery, and she didn't engage with the manager.

Eve quizzed Gemma about the menus for her article and asked about her background.

'I'm not head chef,' Gemma said. 'I'm holding the fort until my boss arrives. I moved here from Cornwall, to be closer to my mum. She's not been well.' She folded her arms.

She wasn't the most forthcoming interviewee Eve had ever tackled. Most people were excited at the idea of featuring in *Icon*. Eve would have expected Gemma to want the publicity. She offered to include more about her career but Gemma shook her head. 'Self-promotion's not my thing. I let the food speak for itself.'

To be fair, it had been sumptuous.

Both Gemma and Sadie seemed to be holding back. If they had secrets, either of them could be the brick thrower's target, despite Nena's slashed tyres. But they could each be the thrower too.

'Have you ever visited Saxford St Peter before?' she asked Gemma.

'Never. My mum only moved to Suffolk recently.'

Eve wondered why the woman had relocated when she wasn't well, but asking felt too intrusive. 'How are you getting on with your colleagues? I found it hard to settle in when I first came here.' It was a lie, but in a good cause.

But again, Gemma shook her head. 'I'm self-sufficient and it's a small community. I'm sure I'll get to know as many people as I want to.'

From her tone, that wouldn't be many.

Eve was taking taster sessions at Saltwater so she could write about a variety of classes. She had her first that afternoon, with Nena's group. The nasty man with the Rolex was there, still in his ridiculous suit.

Nena sashayed up to him. 'The cut is gorgeous.' She touched his sleeve and Eve saw his wife frown. 'I'd hate to endanger a work of art like that. Mr Horace, isn't it?'

It was the first time Eve had seen the nasty man smile – self-satisfied, yet fawning. 'Please, call me Edgar. I work in fine tailoring. I always wear the best.'

'I can see that!' Nena smiled. 'Here, let me get you an artist's smock.'

Eve bet no one else could have got him to don a smock without a murmur. Nena helped him on with it, which Eve thought was excessive. She had the impression Nena found the whole thing entertaining. 'There are enough for everyone who wants them.'

But most people were equipped with more brain cells and had come suitably dressed. There were plenty of worn jeans and hole-ridden jumpers on display.

Eve was curious to see Nena in action. As far as she could make out, the painter hadn't done any teaching for years. Presumably it wasn't her thing, so what was she doing here? Was it because of the affair with Liam? Was he unfinished business? An old flame from when she'd lived in Suffolk? Tutoring was a good excuse to spend time with him.

Whatever the truth, Nena managed her students seamlessly. Not that it was a challenge. They were in awe of her, eager for the smallest crumb of encouragement.

'I'm only here for recreation,' Eve said when it was her turn. 'And for the article, of course.'

'But you're not the sort to be blasé about success.' Nena looked her straight in the eye. 'You're meticulous. Anyone can see that. It would irritate you not to do something to the very best of your ability.'

She could have been a psychologist if she hadn't been a painter. She was reading Eve too accurately for comfort.

She moved on to another woman who claimed she was a no-hoper.

'Nonsense.' Nena's eyes were on her work. 'It's all in the

mind. If you're determined, you can do anything. Get anything you want.'

Eve thought of Liam, and Nena's success at reeling him in.

'Believe in yourself,' Nena said to Eve's coursemate. 'See what happens.'

'She's different when you talk to her one-to-one,' Viv said, after they'd left the room. 'I can't forgive her for causing Simon trouble but on a personal level, I'm warming to her.'

Eve double-took. 'Seriously?'

Viv nodded. 'Didn't you feel the same?'

Eve shuddered. 'Just the opposite.'

When she looked up she saw Nena had left the classroom too, and was watching them. After a moment she gave a very slight nod. The amused look was back.

7

Later on, Eve visited Viv in her room.

'So where are we at?' Viv asked.

'Nena has a secret, obviously – the affair with Liam. If that's what the brick thrower was referring to, I could see it being Tess or Jamie. I'm sure Tess knows about the affair, and Jamie probably does too. I'd say they're possibles for tyre slasher as well.'

'So we think Nena's the most likely subject of the note, after the tyre slashing.'

'I think so. Sadie the manager and Gemma the cook are tight-lipped. They might have secrets. But all the fury I've seen has been directed against Nena.'

'Right. Next steps?'

'To keep watching everyone, but Nena's our priority.' A magnet who'd probably draw the brick thrower close.

Eve kept a careful eye on Nena at pre-supper drinks and when she disappeared, Eve followed.

She didn't go far. Eve almost gave herself away, striding into the foyer. Nena was standing in the centre of the room as Eve tucked herself amongst the coats again.

'Ah, sea!' Nena sounded nostalgic. She smiled at Sadie. 'It's good to be here.'

Sadie's expression was transparent. Fear. Eve saw her swallow. She was reminded of the moment when Nena had touched Sadie's shoulder and the manager had flinched, as though she'd been burned.

'Now,' Nena was still smiling, 'I must settle up with you. I never managed to send you a birthday present. I'd like you to buy yourself something nice.'

Sadie closed her eyes for a moment. 'I don't want anything. You should keep your money.'

Nena took a step forward. 'But I want you to have it. And you must.'

How could an offer of money sound so coercive and threatening?

'You know how much I owe you,' Nena went on. 'After what you did.'

And at that point a new emotion crossed Sadie's face. Pain.

'You did the right thing. You know you did. And I want to as well. I'll never finish paying you back.'

Eve grappled to understand what was going on. Nena sounded like a blackmailer, yet the money was flowing the wrong way.

Sadie looked pale and drawn as she glanced quickly left and right. Eve shrank back in her hiding place.

'What's a few thousand between friends?' There was a glint in Nena's eye.

A few thousand? And how long had they known each other?

'Keep your voice down,' Sadie said at last. 'Please.'

Nena waved a hand and didn't reduce her volume. 'You worry too much.' Her catchphrase. It made Eve's heart beat faster. She was writing a cheque.

When she turned, Eve saw her smile. It was that same smile she'd given when she'd reeled Liam in. Cruel and triumphant.

After supper, Eve and Viv sat in the bar again, chewing over the situation with Sylvia and Daphne.

'Nena and Sadie have a secret connection,' Eve said. 'Nena's claiming she's in Sadie's debt but it's she who seems powerful.' It would keep Eve awake until she understood why.

The bar closed at ten. As Eve and Viv cut along the lane towards their cottage, Eve glanced back and glimpsed Nena flitting across her open-curtained room.

Back in Avocet Cottage, she sat and read. She wanted to switch off. Forget about Simon's predicament and the problems at Saltwater for a while. But as she'd predicted, questions filled her mind and her head was aching. It got progressively worse. She lay down with a cold flannel over her eyes. She hardly ever got headaches, and she had no painkillers with her. Viv might have come equipped but when Eve messaged to ask there was no reply. Perhaps she was asleep already.

Eve hoped she could ignore the pain, but an hour later she gave in, tugged on her coat and boots and braved the dark, windswept lane to reach Curlew Cottage. Whoever was on reception would probably have some medicine.

She found Jamie behind the desk, pink in the face and breathless, his hand shaking slightly.

'Are you all right?' they both said at once.

Jamie laughed nervously. 'Adrenaline rush. Truth to tell, I thought I'd double-booked someone but I was looking at the wrong dates on the calendar. I've never been so relieved in my life.' He gabbled the words out. 'How about you?'

'Horrible headache, I'm afraid, and I've come away without aspirin.'

'Now, there I can help.' He beamed as his breathing gradually steadied. 'One moment.' He unlocked a cabinet, found her a packet and asked her to sign for it.

'Thanks. I might get some sleep tonight after all.'

'Good luck.' He was brimming with bonhomie.

Jamie was always friendly, but it seemed over the top. His relief too extreme.

Eve passed Nena's window as she returned to her quarters. The room was in darkness now, the curtains drawn.

Eve slept eventually, but she woke early the following morning. She hoped she'd be able to concentrate on that day's classes. Gus was awake too, so fresh air was the thing.

Eve wasn't the only one up and about before seven. She passed Liam, who was chopping wood in the chilly morning half-light. His hand was bandaged.

'Hurt yourself?'

His eyes didn't meet hers. 'It's nothing. You'd think I'd know to be more careful by now. It doesn't do to be clumsy with an axe.'

'Sounds painful. I loved the open fire in the bar last night though.'

'First of the season, thanks to a fallen tree. We'll have more wood delivered soon.'

Gus had paused, looking at her over his shoulder. She strode towards him, wondering how you'd injure your hand with an axe blade. She was no expert, but it sounded implausible. It wasn't as though you'd accidentally pick it up by the wrong end and even if you managed to swing it one handed, you'd have to be a contortionist to get the other under its blade. Besides, the resulting injury would be horrific.

In Blind Eye Wood, she soaked up the sounds of nature. A robin singing, and something scuffling in the undergrowth. There was another dog walker in the distance. Gus ploughed through the fallen leaves, nose down. Above them, the foliage that remained rustled in the wind.

'Let's go to the burned oak.'

Gus looked round at her quickly then dashed ahead. It was an old favourite. She remembered meeting Robin there early in their relationship.

Gus was well ahead of her now. He'd stopped again, near the old oak tree.

Something about his stance made her pause but when he let out an eerie whine, she quickened her pace. He was looking at something bulky, lying on the ground. The whining continued, a pitiful, plaintive sound.

As Eve got near, she slowed her pace again. Not wanting to acknowledge what she was seeing.

She swallowed.

Nena Field.

She was wearing an expensive winter coat. A faux fur hat had fallen to one side.

Next to her lay a log, a large irregular bit of bark missing. In her transfixed state, the shape reminded Eve of Scotland.

Very slowly, she pieced the scene together. The bark had been knocked off as the log was used in anger, she guessed. Steeling herself, she looked at Nena properly. Winced at the sight of the blood. Of her matted hair. Her ashen face and unseeing eyes, staring at the sky between the trees.

8

Eve felt sick. It was partly the sight of Nena's body, with her battered head. Partly the shock of it. But though it hit her in the gut, all the signs that Nena was in danger had been there. The slashed tyres. The brick through the window. Both spoke of an anger that could no longer be suppressed.

The brick had seemed like a plea for Simon to act, but how could he, when the thrower hadn't named names? Eve guessed the tyres were a direct warning to Nena. And she'd failed to react. Laughed the whole thing off. Eve could imagine her would-be killer watching, incensed that they'd had no effect. And then, perhaps, their frustration had boiled over. They'd followed Nena to the lonely woods and killed her.

It was horrific. She felt for Nena. She might not have liked her, but no one deserved this. And what about her family and friends?

But to her shame, she was already thinking beyond that. Simon was facing financial ruin. He was desperate to make Saltwater Cottages work and Nena had been his saving grace. Her death might be his downfall. The secluded getaway he was offering would seem isolated and dangerous, and he had lost his star attraction.

She shook herself. Nothing should matter compared with what had happened to Nena. She needed to move. Call the police. Call Simon. Tell Viv. The thoughts spun in her head. How could she break the news? She needed to dial 999 first. Of course she did. But to tear Simon's world apart without even warning him felt wrong. Yet telling Simon when he was alone, with Polly away and no one to help him through it, felt terrible too.

It was only the arrival of another walker that pulled her from the eddy of indecision.

Sadie. Saltwater Cottages' manager. She shouted a greeting to Eve.

'I usually get a breath of fresh air while Jamie's still on duty, before I start my day. And it really is fresh, isn't it?'

At that point, she must have got close enough to see Eve's face. She came nearer, a little unsteadily, and saw for herself.

Eve was still too shocked to respond normally. She just stared at Sadie. The manager's face paled, then tears pricked her eyes. She'd been scared of Nena, but she was emotional now. It struck Eve that she didn't look surprised.

'Dear God,' she said at last.

'I need to call the police. Call Simon. But for a moment I couldn't think.'

Sadie nodded quickly. 'Of course. You call the authorities. I'll ring Simon and find his sister.'

Eve seldom needed someone to tell her what to do, but on this occasion she was grateful. She pulled out her phone and dialled.

Eve had had visions of her and Viv leaving to talk to Simon immediately. To somehow convince him that everything would be all right. But of course, that couldn't happen. The police were on site and she and Viv were waiting to be interviewed. Sadie had gathered the guests and staff in the bar at Curlew Cottage.

Viv was wringing her hands, proving that it wasn't just an expression.

'So help me, Eve,' she said, 'I'm appalled that Nena's dead, but I'm just as furious at the killer for what they're doing to Simon.' She closed her eyes. 'What does that make me?'

'Human. I thought of the consequences pretty quickly too.' It was a relief that she wasn't the only one.

Eve wondered about Nena's final movements. Had she really felt no fear after her tyres were slashed? Her late-night walk in lonely woodland certainly gave that impression. She wondered if she'd gone to meet someone or just to get some air.

'Who do you think did it?' Viv asked, through chattering teeth.

Eve thought of the delight in Nena's eyes as she'd exercised control over Liam. And carelessly laughed at the idea of his wife discovering their affair. 'I suspect there are multiple possibilities. Tess and Jamie have to be contenders. And Liam, even though I thought he was unlikely to have thrown the brick.' Lovers were always high up the list of suspects, she knew. 'He could have lashed out if Nena threatened to tell Tess. He might not know she knows. But there's Iggy too. We saw him follow Nena on Saturday night. If she was seeing both brothers, that's an extra love triangle. And there was the strangest dynamic between Sadie and Nena. I think she had some kind of hold over Sadie.'

Gus was still shivering. The shock had got to all of them. Eve and Viv bent as one to give him a pat and almost knocked heads.

Viv's eyes met Eve's. 'Iggy was in the right place to slash the tyres.'

'It's true, but now I think about it, I'm not sure he'd have had time to get clear before we arrived.'

Viv nodded. 'So back to the other suspects.' For once she'd lowered her voice. 'Could Tess Norland have managed it physically?'

Eve thought of the log. 'I think she'd have been able to do it. I'd say the killer knocked Nena down with one well-aimed swing, then kept going.' It was a horrible thought. 'People are meant to gain strength in the grip of strong emotion, and Tess was desperately upset.' She thought of the way she'd slashed her print. 'The same goes for Tess's brother Jamie. They're very close, I think, and they've dealt with a lot. I could imagine Jamie losing it with Nena for threatening Tess's marriage. And Jamie was close by when the tyres were slashed too.'

Viv nodded. 'You're right, though Jamie's a sunny person, and he was on duty last night. He can't have been on the desk *and* in Blind Eye Wood.'

Eve sighed. She liked Jamie too, but it was no good ignoring facts. 'I went to see him in reception, a little before midnight.' She explained about the headache. 'I found him pink in the face and out of breath.'

'Blimey. You think he could have run to the woods and killed Nena?'

'I don't want to believe it, but I'm pretty sure he was up to something. Still, we don't know the time of death yet. I saw Nena cross her room when we left the bar just after ten. Jamie was on duty by then.' Fifteen minutes to the burned oak at a run. Fifteen minutes back. Some time to get cleaned up... 'Leaving the desk would have been a risk, but it's not impossible. I doubt he had many visitors other than me last night.

'As for motive, as well as protecting Tess, he might have feared for his future. If Liam and Tess had split up, Tess might have resigned. And without her salary as well as his I'm guessing they'd be sunk. Then again, the whole future of Saltwater Cottages is under threat now. They might both lose their jobs. But maybe he didn't think that far ahead.'

'And what if it was Liam who did it?'

Eve thought it through. 'He could have followed Nena, or arranged to meet in the woods. Maybe he'd made up his mind to finish it. Really make it final this time. And then once again, Nena got round him. He could have been frustrated with himself but blamed her. Or maybe she threatened to tell Tess. He might have picked up the nearest thing to hand and lashed out. It looks like a spur-of-the-moment killing, using the log as a weapon.'

'True.'

'Liam's hand was bandaged this morning. He claimed he'd been careless with his axe but a graze from a bit of bark feels more realistic. I hope the police will ask him about it.'

Viv put her head in her hands. 'They all seem like strong candidates, but I'll bet there are others. Any of the guests or staff could have motives; Nena was the sort to make enemies.'

'True. But I think the guests are unlikely. The new batch only arrived on Saturday – after the brick was thrown. There's also motive to consider. If any of them have existing links with Nena, the police will find them, but other than that, deciding to kill her within thirty-six hours seems like a stretch.'

'Right. That makes things simpler.'

Eve was distracted from her thoughts by raised voices across the room.

'I expect the police will assume you lost your temper, Edgar.' A stocky, sandy-haired man was standing opposite the unpleasant Rolex-wearer, grinning. 'We all heard Nena laugh at you behind your back. She said what an idiot you looked in that smock.' He guffawed. 'She said a bear could paint a better picture than you.'

'You were saying?' Viv said.

Eve grimaced. 'You win, but I'd say he's an isolated case.

And can you imagine him wielding a log? It would muck up his smart clothes. There's one other possibility, though. Nena could have thrown the brick, then been killed to stop her revealing the secret in the note.'

Eve thought of tight-lipped Sadie. What had given Nena power over her?

9

Thoughts of Simon's misery filled Eve's head, but she made herself focus on the hubbub in the bar. Everyone was talking about when they'd last seen Nena and she needed to take notes. As soon as she had the time of death, she could look at who'd had the opportunity to kill.

She heard four people say they'd seen Nena through her window, later than Eve had. Sadie had seen her just before 11.15, but the final sighting was at 11.20 p.m., by a guest with no known connection to Nena. Nena had been sitting reading with her curtains open. Waiting for someone maybe? Just after midnight, Eve had noticed her light was out, her curtains drawn.

So she'd left her room sometime after twenty past eleven. And she'd have passed the reception desk unless she climbed out of her window. Jamie should have seen her go.

Eve imagined him watching her. Wondering if she was meeting someone, or if she'd be alone. Considering following her, just to talk. To make her realise the damage she could do to his sister. Maybe he'd left his desk at last and tailed her to the woods. Perhaps he'd confronted her and she'd laughed. It would have felt like a slap in the face...

But it might not have been like that.

Liam was telling everyone he was back in his room by eleven fifteen after doing his rounds. Eve watched as he made the claim to yet another member of staff. 'And Tess was in our apartment all evening,' he said.

Sadie looked up sharply, then glanced quickly down again, her cheeks pink. What was that all about? She knew something, Eve was sure. She'd have to ask her when she got her alone.

Iggy approached Eve.

'Are you all right?' His eyes were full of concern. 'Sadie told me you discovered the body.'

She nodded and took a deep breath at the memory. 'I'm okay.'

'I still can't believe it. I mean, I know Nena rubbed some people up the wrong way, but to kill her?' He shook his head.

Gemma the chef was standing close by. Her knuckles whitened on the mug she was holding. It seemed to be in reaction to Iggy's words. Eve caught her eye and held her gaze.

'It's a terrible thing to happen,' Gemma said.

It was true, of course, but something was off.

'People are saying Nena left her room after eleven twenty.' Iggy shook his head. 'It's horrible to think she was heading into danger when we were relaxing. I went to the bar at around eleven fifteen to see if anyone was around. It was closed of course, but the staff sometimes gather for a nightcap. I found Gemma there. Sadie came in too.'

'But not until later,' Gemma said. 'At a quarter to midnight maybe. We were getting settled in by then. I'd just decided to nip to the staffroom for a bottle of gin, but I heard her arrive as I left.'

Iggy sighed. 'Sadie said we ought to get to bed, but inertia had set in. In the end, all three of us stayed up chatting until two or so.'

Like everyone else, he was reliving each moment of the evening aloud. A way of coming to terms with what had happened, and maybe from nerves too. The police would ask. He, Gemma and Sadie might be in the clear if Nena had been killed before two.

Eve was surprised they'd stayed up so late. You'd think they'd be tired after a long day. 'What about you, Gemma?' she asked. 'You didn't see anything odd when you went to fetch the gin?'

The cook shook her head. 'I used the staff door off the bar. It's a shortcut. The corridor to the staffroom was deserted. I stayed there for a while to take a call, but no one came by.'

She couldn't vouch for Jamie on reception, then.

'What about before you went to the bar?' Nena had still been in her room, but someone could have been hanging around. 'You're based here in Curlew Cottage, aren't you?'

Gemma nodded. 'My suite's next door to Liam and Tess's, along the corridor from Iggy's. I didn't see or hear anything. Or nothing relating to Nena anyway.'

Eve held her breath. 'You noticed something else?'

She pulled a face. 'Yes, but well before Nena drew her curtains. Someone rapping on Tess and Liam's door just after ten thirty-five.'

'You remember the time?' Eve would need to note the details and make sense of them later. For now, she focused on the gist.

'I checked because it seemed late to go calling. There was no reply. I'd heard Liam leave a few minutes before that, then Tess crying but she went quiet after a minute or two.' Her eyes were fixed on Eve's. 'It would be interesting to know what upset her. She must have gone out as well. She only just missed their caller.'

Gemma was being remarkably forthcoming. It felt as though she was stirring up trouble. But as she'd said, whatever the Norlands had been up to, it was too early to relate to the murder. 'Wouldn't Tess and the visitor have bumped into each other?'

Gemma shrugged. 'There are two sets of stairs. I wondered afterwards if it was Sadie who'd knocked. She was on the landing, having a word with Tess and Liam when I left for the bar at eleven fifteen. Tess still looked upset.'

That was interesting. If Gemma was right, it was no wonder Sadie had looked surprised when Liam claimed Tess had been home all evening.

She was called for her interview at that moment. She was hoping it would be with Robin's cousin-in-law, Greg Boles. He was worth a thousand of his lazy, blinkered boss Palmer, though talking to him felt awkward. She knew him quite well now, but they kept the association under wraps. The information Greg shared with Robin would be a sacking offence. Eve had to play-act when they spoke officially. It would be terrible if Palmer started to ask questions.

As a uniformed officer escorted her to one of the teaching rooms, she thought about Gemma's account. If Liam had lied about Tess not going out, it was odd. Nena hadn't left her room until after eleven twenty. Establishing his wife's whereabouts before that seemed pointless. Why would he try? Still, if he had, it was interesting. It looked as though he was prepared to cover for her, despite his affair. But of course, he'd started to realise how poisonous Nena was. Now she was dead, perhaps he'd remembered that Tess was precious to him. Or maybe he wanted to distance the pair of them from any involvement for selfish reasons. But the question remained, why worry about the earlier part of the evening?

The uniformed officer knocked on the door of the teaching room.

'Come!'

Eve's heart sank. It was Palmer. How did he manage to stuff that one word with so much self-importance?

'Ah, Ms Mallow.' He stared at her as she entered the room. 'We meet again. I might have known I'd find you here. Where there's trouble you're never far behind.' He motioned her to a seat.

Eve took a deep breath. She could irritate him best by keeping her temper. 'I'm here because my best friend's brother runs the venue.'

He looked at her narrowly. 'Yes. The involvement of your close friend has been noted.'

He made 'involvement' sound criminal.

'I've heard you're trying to drum up publicity for this place. You've got it now.' He spoke as though he'd caught her out.

He surely didn't think she'd murdered Nena Field for press coverage. 'I wanted to pitch Saltwater as a rural retreat, away from the stresses of everyday life. In the wake of this tragedy, my chances of doing that have dropped to zero.'

He grunted and shifted in his chair, looking at her with dissatisfied eyes.

'So you found the body.'

She nodded. 'It must have been around a quarter to seven this morning.'

His eyebrows rose and he leaned forward. 'What were you doing in the woods at such an antisocial hour?'

Surely a detective inspector should have more imagination? 'I was walking my dog. It's a well-known early morning pastime.'

He got her to recount her movements and interactions with Nena, seizing on the most innocuous elements as though they were incriminating.

'And what can you tell me about the other staff and guests?'

He waited until she started to speak, then interrupted her. 'Please keep to the pertinent points, not idle gossip.'

Her blood pressure was probably through the roof. Gus's presence was comforting. He was looking daggers at Palmer.

But what to tell him? Pointing the finger in a murder enquiry was serious, and Palmer was apt to put two and two together to make five. In the end, she told him everything, but blandly, without any of the thoughts she would have shared with Greg. She could always fill him in later.

She had to tell him about Jamie's breathlessness, but coupled with his explanation, Palmer didn't leap on it as significant.

At last, the inspector sat back in his chair. 'I'll have a statement prepared for you to sign. We may need to talk to you again.' He said it like a threat. 'For the time being, you're free to go, but make no mistake, I will come down on you like a ton of bricks if you interfere in my investigation. Is that understood?'

She gave him the sweetest smile she could manage. 'Absolutely. I'd hate to tread on your toes when you're so good at your job.'

He looked at her suspiciously as she stood up to leave.

It was frustrating. Palmer hadn't given away any details about Nena's death. Still, Eve would get them in time. Greg Boles would chew it all over with Robin and Robin would check in with her. She'd texted to let him know what had happened. It wasn't ideal, adding worries to his load, but he'd want her to be honest.

She'd contacted *Icon* too. She still wanted to big up Saltwater Cottages as best she could, but she'd asked to write Nena's obituary as well. She hoped to goodness interviewing her contacts would lead to her killer. She certainly wasn't going to leave it to Palmer. The sooner the case was solved, the quicker everyone would feel safe. And the more chance Simon had of saving Saltwater. Not to mention the stables and his and Polly's home. The thought of him losing all three was devastating.

10

The Saltwater Cottages guests gradually dispersed. Viv was heading straight to Simon's.

'Are you coming?'

'Soon. But I want to catch Jamie. I didn't emphasise his odd behaviour to Palmer – you know what he's like – but I've just texted Greg about it. I felt I had to. He's promised he'll treat the information sensitively. I'd like to talk to Jamie before the police put him on his guard. Being on the desk is his alibi last night. If he left, I need proof.'

Viv nodded. 'All right.'

But when Eve reached the front desk, it was deserted. She looked left and right. Maybe Jamie had nipped to the bathroom. Taking a deep breath, she dived behind the counter and looked around, trying to stay calm. If he'd been away from his post last night for half an hour or more, what might give him away?

She whisked through the pages of his notebook, taking photos to analyse later. There was no time now. He might return any second. She doubted there'd be anything telling, but she was desperate to do something concrete.

As she closed the pad, she noticed indentations on the top page. Two numbers, four and six. She sighed quickly. It probably meant nothing. He might have rested a sticky note there to take down a phone number. She recorded the information anyway.

Under the counter, she could see several sets of keys. Bunches for each of the cottages, the bar and restaurant, and the offices. It was hardly the most secure set-up. She'd have to warn Simon.

She heard a creak. The door to the men's bathroom was opening. Eve caught her breath and ducked out from behind the desk.

Just in time. It was Jamie, on his way back. His face was pinched and troubled.

He rushed up to her. 'I'm sorry, are you all right?'

He looked just as concerned as Iggy.

Eve nodded. 'It's a horrible shock, but I'm okay, thanks. How about you?'

'Yes, me too.' He put his hands over his face. 'You know how I felt about her. I wish I hadn't had that outburst.'

His words came back to Eve. *If there was any justice in this world, she'd get what's coming to her.* He'd called her an abomination.

When she didn't reply, Jamie stumbled on: 'Not liking her doesn't make it any less shocking, somehow.'

'I know she used to live around here. Did you grow up together?' She wondered how long he'd hated her for. It was probably down to her affair with Liam, but you never knew.

He glanced away. 'I'm a bit younger than she was. We didn't really overlap. Tess knew her a bit. I was the kid brother no one wanted hanging around.' He laughed but it sounded unnatural.

'I've pitched to write her obituary. It'll be useful to get everyone's memories. Speaking to people who disliked her is just as important as talking to her fans. It means I can paint a truer picture.'

His eyes were far away. 'She was a wild child. Allowed to get away with a lot, which probably explains the way she behaved as an adult.' His voice shook slightly as he spoke. He couldn't disguise his feelings, even now she was dead. 'When her parents split, they both wanted her love. They gave her everything and more.'

'She was a poor little rich girl?'

But Jamie shook his head. 'No. She didn't have that excuse. The material goods weren't in place of affection. Her parents adored her. But I remember Mum saying there was a bit of desperation about it. They'd buy her expensive presents, take her on foreign trips. Each of them trying to trump the other.' He closed his eyes for a second. 'Mum said it was unhealthy. Of course, there was no way she could do the same for us, and Dad was never going to.'

It was hard if you didn't have enough, but Eve agreed with Jamie's mum.

She could see how emotional he was. It made her all the keener to know if he'd lied about the cause of his breathlessness.

She smiled and watched him closely. 'No more double-booking scares today?'

Confusion. 'What?' But then his expression cleared. 'Oh. Last night, you mean? Of course. No, no more.'

He'd been thrown, but he could have forgotten, given the momentous events since. She'd get back home. Have a look at the photos she'd taken of his notes. Work through what she knew and see if anything came clear.

'You must have seen Nena leave last night, I suppose?'

Jamie turned a shade paler. 'I guess I went to the bathroom at some point. I didn't see her.'

It might be a coincidence, but if so the timing had been lucky. More likely Nena had wanted to depart in secret – which would make sense if she was meeting Liam – or Jamie *had* seen her, followed her and killed her. She looked at his boyish face, which morphed between friendly openness and a fierce fury each time Nena was mentioned. It would be terrible, whoever had killed her, but she really hoped it wasn't him.

'You weren't away from your desk for a stretch at any point?'

He flushed.

She was pushing it now. She hoped he wouldn't guess her thoughts. 'I'm asking for Simon really. Trying to find anyone who went further afield and might have seen something.'

He swallowed. 'No, I'm afraid not. The only time I was gone for longer was around half ten, after the bar staff left. It's my job to check everything's in order and lock up. But I can't have been away longer than ten minutes. The bar was deserted at that point. Gemma, Iggy and Sadie went in later for a nightcap.'

She was sure he was hiding something. He'd never win at poker. 'Did Nena often go walking late at night?'

Jamie shook his head. 'Not after eleven, like everyone's saying. Not that I saw.'

Perhaps she had been meeting someone, then. Eve turned her attention to the other key players. She ought to have the time of death by the following day. Greg and Robin would see to that. She'd need to check alibis and disprove them if she could.

'I'd love to talk to Liam and Tess. Do you think you could book me in for provisional appointments tomorrow morning? As old friends of Nena's they'll be invaluable for the obituary. I'd like to interview Sadie too.'

Jamie frowned. 'Of course. I've got your number if we need to rearrange. But Sadie didn't know Nena well. She's new to the area.'

But Eve knew better. The secret link was high on her list of things to investigate. 'I want to ask her some questions about the courses for the other article I'm writing. But I'd like to talk to everyone who knew Nena. Iggy's another to add to the list.' If he and Liam had both been sleeping with her, it would be highly significant.

'Okay. I'll let them know.' He spoke slowly, as though the situation was sinking in. 'Poor Simon. This will hit him hard.' He swallowed. 'And the rest of us too, perhaps.'

If he'd killed without thinking of that, it had clearly hit home now. Crowds of journalists were amassing at the entrance to Saltwater End, held back by the police.

11

It was mid-afternoon by the time Eve and Gus got back to Elizabeth's Cottage. The Saltwater staff with rooms at the venue were staying put. Everyone else had been asked to go home. Jamie would be stuck with his spendthrift dad 24/7, leaving Tess with Liam at Saltwater End. Eve's neighbours, Sylvia and Daphne, had never been residents. They were in Hope Cottage as usual, the only other dwelling on Eve's tiny road, Haunted Lane.

Viv and Robin had both been on the phone. She'd heard the tension in Robin's voice. She knew he wanted to be in two places at once, but the case in London was reaching a climax. If they wound up the gang it could save hundreds of lives. He promised to pass on news from Greg as soon as he had it.

Viv's was the hardest call to take. Simon was in bits. He'd had to tell the bank that all his clients were being sent home and there was no firm date for Saltwater to reopen. And of course, he still needed to pay everyone.

'*He was crying.*' Viv was too. '*Full on sobbing. I've never seen him like that. I feel so helpless. He still hasn't told Polly about the financial problems either. I can see it's hard when she's away, but he's left it too long now. The secret's got out of hand.'*

Eve had been worried that might happen. She refused to let this ruin Simon and cause misery for Viv. 'What do you say to bringing Simon round here? We could invite Sylvia and Daphne too, if he doesn't mind them knowing the trouble he's in.' She might have news from Robin before they'd finished. She'd finally admitted to Viv and her closest friends that he got inside information. She knew she could trust them. 'We won't let this beat us.'

Gus, who'd simply heard her list his favourite people, was skipping about as though she was planning a party. Outside, pounding rain lashed the window, mirroring Eve's inner feelings.

She heard a text alert from down the line. *'That's Simon,'* Viv said. *'He's keen. He says you can tell the others about his debts.'*

'I'll get the kettle on.'

Eve rang Sylvia and Daphne next. They offered to bring cakes from Monty's. *'I only wish we could do something more meaningful,'* Daphne said, before hanging up.

Viv would argue that there were few things more meaningful than cake.

When they were assembled, Eve felt bad for making Simon sit amongst them. As though she'd exposed him – someone who never normally ran into trouble.

'We need to work together.' Eve poured them drinks, handing around the sloe gin spice cakes her neighbours had brought. She'd heated them in the oven. They were comforting like that. 'The sooner this is solved, the sooner you can get back on track, Simon. I'd guess this killing was very personal and once the truth comes out, it won't reflect on your business.'

He took a deep breath. 'Thanks. It's ironic to think I wanted Saltwater Cottages to be on everyone's lips.'

They discussed everything they knew. 'We need the time of death,' Eve said. 'Then we can zone in on people whose alibis look shaky. Anyone at Saltwater could have killed her but my money's on one of the key contacts we've identified.'

'You're writing off Edgar Horace?' Viv asked.

'I guess it's possible he was angry enough to kill if he'd heard Nena ridiculing him, but my instinct says no. He might have demanded a meet-up so they could have it out, but the murder looks impromptu. And if he didn't set out to kill, why see her in the woods? My hunch is none of the guests are likely because they'd only just met her.'

Viv nodded.

'The latest information I've got is on Jamie.' Eve relayed their conversation.

'I suppose we can't discount him,' said Viv.

Eve WhatsApped them the photos she'd taken of his notes. She warned Simon about the keys behind the front desk too, vulnerable whenever reception was empty. 'The evidence I gathered was a bit random. I was working at speed, but I'm uneasy about Jamie. He told me he was panicking last night because he thought he'd made a double-booking, but the excuse is odd. He's the night manager. How many people call between ten p.m. and seven a.m. to register for a course?'

'Maybe Jamie transfers online reservations into a booking calendar?' said Daphne hesitantly.

But Simon shook his head. 'It's automated. The system would prevent a double-booking.'

'So it is odd,' Viv said.

'Some people clearly call late, though.' Sylvia was peering at her phone. 'There's a note about a potential booking in the pictures you just sent. The details were taken down last night, according to the date and time.'

Eve scrolled through. She hadn't had time to look. There it was.

12th Nov, 23.35 – Melanie Blomquist (??) interested in print-making course.

It was followed by a London phone number and the words 'from 15/11'. If Jamie had taken that call, he couldn't have made it to Blind Eye Wood afterwards, killed Nena then arrived back breathless by 11.55 or so, when Eve had seen him.

But had he taken the call? 'I wonder why he didn't check the spelling of her name. You'd think he would, if he spoke to her in person.'

Daphne leaned forward, looking all the more worried. 'That's a point. And it's not like him. He's bright. Helpful and considerate too.'

Eve turned to Simon. 'What do you think of Jamie?'

He pulled himself from his reverie. 'He's a true professional.'

Sylvia shot Eve a sidelong glance. 'You think he might have taken the message off the answerphone?'

Eve nodded. 'I wondered.'

'But it doesn't help much.' Simon sank down in his chair again. 'He could have nipped to the loo and missed the call.'

Eve sighed. 'The time of the message was twenty minutes before I found him out of breath, but you're right. It doesn't prove anything.'

'And I can't believe he'd kill anyone,' Daphne said.

Eve met her gaze. 'Not even on the spur of the moment? After trying to reason with Nena over her affair with Liam? He and Tess are very close, and I'm afraid he hated Nena.' She repeated what he'd said about her.

Daphne looked uneasy.

At that moment, Eve's mobile rang. Robin. She took the call

up the cottage stairs so they could talk privately. After that, they exchanged everything they knew. Eve cross-checked her findings with what Greg had told Robin and they tossed out theories. When she finally managed to ask about his case, he was tight-lipped. '*We need more information.*'

'You will be careful, won't you?' The crimes he was investigating involved vast sums of money. The criminals would kill without a second thought to avoid losing out, never mind jail.

'*Always. But it's you I'm worried about.*'

Back downstairs, her friends looked up as she appeared in the doorway.

'The pathologist says Nena died between ten p.m. and two a.m. She was last seen in her suite at eleven twenty, and it takes fifteen minutes to jog to where she was killed, so in reality, she must have died sometime between eleven thirty-five and two.'

'The upshot is, Sadie, Gemma and Iggy are out of it. They alibi each other and they're not closely connected. There's a back door and Iggy went out for a cigarette at around one, but he says he wasn't gone for more than a couple of minutes and the others back that up. I've noted all the timings and they agree with the gossip I heard earlier.

'So our mission's quite clear. Liam, Tess and Jamie are the most likely killers. We need to break their alibis.

'It'll be hard when it comes to the Norlands. They were holed up in their suite, according to them. And despite the affair, I believe I've already heard Liam lie for Tess. I doubt I'll be able to change his story if the police haven't managed it. I don't know about Tess, though. She might come clean eventually if he's guilty.' She thought of her lacerating the print of Liam and Nena. 'Either way, they're telling the same story at the moment. If one of them did it, perhaps they want to stay together despite everything. Or it could be self-interest, or because they were in it together.'

Viv leaned forward. 'And the timings?'

'Either of them could have left their room after Gemma saw them with Sadie at eleven fifteen. Or maybe it's Jamie and he left the front desk. I'm now seriously wondering if he did.'

Viv's eyes were round. 'How come?'

'Gemma said she remembered seeing him on her way to the bar at eleven fifteen. So far so good. But after that there's a question mark. Sadie passed reception at around eleven forty-five, also en route to the bar. She claims she can't remember if Jamie was there.' Eve had been suspicious when Robin relayed this, but Sadie had claimed that sort of detail wouldn't register. 'And a witness has come forward to say he found the front desk empty at that time. So, Jamie was definitely missing ten minutes before I arrived and ten minutes after the phone call from Melanie Blomquist. If I'm right, and that was an answerphone message, then he could have been away for a stretch.

'If Jamie killed Nena, he'd have to have left reception by around eleven twenty to get back in time to hand me my aspirin. It would fit with him following Nena if she'd left her room just after she was last seen.'

They all looked at each other.

'Another thing of note is that the police don't believe Nena climbed out of her window. It was locked when they examined her room. And there's one more thing, too. Liam's changed his story about the cut on his hand. He must have realised the excuse he gave me was questionable. He told the police he caught it on a Stanley knife in his toolbox.'

The lie had to mean something.

12

Early on Tuesday morning, Eve walked Gus on the beach. She'd wanted to wake herself up after a patchy night, but it was almost too much of a good thing, with gale-force winds blowing.

Back at home, she rejoiced in the warmth of Elizabeth's Cottage. Her safe, snug bolthole. It made her think of Simon and the threat to his home. It was time to get to the bottom of this terrible episode.

She took her tea and toast to the dining room and got to work on some background research. In the past, she'd found digging into a victim's life, their friends and foes, joys and fears, had unlocked clues as to how they'd died.

Eve was already intrigued by Nena's upbringing. She was a child who'd been deeply loved by her warring parents according to Jamie. They'd been scared to lose her and had vied for her attention with extravagant presents alongside love. How must that have affected Nena? Had they tried to keep their fear-driven rivalry from her? Either way, Eve was sure she'd have sensed it. Children weren't fools.

She looked back at the notes she'd made. If Nena's parents

had been so desperate to hold on to her, why had she ended up with that friend of her mother's for six months?

She reread the article she'd found previously but there were no details. She'd want to talk to Nena's parents anyway, as well as close friends. She began to search for leads, and found that Nena's father was dead. He'd suffered a heart attack when she was twenty-two. Her mother was still living though, and still in Suffolk. She'd reverted to her maiden name, Lamb, following her divorce. Eve found photos of Nena in *Vogue*, pictured at the mother's home, just outside the village of Great Glemham. It wasn't far. Thoughts of the police, passing on the worst possible news, filled Eve's head. Losing a child was too painful to contemplate.

She closed her eyes for a moment, shook her head, and ploughed on. Work was a good antidote. Ms Lamb's house was easy to find.

She glanced down at Gus, who sensed her attention and shifted to meet her gaze, his collar clinking. 'There's no privacy any more. I bet Ms Lamb is being doorstepped by journalists as we speak. She'll be fed up with the entire breed by the time I get to talk to her. But at least I've got her address.'

Eve wrote the poor woman a letter expressing her sympathy and asking if she might be willing to share her memories of Nena. She included links to her work, in the hope of showing she wasn't gutter press. She'd send the letter first class that day. Give her time to consider her response.

After that, Eve searched for old friends of Nena's. She wanted someone who'd seen her transition from a youth into an adult. Iggy, Liam, Jamie and Tess fitted the bill of course, but it would be useful to speak to someone from a different setting.

After trawling Facebook and Instagram, she lit on an art-school friend who looked promising. She was a professional now, and could comment on Nena's career as well as her character. One call told Eve the friend was out of the country, but her agent promised to contact her as soon as they could. Eve hoped it wouldn't be long.

After that, she mapped out a trajectory of Nena's life, from her comfortable childhood at a grand house just outside Saxford, to her parents' split when she was five, to her art-school days and leap to fame. Her drink- and probably drug-fuelled parties. The strings of awards and lovers. The blazing headlines and camera flashes reflected in Nena's dark glasses. Eve couldn't imagine the pressure of living like that, but she wondered if Nena had enjoyed it. She'd welcomed the publicity that went with having her tyres slashed. She even looked amused in photos captured with a long lens. As though she'd known the paparazzi's game and was one step ahead of them.

As Eve worked, she got a text from Jamie.

I've told Liam and Tess you'll want to talk to them for Nena's obituary. They should be around if you want to head over. Sadie can't see you today. Police and legal stuff. Iggy's helping her, though you might catch him in passing.

It made sense that Sadie would be busy. All the same, Eve could imagine her trying to avoid the interview, given her secret connection with Nena. Eve would request an appointment for tomorrow. Sadie might have an alibi but she also had some explaining to do. Whatever she was hiding could be relevant. There was still a chance that Nena had thrown the brick and the secret had been Sadie's. She'd liked mind games. But of course, Sadie couldn't have killed her.

No. Talking to Liam, Tess and Jamie was most pressing, given the time of death. If she could break their alibis, she'd be much further ahead. She might not rate her chances with the Norlands, but Jamie was another matter. She texted him back, asking to interview him too. She offered to call on him at home.

There was a long pause before he replied.

It might not be the best day to visit.

He could be stalling, like Sadie, but perhaps his dad made things awkward. Simon had called him a dysfunctional drunk. Poor Jamie.

Perhaps I could buy you supper at the Cross Keys? Any time will do.

He must be shattered. He'd been working overtime on Monday, after being up all night on duty. But she had to push. It was too important not to.

After another long pause, Jamie replied.

Okay. Thanks. A drink at the Cross Keys will do. I don't need you to buy me a meal. Six okay?

She texted back to confirm, squirming. It looked as though she'd offended him with the offer of free food. Once again, she thought of the future. Of Simon having to make his staff redundant. What would Jamie do then?

13

Eve walked to Saltwater Cottages. It wasn't far and she needed time to get her thoughts in order. She was planning to target Liam first. She couldn't get past the cut he'd lied about on his hand. There was a thin line between love and hate and she sensed he'd been teetering on it. She wanted to push him further, get him talking about his movements on Sunday night, see if she could catch him out.

She was focused on the second anomaly she'd identified too: the unanswered knock Gemma had heard on Tess and Liam's door shortly before 10.40. Liam had said categorically that Tess hadn't left their rooms that night.

In reality, he couldn't know if he hadn't been there himself. And Nena couldn't have been killed before 11.35 anyway, so why lie about it? Either of them could have committed murder after their chat with Sadie at 11.15. That was the key time. Lying about their comings and goings beforehand was an unnecessary risk.

Eve could only conclude Liam's reasons for doing so must be pressing. Maybe he and Tess had been up to something together, despite their differences. Tess had hated Nena and perhaps Liam had too, by the end.

As she neared Curlew Cottage, she bumped into Tess.

Her loosely waved blonde hair was covered in water droplets, thanks to the air, thick with damp. She let it fall over her face and behaved as though she hadn't noticed Eve, but Eve had seen her flinch slightly.

Jamie would have explained Eve wanted to interview her about Nena. Guilt could explain her reluctance.

'Hello, Tess.'

The print teacher looked up at last. 'Oh, hello.' Her surprise was badly acted. 'Are you on your way to reception?'

'I was, but I'd love to talk to you, if I may? I expect Jamie explained that I'm writing Nena's obituary. It would be great to hear from everyone who knew her. Can I buy you a coffee if the bar's open? Or we can just sit there and chat.' Whatever happened, she couldn't let Tess wriggle out of it.

She hesitated, but then her shoulders drooped. 'The bar staff are taking paid leave, but you can come to our suite. We've got coffee.'

'Thanks. I'm sorry to bother you when things are so awful. It's always hard, having to go in with questions when a tragedy is so fresh.'

Tess shook her head. 'Nena and I weren't close.'

No surprises there.

'But this job seemed like the answer to my dreams, and now...'

It was a powerful reason for her *not* to have killed Nena, but Tess's passion could have overridden practicality. She'd been consumed by it; you could tell that from the print she'd destroyed. She might have arranged to have it out with Nena in private then lost control. If Liam had guessed what she'd done, he might lie for her. He wouldn't want his affair to come out or to lose his job and accommodation.

Eve imagined a stand-off in the woods. Nena laughing at Tess's distress. Telling her she could make Liam do anything she wanted. Tess cracking. Snatching up the log and in one movement swinging it up, smashing it against Nena's head. Catching her on the temple, bringing her down. Quaking with fear and horror at the damage she'd already caused. Then finishing the job in desperation.

Tess led Eve into Curlew Cottage and up the stairs. She opened the door to a set of rooms: a smartly finished sitting room with a kitchen-diner off it. Through another doorway, Eve could see a king-size bed with crisp white linen and a slate-grey throw. Simon had taken care over the staff quarters.

Tess made espressos and they sat on a stylishly low sofa. Eve thought it was impractical, but each to their own. A tall side window looked out over the adjacent cottage. The oppressive, grey day had settled like a blanket over Saxford.

'Like I said, I didn't know Nena well,' Tess began.

'I wondered if she'd sat for you.' Eve had to say it. 'Wasn't it Nena in the print you destroyed?'

Tess went very still. 'You're mistaken.'

But Eve knew she wasn't. Nena's hair and bone structure had been distinctive and Tess was too good an artist. 'Your brother mentioned you and Nena were contemporaries.'

'It's true, we hung around in a group in the school holidays. We were all of an age, though Nena went to a fee-paying place nearby, unlike the rest of us. Our gang divided up into the more conventional sorts and the hellraisers.'

'And Nena fell into the latter category?'

Tess nodded, her nails digging into the palm of her hand. 'She and Liam used to dare each other to do outrageous things.'

'What kind of stuff?'

'Selfish, stupid adventures. Stealing someone's boat from the yacht club. Climbing the church tower at Wessingham. On the outside.'

It was one of the highest locally. It would be Eve's idea of hell.

'Joyriding.' She cast her eyes down. 'The first time, I was terrified Liam's dad would blow a fuse. But in fact, he egged Liam on, as though it was a manly way to behave. Iggy got more flak for being less of an idiot.'

It sounded as though the dad had driven a wedge between the brothers back then, building on their differences.

Tess sighed. 'It was my mother-in-law who worried over Liam. She and his dad are both dead now. They had their kids late.'

'I guess Liam's wild side appealed to you?'

Tess flushed. 'I was young when we first went out.'

But she wasn't so young now. 'I'm glad it worked out for you.' Eve let the sentence hang.

'Liam's grown up, of course. He's different now his dad's not around. Not so much to prove, I guess.'

He might not go joyriding these days, but he was still after thrills and Tess knew that. 'Were Liam and Nena dating back then?' It was a natural question.

'Not according to them.' She took a deep breath.

'But they were close childhood friends, obviously. And they were still close these days.' She had to push it. She needed Tess to give herself away.

'Nena didn't have friends. You have to treat people as equals for that. That certainly didn't apply to Liam!' She took a sharp breath.

Eve thought back to her husband trying to distance himself from Nena then falling for her charms all over again. She could see him losing patience with himself and taking it out on her. If he hadn't cared about upsetting his mother, nor about cheating on Tess, then he probably wasn't a very nice person.

'But I'm not saying Liam and Nena were enemies,' Tess put in, her words hurried.

'I wasn't imagining Liam might be guilty for a moment.' *Like heck.* 'But I do wonder who killed her. It's scary, interviewing for an obituary after a murder. I know I'm likely to quiz the killer. I was in the bar until it closed, so I didn't see anything suspicious in the run-up to the death. Did you spot anything? When you went out earlier that night, I mean?' Nena had been killed later, but she wanted to know why Liam had lied about that earlier part of the evening.

Tess appeared to make every effort to look confused. 'I didn't go out earlier.'

Eve feigned surprise. 'Oh. Only someone mentioned they'd knocked on your door and there was no reply.'

There was a long pause. She saw Tess swallow. 'That's odd. Who told you?'

'I can't remember now.' She sensed Gemma wasn't the sort to forgive if Eve dropped her in it. 'It was during the hubbub as we waited to talk to the police.'

Tess's frown deepened. 'I'd taken a sleeping pill. I do remember hearing the knock now, but I let it go. It must have been late-ish?'

There was a definite questioning note to her voice. She was feeling her way.

'Around twenty to eleven, I think they said.'

'It was an odd time to call. I didn't feel like getting up to answer.'

Eve agreed about the timing, but Tess taking a sleeping pill sounded unlikely. It would explain her going quiet, as reported by Gemma, but she'd have to have settled down the instant Liam left, which seemed odd given Tess's upset. Besides, she'd been up again thirty-five minutes later, talking to Liam and Sadie on the landing.

Eve mentioned it.

Tess looked defeated. 'It wasn't a restful evening. Sadie's lovely, but she lives the job. She wanted to ask about an equipment request I'd put in. Liam will have to sort the installation, so it involved both of us. I went back to bed as soon as she left and stayed there.'

How could she disprove that? There was no obvious way to trip Tess up. She needed a witness who'd seen her later on, or some other leverage.

As for Sadie's visit, the whole thing sounded utterly fictitious.

Eve had Sadie pegged as the caller who'd got no answer, too. If so, she'd made two urgent attempts to talk to Liam, Tess, or both. There had to be a reason behind it, but Eve couldn't see it yet.

They were interrupted by a knock at the door. Sadie. Her eyes met Eve's briefly over Tess's shoulder, then she whispered something and Tess moved onto the landing, pulling the door almost shut behind her.

Eve hesitated a moment, still bothered by Tess's story of the sleeping tablets. Gut instinct said it was baloney, but she'd rather know for sure.

She peered at the almost-shut apartment door. Delaying would only make it worse. Decision made, she rose and slipped through to Tess and Liam's bedroom. Her breath shortened as she went, adrenaline kicking in immediately. She wished she could stay calm.

No sign of sleeping tablets on either of the bedside tables.

She glanced back through the doorway but she could still hear Tess and Sadie murmuring outside.

Checking the en suite felt like a big risk, leaving more distance to cover if Tess came back. She could say she'd needed the bathroom, but the excuse would feel transparent.

She went for it anyway and slid the medicine cabinet door open. No sleeping tablets there either.

Darting back to the bedroom, she pulled open the drawer of the bedside table with night cream on top. Another dead end when it came to the pills. But there, underneath a paperback, was Tess's diary.

Eve swallowed. With every second, the chances of being discovered increased, and it would be horribly intrusive to look.

But justice was at stake, as well as Simon's business, his future well-being and that of every member of staff, from the stables to the cottages.

She grabbed the journal, flicking to the correct month, then fumbling for the right date.

The pages for the last ten days were blank. Before that, the entries were enthusiastic. All about lesson planning and interactions with her students. The only signs of trouble were mentions of her parents. Concern for her mum and how challenging the nursing home fees were. And regret for Jamie at having to lodge with his dad while she stayed in comfort at Curlew Cottage. And then suddenly, the entries had stopped.

She might have been busy, but Eve guessed that first blank day was when she'd found out about Liam and Nena. She'd probably felt too upset to note her feelings. It was only a hunch, but it was how Eve had felt when her husband walked out.

She was putting the diary back, on borrowed time, when she noticed something further down in the drawer. The edge of a photo. She pulled it out.

It was of Iggy. How many women kept a photo of their brother-in-law in their bedside drawer?

Eve caught her breath as she realised the tone of Sadie and Tess's words had changed. Their voices were louder, less guarded. They were winding up their chat.

Eve replaced the photo, pushed the drawer closed with her hip and darted back to the sofa. She probably looked as breathless and pink as Jamie had, the night of Nena's murder.

14

After her interview with Tess, Eve walked up and down Saltwater End, looking for Liam. Trying to find him was frustrating, though it gave her the chance to work off her adrenaline. She'd caught Iggy on reception, who'd directed her to the end cottage, which apparently needed maintenance. She hadn't found Liam there, and had a sneaking suspicion he was avoiding her on purpose. The fact made her more determined. She didn't ask Iggy to call him – it would only give him a chance to make excuses.

In the end, she walked Gus up the lane as though she was going home. She managed to get him to sit quietly in the staff car park and watched from there. Liam appeared two minutes later.

Ha! Got you! She intercepted him. 'Hello! I was just giving Gus one more walk round before we tried to find you again.'

There was a brief flash of anger in his eyes but after a moment he gave a grunt of resignation. 'We might as well sit in the bar.'

Iggy made them coffees, smiling at Eve as he set them down. Eve was grateful for the drinks. It made the situation feel slightly less formal. Once Iggy had retreated, Eve saw him through the doorway, talking to Gemma.

She turned her attention to Liam. Gus had rolled over to have his tummy tickled and, unexpectedly, the custodian obliged.

'We had an Alsatian at home. Dad's. He was an old softie. Just like this one here. Iggy was scared of him when he was little.' He laughed. He couldn't seem to resist being mean about his brother. A moment later, he gave Gus a final pat and sat up straight, his eyes cold as he faced Eve. 'What do you want to know?'

Eve started with non-controversial questions: what Nena had been like growing up, and what they'd got up to together.

As he talked, her attention was momentarily caught by Iggy and Gemma again. They were still visible down the corridor and Sadie had joined them. She'd bustled up, her mouth moving quickly, her expression intense. She couldn't be nagging them for slacking; they'd only been there a couple of minutes. Iggy looked serious and a moment later they dispersed.

Eve's attention snapped back to Liam. 'Do you remember Nena's boyfriends? It would be good to speak with anyone who's still local.'

Liam gave a hollow laugh. 'There were countless conquests.'

'Who was her favourite? Anyone she really fell for?'

Eve could see the hard look in his eye, as though he was reining in his feelings. She guessed he'd been jealous of each and every one.

'No one who lasted, so she couldn't have been that keen. I can't remember their names now. They weren't the sorts to stick in my mind.' His voice was full of derision.

'Not to worry, it was just a thought. It must have been fun to discover you'd all be working together.'

Liam nodded, his jaw tight.

She felt the strength of their love–hate connection. 'Was it you who suggested inviting her?'

'Good grief no.' The moment he said it, he snapped his mouth shut, as though he regretted his words.

'Why? You didn't like her?'

He took a deep breath. 'It wasn't that. Someone put her forward before I arrived. But she tended to complicate things.'

No more than you did, when you embarked on your affair. Eve thought of Tess's anxious eyes and her own ex-husband's betrayal. She wanted to hold Liam to account, but it would be counterproductive at this stage. 'I had the impression you were quite close.'

He glanced at her quickly. She could feel his dislike. 'I don't know what gave you that idea.'

She was longing to say it was the kissing. 'You know what Saxford's like. Gossip is rife.'

He grunted.

'So you don't know who suggested inviting her?'

Liam shrugged. 'Sadie maybe?'

Sadie, who'd seemed in her thrall. But she had an alibi.

'It's a horrible thing, isn't it? Utterly appalling for Nena and her family, and hard for Simon and all of you too. Do you have any idea who might have wanted her dead? Simon's desperate to get a handle on it all. He's my best friend's brother. We're both trying to lend a hand.'

Liam's steady gaze met hers. 'I couldn't say. She sailed close to the wind. I suppose someone lost control and that was that.'

Implying it was her fault. Plenty of people could be aggravating, Liam included. It wasn't normally considered acceptable to hand down a death sentence in response. Eve's blood was simmering nicely. 'You didn't see anything earlier in the evening, I suppose? Where did you go when you did your rounds?' She was convinced Tess had lied about that period. She wanted to know if Liam would too.

He twisted his signet ring. 'I went from Sandpiper Cottage, along the row and then back to Curlew Cottage at the end. I didn't see anything unusual.'

Eve sighed and tried to come across as grateful and trusting. 'I knew it was a long shot. What about Tess when she went out?'

Liam stiffened. 'She didn't.'

Eve feigned surprise again. 'Oh, sorry. It's just that one of your neighbours mentioned you were both out.'

His frown deepened. 'And how would they know that?'

'They heard someone knocking on your door, and no one answered.'

Liam leaned back in his chair and folded his arms. 'Tess mentioned someone knocking,' he said, after a long pause. 'She was in the shower, that's all. She couldn't come to the door.'

They had to be lying. 'Ah, I see.'

She mentioned Sadie's chat on the landing next. Liam told the exact same story as Tess. Could Sadie really have been asking about printing equipment? She couldn't see it. But she assumed Sadie would back their story. They wouldn't tell it otherwise. So either it was true, or all three of them had agreed to lie. *Very odd.*

She looked pointedly at Liam's hands. He was still twisting his ring, over and over.

He stopped. 'It was my dad's,' he said at last. 'I'm forever fiddling with it, but I like to keep it on. Good man, my father.'

'It's a lovely ring.' She had to try to find common ground. 'My partner wears one of his dad's too.' Liam still had the bandage on his hand. She nodded at it. 'How's the injury?'

His knowing look made her feel uncomfortable. 'Almost healed. Thanks for asking.'

'It must be hard, working with an axe. So heavy.' She visualised him lifting it. He'd hoisted Nena's huge rug as though it were a roll of wrapping paper. He was strong. He'd pick up a branch and swing it as though it were a twig.

'It keeps me fit.'

He could probably run to and from the burned oak in Blind Eye Wood without breaking a sweat. But if he was the killer, she still couldn't see him throwing the brick. How did it all fit together?

'So you didn't see anything odd near the car park when you began your rounds? Someone loitering or anything like that? Someone could have approached along the heath path if the killer's an outsider.'

'No.' Liam's eyes darkened. 'I told you. Nothing.'

'And you didn't leave your room later – and see anyone then?'

He didn't break eye contact. 'Absolutely not.'

Her adrenaline was going again as she left. Liam had only just kept his temper, but the interview had been useful.

She was almost certain he hadn't done his rounds the evening Nena died. When he'd talked her through them, he'd said he'd started at Sandpiper Cottage. That was at the far end of the lane from the car park. Yet when she'd reiterated the route, deliberately reversing it, he hadn't noticed.

Great. She'd done well at shaking his and Tess's alibis, but not for the time when Nena had died.

Eve could imagine either of them losing their temper later that night, but what had they been up to earlier, and why did it matter?

15

While Eve was with Liam, she'd had a text from Simon. The police had vacated Nena's room and would she like to see it?

She texted back immediately to tell him she was on site. He said he'd meet her there in ten minutes.

While she was waiting for him, she found Iggy on the front desk.

As they talked, the photograph she'd discovered in Tess's drawer filled her head. Were they lovers? If so, it might make Tess less likely as a suspect. Presumably Liam's infidelity would lose some of its sting. But the way she'd slashed her print fought with that idea. She'd minded about the affair all right.

'You must all be in shock,' Eve said, 'and I know Sadie must be having an awful time. But I'd still value an appointment with her. Jamie explained today's no good – which I can totally appreciate. But perhaps tomorrow might work. Or any day. Any time.' Maybe she'd agree, once she realised Eve wasn't going anywhere.

Iggy looked tired but he gave her a sad smile. 'Of course. I'll ask her.' He glanced at his screen. 'Things ought to be less frantic tomorrow.'

'It would be great to ask you about Nena too.'

'Sure, if it'll help. Just come and find me here when you're ready.'

'You must be busy as well.'

'I've been ringing around, postponing bookings and fielding cancellations. It would be nice to take my mind off the situation.' He leaned forward. 'We're all wondering what the future holds.'

He fell silent as Simon walked in and Simon was awkward in turn, stumbling over his enquiries after Iggy's well-being. Eve wished they weren't stuck in this situation and that Nena was still alive and strutting her stuff.

Simon gave Eve a quick hug. 'It's good to have so many supportive people around. So, you'd like to see Nena's room for the obituary?'

She smiled at his tact. 'That's right, if it's not too intrusive. I know Nena travelled a lot, but this will give me an idea of the way she lived. Her style.'

'Of course.' Simon led the way, using his keys to open the door to the artist's suite.

'Thanks for coming up with a cover story,' she said, after they'd closed the door.

'I'm afraid the entire staff probably know you've helped the police before.' Simon sighed. 'I heard someone mention it when I came to talk to Inspector Palmer on Monday.'

Not good news. It would make everyone twitchy.

Simon was staring at Nena's bed through an open doorway. 'The police have taken her sheets and pillows.'

Eve wondered about DNA, if they suspected Nena had had a lover, but would she have entertained Liam or anyone else in her suite? She was right opposite the reception desk. Whoever visited stood a good chance of being seen.

Like Tess and Liam, Nena had a sitting room and a kitchen–

diner at her disposal, as well as the bedroom. Gus was making a thorough examination of the place, sniffing in corners, pottering to and fro. The suite was in the oldest part of the building, the sitting-room window in a recess in the wall, a small window seat in front of it.

The decor was different to Liam and Tess's suite too. Opulent. Nena had some period pieces, including the grand but foxed old mirror Viv had mentioned. There was a classic wing-backed armchair too, facing into the room at an angle, close to the mirror. Nena must have been sitting in it when the witnesses spotted her, the night she died.

Eve walked over to the fireplace. She could smell it had been used recently and there was a spent match on the mantelpiece. In an ideal world there would be a half-burned letter in the grate, containing a vital clue, but there was nothing. The fireplace had been cleaned out.

'That's odd.' Simon frowned and Gus looked up. 'The firewood hasn't been delivered yet. It's due in a week. I was worried they couldn't get here sooner. Now I wish I could cancel, but it's too late.'

'Of course, I remember now.' Liam had told her the only firewood they'd had had come from a fallen tree. She gave Simon's arm a squeeze. 'You might need the delivery soon. You'll want to go full steam ahead once Nena's killer's found.'

'If people still want to come.'

'I'm sure they will.' She hoped to goodness she was right. 'So unless Nena brought her own fuel to keep warm, she lit the fire for another reason.'

'I'll ask the cleaners if they remember what was in the grate. Just in case.'

'Good idea.' The answer would probably just be ashes, but you never knew.

She looked down at the wooden floorboards, which were marked with the ink Nena had spilled. If the rug had matched the rest of the room's contents it had probably been expensive. She asked Simon.

He grimaced. 'It's the least of my worries right now, but yes. We took care over this room. I asked for Nena's preferences. Not that she would have been here full time, but she was worth a lot to us for the handful of courses she'd run. I had the impression she'd expect special treatment and I provided it.'

'Fair enough.' Eve wasn't fond of prima donnas, but she could understand Simon's thinking. And of course, Nena had been used to kid-glove treatment from when she was a child. 'Can you remember who suggested inviting her to teach here?' She wondered about Liam, though he'd denied it, or Sadie.

Simon's eyes were anxious. 'No. A whole group of people threw out suggestions over a drink at the pub. And now it seems significant. It felt so unlikely she'd say yes that I wondered why she'd been put forward. But I decided there was no harm in trying.'

Eve wondered if someone had wanted her here to kill her, but the use of the log made the murder seem impromptu and besides, she'd been on site for four weeks already. Why wait until now, if someone had planned her killing back then? 'She's got lots of paints, I see. And an easel.' They were stored in a corner of the large room.

Simon nodded. 'She ordered them in.'

'I wonder what she was working on.' Eve wandered over to two framed paintings on the wall. Oil on board. 'These are hers, aren't they?'

Simon nodded. 'But they don't look like local scenes.'

Eve photographed them for reference. 'And you wouldn't think they'd be up and framed if she'd only just finished them.' She wondered if it was normal for an artist to travel with their works. Perhaps she'd wanted them there for guests to see. 'She didn't ask to have them added to your insurance?'

Simon winced. She could tell she'd added an extra layer to

his anxiety. 'No.'

'I guess she wasn't the type to get bogged down over details. Or maybe she had her own cover.'

The question was, what had she been working on right now? There was no sign of any other oil painting. Yet the oils had been used; the tubes were almost empty. There was no pen and ink drawing she might have been completing when she'd had her spillage either.

Of course, she might have used the ink for letter-writing. Eve suggested it to Simon and they searched the room, but the only notes they found were written in ballpoint. There was no sign of a fountain pen.

'I wonder if the police are considering theft as a motive.'

'You think the killer might have attacked her then come back to steal a painting?'

'It's possible. Of course, she could have sold what she was working on, or given it away, but her works are a big deal. You'd think there'd be gossip about it if she'd made a recent sale or gift. It would be worth asking around.'

'Could she have burned it, if she was dissatisfied with the end result? It would fit with the recent fire. Or she might have destroyed it some other way.'

'I'd imagine she'd have painted over it if she didn't like what she'd done. And I've never tried burning an oil painting, but I'm guessing someone would have noticed the smell. All I can detect here is standard woodsmoke. But she could have got rid of it some other way, I suppose.' Instinct told her it was unlikely.

Simon let out a long breath. 'It would certainly make the killer a lot of money if they stole it. Assuming they could find a buyer.'

'If it was a painting which had never been seen, perhaps they could keep it under wraps for a year or two, then sell it on, without anyone relating it to her murder. I imagine they could fake a receipt or something.'

Nena's latest works had sold for millions.

Simon frowned. 'But if the killer took it, how did they get the painting past Jamie?'

Eve lowered her voice. 'Unless Jamie stole it. You said he and Tess are short of funds, and there's their mother to look after.'

Simon's face fell. 'And their no-hoper of a dad. I've heard in the village that Jamie cleans up after him each morning but by nightfall he's destroyed the place again. Bottles everywhere. Cigarette burns on the furniture. I think Iggy passed Nena's wrecked rug on to Jamie. It might have been damaged but it was better than what he had.' His eyes met Eve's. 'But I know Jamie, Eve. I can't believe he'd kill Nena for money, or for any reason. Can you?'

Eve pictured Jamie's cheery face, then his expression as he'd called Nena an abomination.

'Not if he'd planned it. But what if he followed Nena to remonstrate with her over her affair with Liam? I could imagine him seeing red. He could have picked up the log and lashed out without ever meaning to inflict serious damage. And then, when he realised how badly he'd injured her, he could have finished the job. After that, he might have wondered what he'd find in her room. He's on the desk. He's got master keys, just like you.'

Simon was silent.

'I really like him, but Robin's always telling me likeable people can do terrible things. And he's probably sleep deprived, unless his dad's as quiet as a mouse all day.'

'That I doubt.' Simon rubbed his forehead. 'He's as selfish and volatile as they come.'

'Anxiety might keep Jamie awake too, what with the care-home fees.'

'And his dad's debts.'

He seemed almost primed to snap.

16

After they left Nena's room, Simon took Eve to the deserted bar, found a bowl and some water for Gus, then fetched sandwiches from the fridge. It was late for lunch.

'All this stock will be out of date by the time we can have people back. I'll take the rest to the church hall and put it in the fridge there. The villagers can come and help themselves.'

'That's kind.' It was just like Simon to think of it, despite the trouble he was in. 'Have you heard from Polly recently? How's the US trip going?'

He put his hands over his face. 'Fine. She's worried about Nena's death of course, and we talked about that. But it's just so hard to tell her about the money, Eve. I need to see her face to face so I can gauge her reactions.' He looked so miserable.

'I understand.' She did, yet she knew she'd tell Robin if she were in Simon's position.

After they'd eaten and Eve had updated him on her interviews, she went to find Iggy. She wanted to understand his relationship with Tess. Perhaps Iggy had been comforting her and things had got out of hand. Relationships were complicated. She could still love Liam, yet be involved with his brother too.

But Eve needed facts. Were they in a relationship and had they talked about her leaving Liam? It wouldn't be easy, when they all worked under the same roof, but if they had, then Tess killing Nena from jealousy might be less likely, despite her misery and the print slashing. On top of that, she needed to know why Iggy had followed Nena on Saturday night. It was still possible he was involved with her, instead of, or as well as, Tess. The thought made Eve's head spin.

She found him on the front desk.

'Is now a good time to talk? Unless the phones are busy?'

He gave a rueful smile. 'I'll be glad to switch the system to voicemail for a bit. Let's go to the admin office and talk there.'

They sat in the comfortable padded chairs Simon had provided on either side of a large desk. Gus settled himself at Eve's feet.

Iggy leaned forward. 'What can I tell you?'

She opted for the same approach she'd taken with Liam. Easy questions first.

'It would be great to hear about Nena growing up. And how she'd changed, if she had.'

'You've probably heard she was a wild child.'

Eve nodded. 'And that Liam went to the same extremes she did.'

Iggy's expression hardened as she mentioned his brother. 'I was the "sensible one". A right little goody two-shoes, in my dad's judgement. Most parents would have been glad I wasn't out stealing cars and boats.'

'Did Nena make you feel left out?' His dad clearly had.

'Not really. She tried to include me. She'd have loved me to rebel. She probably saw me as one of her failures.' He laughed. 'She liked everyone dancing to her tune. She'd have admitted that herself.'

'She was very beautiful. Both now and back then, I imagine.'

'For sure. Almost all the guys ran after her.'

'But not you?'

He took a deep breath. 'She wasn't my type.' He shook his head. 'I'm sure that'll sound unbelievable. I don't reckon she'd have looked at me twice anyway.'

'I'm not sure about that. I had the impression she had a soft spot for Liam, and you're very alike.' She saw his expression darken and added quickly, 'Visually, I mean.'

Iggy shrugged. 'Liam and Nena were always close, but as partners in crime, not romantically.'

Did he really not know about their affair? Eve was certain Tess would have told him if she and Iggy were involved. But of course, he might not admit to it if he cared for her. It gave her a prime motive. She let the silence ride.

'Liam's marriage to Tess is a happy one, as far as I know.' The words sounded acted.

'I thought Tess seemed a bit subdued when I turned up.'

He sighed. 'That'll be down to her family situation. Her mum has dementia and her dad... Well, her dad's not the easiest.'

'Tess is an old friend of yours too, I suppose? You grew up together.'

'We did. We went out for a bit. It didn't last, obviously. We were almost too close. Like brother and sister.' His smile had been fond, but now it became grimmer. 'Liam got right in there when we broke up. As you said, similar looks, different personality.'

She sensed it was his brother's behaviour that made him angry, not the split itself. There'd been easy affection when he'd talked of Tess – nothing passionate or intense. Perhaps they weren't involved after all.

Even the photo of Iggy might not be significant. Tess could have been reminiscing after discovering Liam's affair. Thinking how nice it had been to be involved with someone steady and reliable. Eve still believed she could have lashed out at Nena.

'Liam said Nena christened you Iggy.' She sprung the statement on him to get an unguarded reaction. He couldn't have killed Nena – and it would hardly count as a motive – but it was relevant to the person she'd been. And if Iggy knew who'd committed murder, her unkind words might make him more inclined to keep quiet.

Iggy's look turned cool. 'Seriously? Liam managed to slip that into conversation since you got here?' He seemed angrier with Liam than with Nena. But after a moment he sat back in his chair. 'Brothers. Who'd have them? But yes, that's right. Iggy the ignoramus. I suppose he told you he blackmailed me not to tell everyone at uni.'

Put so starkly, it sounded more sinister. Eve nodded and Iggy shook his head.

'It's all true. The girls there loved it, for some reason. The nickname stung at the time, but it's stood me in good stead, bizarrely.'

They talked a little more about Nena's parents, her rise to fame and her approach to teaching.

'Can you remember who suggested inviting her?'

Iggy frowned. 'I think it was Sadie.'

Sadie, with her secret connection to Nena. Why would she invite someone she seemed scared of? But if she'd put her forward, she hadn't done it so she could kill her. Her alibi was unbreakable. And in any case, it was as Eve had thought before – why wait four weeks before going ahead?

'By the way,' Eve met his eye, 'you didn't see anything the night Nena's tyres were slashed, did you? Only I noticed you were following her up Saltwater End when Viv and I found her car had been vandalised.'

Iggy's hesitation was infinitesimal. 'No.' Then after a

moment, he sighed. 'It's frustrating. I was on the lookout, but I was focused on her, not her car.'

'How do you mean?'

At last, he spoke. 'I was uneasy. Nena and I used to chat quite easily. Maybe because we didn't fancy each other. She told me she'd received a note. Typed. Slipped under her door.'

'What did it say?'

'That she deserved to be dead. She didn't take it seriously. She was laughing, if you can believe it.'

Eve swallowed. 'You told the police?'

He reddened. 'I need to. I know that.'

'Who do you think sent it?' If the story was true, she guessed he was protecting someone. She couldn't see it being Liam, given their relationship. Perhaps he thought Tess was responsible. He said they'd been as close as brother and sister.

He didn't meet her eye. 'I've honestly got no idea.'

Eve waited, but he didn't add anything, even in the awkward silence.

'Thanks for talking to me.' She left the room.

She found Gemma standing in reception.

Eve greeted her. 'Can I grab a quick word while I'm here? I'd love your impressions of Nena, as an incomer who hadn't known her long.' That sort of interviewee was always useful. You got a fresh perspective.

Gemma looked as guarded as Liam had. 'Okay. If it's quick.'

The time pressure seemed suspect, given the lack of guests, but she nodded. 'We could take a stroll up the lane if you like. Get some fresh air.' She could tell Gus was getting fed up. He was shooting her accusatory glances.

Gemma sighed. 'All right.'

It wasn't the nicest of days. The wind was high and beyond the heath the angry sea was a roiling mass of grey. They walked up the rutted lane, avoiding the puddles from yesterday's rain.

'I hate this time of year,' Gemma said. 'It feels like everything's dying.' Then she paused. 'Bad choice of words.'

'But true.'

Gemma nodded.

'What did you think of Nena? I'm getting lots of input from people who've known her for years. It's interesting to speak with someone who saw her with fresh eyes.'

Gemma stared towards the woods. 'I didn't take to her. I've been brought up to stand on my own two feet. Fight my corner. Not have everything given to me on a plate by lenient people who fall over themselves to cushion me from life's knocks.' Her tone was brutal.

'Her parents, you mean?'

'Most people, I'd say. Are you asking as a journalist? I've heard rumours about you.'

Eve could imagine. 'I sometimes turn up useful evidence when I write about murder victims, that's all. But you're in the clear. You've got two people to vouch for you.'

Gemma said nothing.

'How do you like Suffolk?' *Why does this have to be so awkward?*

'It's beautiful in a wild sort of way. Especially here on the coast.'

'You've never lived here before?'

Gemma shook her head. After a pause she added, 'My mother moved to the county, like I said before. I wanted to be closer to her, so this job was perfect. Or it seemed that way.' Her tone was ironic.

'I hope the murder's solved soon so that you can—'

Eve was interrupted by Liam, driving towards them, too fast for such a quiet, rough track. His front right tyre hit a puddle and sprayed muddy water over Gemma's trousers.

'Of all the—!' She tugged up her sopping trouser leg.

It was then that Eve saw it. A wound that looked remarkably like a dog bite.

In an instant, Eve was back in Simon's kitchen, with the brick, its message and Simon's neighbour's dog, snarling at the intruder. The dog had got loose, been in Simon's yard, and found a stranger there. Simon had described it as a brute. What were the chances the intruder had escaped without injury?

17

As Gemma wrung out her sopping trousers, Eve asked her about the wound on her leg.

'Some idiot left their crazy dog unattended on the footpath between here and Wessingham. It bounded up out of nowhere, bit me and dashed off.'

The wound had looked angry. 'You got it seen to okay?'

She nodded. 'It didn't need stitches. They just cleaned it up and dressed it. They said to give it some air after a day or two. I'm going to go indoors and change my trousers.'

Eve watched her retreating back. She could have thrown the brick, despite being innocent of Nena's murder. She'd gone into detail about Tess and Liam's movements before Nena was killed. Maybe she'd hoped to hint at some wrongdoing which related to the anonymous note. Liam's affair with Nena perhaps. Tess's upset would fit with that.

Eve wondered who'd tended her wound and when the appointment had been, but pushing further would look odd. She'd visit the doctors' practice instead. Chat to the receptionist. They'd never break confidentiality rules, but she had an idea to get round that.

For now, it was time to nip home. She needed to prepare for her talk with Jamie at the Cross Keys. She was glad that he'd refused dinner now. Viv had texted, demanding a debrief, and they'd arranged to eat together. It would be a relief to relax and bounce ideas around after seeing Jamie. She wasn't looking forward to such a delicate conversation with a likeable neighbour.

She set off up Saltwater End in the dark of early evening, with Gus by her side. The breeze worked its way inside her collar, making her shiver. Looking back at the row of cottages, she wondered about the inhabitants. Thoughts of Sadie's late-evening visit to Liam and Tess crowded her mind, but she was distracted by movement at one of the windows. Gus stilled, his head up. A curtain fell back, but in the split second before it did so, she recognised Iggy. She watched his silhouette dart away, then followed the direction of his gaze and saw Gemma, walking towards the beach. She must have changed her trousers and reappeared. Had Iggy been spying on her?

What was he up to? Something better done when Gemma was out of the building?

On instinct, she skirted Curlew Cottage until she was round the back, below Gemma's windows. Her curtains were closed but the light was on. Eve shivered. Behind the drapes a shadow dashed to and fro. Tall. Sometimes at full height, sometimes bending.

It looked as though Iggy was conducting a frantic search.

An hour later, Eve had showered, changed and checked her messages and emails.

The agent of Nena's art school friend had been in touch. He'd managed to make contact and she could see Eve on Saturday afternoon.

Now, she was ready to tackle Jamie. She'd done plenty of

planning, though thoughts of Iggy, Gemma and the other key players fought for her headspace. She wondered if Iggy had sensed something off about Gemma. Perhaps, like her, he thought she'd thrown the brick through Simon's window. Resolutely, she closed her mind to everything but her next interview.

'I've got more of a chance of breaking Jamie's alibi than Liam and Tess's,' she told Gus. 'At least he was up and about and somewhere public. I want to find out if he took the call from Ms Blomquist, or if he was away from his desk. A witness says he was absent at quarter to midnight and the call came in ten minutes earlier, according to his notes.'

Gus was firmly focused on his supper and gave no sign of listening to a word she said.

'If he was gone for ten minutes, it needs explaining. It's not enough time for him to have killed Nena, but who's to say he didn't dash off for longer? It would be risky, but the murder looked impromptu. It's not as though he'd have been thinking of alibis.'

Gus was pursuing one last bit of food around the bowl, which was now skidding on the kitchen tiles.

At last, he looked up. 'Shall we go and see Hetty then?' She was the pub schnauzer, and the love of Gus's life.

Gus sprang towards the door.

Eve's mind was on how to tackle Jamie. She only knew about the Blomquist call by spying on him. Some creative thinking was called for.

Jamie was sitting at the bar when she entered the Cross Keys. Gus dashed off to greet Hetty, so she was on her own without an appealing dachshund to oil the social wheels.

'What can I get you?' Jamie asked.

She'd been intending to buy but she didn't want to offend him again. 'A Coke would be great.'

He had the same and they decamped to a table.

'Will you be working tonight?'

He shook his head. 'I'm on paid leave until we know what's what. The answerphone will cover any late calls and everything's locked up tight. I don't know what to do with myself, to be honest. I couldn't sleep last night and catching up in the day's no good. My dad's not the quietest of men.' There were deep shadows under his eyes. 'So, you had some extra questions?'

As Eve trotted them out, she was sure he must be wondering why she felt they were so important. The answer, of course, was that she didn't. She was just building up to finding out about the phone call.

'Oh, by the way,' she said at last, 'have you heard from a Melanie Blomquist at all?' She watched Jamie's eyes. There it was. A definite wariness.

'The name does ring a bell.' He was treading carefully, she guessed. Not sure what he was dealing with.

'She's a friend of my mother's.' Eve didn't like lying but murder was a reasonable excuse. She remembered the note in Jamie's log. 'She's in London from tomorrow. Mum said she'd left a message on the Saltwater Cottages answerphone at some weird time of the night.' Eve smiled. 'She's a bit of a character.'

It had to be worth a bluff.

Jamie was frowning. He took a long swig of his Coke before he answered. 'I remember now, but she didn't leave a message. I spoke to her.'

Eve kept eye contact. 'Oh, sorry. I must have misunderstood. I thought she'd asked someone to call her back.'

Jamie shifted in his chair. 'Well, she did. I mean, she needed more information.'

'I thought you knew everything about Saltwater Cottages.' She said it teasingly, in a complimentary way. She was sure she sounded weirdly arch.

He smiled uneasily. 'No offence to Ms Blomquist or to you, but she was a little tricky to deal with. I said I'd pass her query on to Sadie.'

Eve let it go. She'd got the answer she'd been after. Chewing it over with Viv would come next.

18

A short while later, Toby, one of the three co-owners of the Cross Keys, was delivering platefuls of game pie to Eve and Viv.

'Jo's given you extra veg and gravy,' Toby said. 'She says it's because of what happened at Saltwater Cottages.' He smiled and shook his head. 'I think she is aware, deep down, that food can't cure all ills, but it's all she's got.'

Jo was Toby's sister-in-law and fiercely passionate about the food she cooked. In fact, fierce full stop.

'There's a lot of strength to be gained from things like game pie,' Viv said. 'And cake, obviously.'

The food smelled like heaven, and the robust glasses of red they each had were the best accompaniment.

'Have you heard much about the death?' Eve wanted Toby's gossip. It could be valuable.

'People have talked about nothing else. We had the press in here, sniffing around. Jo gave them short shrift, though Matt managed to sell them quite a lot of beer before she sent them packing.' Matt was Jo's husband and Toby's brother. A practical sort. 'We've even got a couple of the Saltwater guests staying here.' Toby lowered his voice. 'A husband and wife. I don't think much of him, to be honest. He's terribly well-to-do, as he keeps telling everyone, but as rude as they come.' He sighed. 'They were due here next week anyway. Now we get them for two! Snob though he is, he's got a thing about traditional country pubs. The whole trip was a birthday present for his wife.' He glanced up cautiously. 'Don't look now. He's coming down the stairs. They'll probably want supper and find something to complain about.'

It was Edgar Horace, who had possibly heard Nena mocking him.

A moment later, he and his wife took a table by the window. Eve was glad they weren't sitting too close.

'So tell me again,' Viv frowned, as Toby left them, 'you think Jamie's lying? That he definitely took Melanie Blomquist's message off the answerphone?'

Eve nodded. 'What's the first thing you think of, when you think of Jamie?'

Her friend shrugged. 'Eager? Helpful? Friendly?'

'All of those things. Yet his notes show he didn't bother checking he'd spelled Ms Blomquist's name correctly. And he told me she was "tricky", so he decided to leave her to Sadie. Can you imagine him doing that? Or even complaining about Ms Blomquist to me? Especially when he thought she was a family friend.'

'In all honesty, no.'

'I believe he was thinking on his feet, but he was too exhausted to manage it well. He certainly wanted me to think he'd spoken to her in person.'

'Why wouldn't he call her back himself?'

'I'll bet he tried. Perhaps he failed to catch her or decided it was too late and would have to wait until morning.'

'So he's trying to hide the fact that he was away from his desk then, as well as ten minutes later?'

'I'm fairly sure of it. So it could mean he was absent from

eleven thirty-five until eleven fifty-five, when I went to reception. It's not enough time to kill Nena, but he could have left earlier. He's certainly acting like someone with a guilty conscience. I'll cross-check what he said about Melanie Blomquist when I speak to Sadie.'

'Good plan. So, Jamie's high on the suspect list.'

'I'm afraid so. He could have stolen a painting too, if one's missing. He needs the money and he, Liam, Sadie and Iggy all have master keys. To say nothing of the sets behind the desk. Though where would he put it?' It was the aspect Eve was least happy with. Nena's pictures were normally large. 'Either way, we know Nena was working on something and assuming it wasn't one of the paintings on the wall, it's disappeared. Sold, gifted, stolen or destroyed? That's the question.' She texted Greg Boles to make the point.

'And what about the other suspects?' Viv said, when she'd finished.

Eve sipped her drink. 'The same motives still stand. Liam, if Nena was threatening to tell Tess about the affair. Tess, from jealousy. She has a photo of Iggy in her drawer, by the way.' Eve explained the discovery. 'But unless the pair of them are in love, I don't think it makes a difference. They went out when they were younger. I could imagine Tess hankering after the old days, having realised what a toad Liam is, but I don't think she and Iggy are involved. His feelings towards her seem fond and calm. I believe it's Liam's behaviour that gets his goat, not losing Tess.

'I'm certain all three suspects have lied to me. Liam about the injury to his hand and the rounds he supposedly did the night Nena died. Tess about not leaving her apartment, and Jamie about the call.' She shook her head. 'I still don't know why Tess and Liam would lie about their movements before Nena was killed. And Sadie's reason for visiting them at quarter past eleven is odd too.' She related Liam and Tess's version of events. 'You'd think a query about printing equipment could wait until morning.

'I wonder now if it was Liam who slashed Nena's tyres, given the cut on his hand. He was angry and finding it hard to break up with her. She received a poison pen letter too, according to Iggy. That could have been part of the same campaign. Perhaps he wanted to frighten her away but it failed. Then his fury spilled over catastrophically the following night in the woods.'

She thought of Iggy and Nena's cosy chats and filled Viv in. 'Iggy claims they could talk easily because there was no sexual tension. That might be true, but it's also possible they were involved, just like Liam and Nena were.'

'Blimey,' Viv said. 'Talk about a tangled web.'

A text sounded on Eve's phone. She pulled it from her pocket, glancing up to check Jo wasn't watching. She hated customers mixing her exquisite cooking with technology. Or with anything, really.

'What? What is it?' Viv must have seen her expression.

'It's Simon. With news.'

'Tell me then!'

Eve explained what they'd seen in Nena's fireplace. 'She'd been burning something but the grate had been cleared out. Simon asked the cleaners if they'd noticed anything interesting in the grate.'

'And had they?'

'They never cleared it. Which means Nena made a very neat job of cleaning it out herself.'

'And she didn't look the domestic sort.'

Eve nodded. 'She must have had good reason to handle it personally.'

What had she been hiding? Nena might have been burning private correspondence, but if it was that sensitive it would be easy enough to make sure it was properly destroyed. She wouldn't need to clear the grate. It was a puzzle. She texted Simon back. 'I've asked for permission to search the bins at Saltwater. If Nena used the fire recently, we might still find traces of what she burned there.'

'Good idea. Though I don't know why you're bothering to ask. He's not exactly going to say no.'

'It's called being polite.'

Viv rolled her eyes. 'You really should loosen up.'

They were finishing their meals when Sylvia and Daphne entered the pub. The pair ordered glasses of brandy, then Eve waved them over.

'What news?' Sylvia loosened her red and green scarf as she sat down.

Eve filled them in, finishing with what she and Simon had seen in Nena's room. 'Could you keep your ears to the ground, see if you hear anything about a recent sale or someone who's been given one of her paintings?'

Sylvia frowned. 'Of course. But if it was gifted, we might never find out.'

Greg could probably determine if she'd sold it. Nena ought to have a very large deposit in her bank account. 'What about if someone stole her painting, do you think they'd manage to sell it?'

Her neighbours might not be painters, but they both belonged to that world.

Daphne's delicate features formed into a frown. 'I'd say so. Generally, you'd need someone who wanted the painting for its own sake, not as something to show off. It would be risky to advertise that they'd got it.'

Sylvia nodded. 'If Nena hadn't yet shown the painting publicly it would be easier. Experts might be able to guess when she'd completed it, by looking at the materials she'd used, the style and so on. But no one would know for certain. The buyer would have to be criminally minded to buy it in the wake of the murder, but people like that exist. Nena's paintings will go up in value now she's dead.'

'And they were already worth a small fortune,' Daphne added.

'How would the new owner explain the painting if they did admit to it?' Eve asked.

'They'd have to say it had been a gift, I'd imagine.' Sylvia sipped her drink. 'Or they could fake papers and claim it was a private sale, especially if they waited a few years till all the hoohah had died down.'

'Of course, at the moment no one's talking about a theft in the wake of Nena's killing,' Daphne added. 'If the police publicise a missing painting, that will be different.'

'They seem focused on her personal life.' Though that might change.

'Even though the landscapes in her room weren't local, she could have completed them in Suffolk,' Sylvia said. 'Perhaps she worked from photos or preliminary sketches.'

'True.' Inspector Palmer would probably say the same. But to Eve, they hadn't looked new, somehow. And they hadn't smelled of paint. 'I took photos of them when I was in Nena's room. I'll put them on the WhatsApp group so you can see.'

'It's interesting that they're on board,' Daphne said as the message pinged through. 'She normally painted on canvas. I'll see if I can find out more about them.'

'Thank you. Leaving paintings aside, there was no pen-and-ink drawing either, yet she had ink in her room. And every example of her writing I saw there was in biro.'

Daphne frowned again. 'That's odd. But I do find it hard to imagine Jamie stealing anything, let alone attacking Nena. Perhaps she sold both works.'

But Eve could still envisage Jamie lashing out, then seeing a terrible opportunity to make his mother's final days comfortable and pay off his dad's debts.

'In other news, I wonder if Gemma threw the brick through Simon's window.'

Viv sat bolt upright. 'Of all the— Just wait until I talk to her!'

Eve put a hand on her arm. 'No haranguing. It's not certain. But I think Iggy suspects her of something.' She explained about the dog bite and the apparent room-searching, then stood up. 'Can I get anyone another drink?'

Viv asked for a glass of wine and Sylvia and Daphne for refills. At the bar, Eve found herself next to Mr Horace. He was tapping a credit card irritably on the counter as he waited for attention. Both Matt and Toby were serving other customers as quickly as they could. Gus came to join Eve and she bent to stroke his head as she waited.

As she stood up again, she glanced to her right. Edgar Horace was tapping faster now. What a jerk. But as she looked, she noticed something odd about that precious watch of his – the one he'd made such a song and dance about at Saltwater Cottages.

A moment later, Matt served him. Just as he was taking his payment, Toby was free to help Eve. As soon as Horace had left the bar, Eve leaned forward.

'I think Mr Grumpy I'm-so-well-to-do Horace is a phoney.'

Toby frowned. 'How do you mean?'

'His watch is an imitation. Rolexes have a magnifying glass over the date. I remember reading that you can tell a fake if the date looks the same size whether you view it side on or from the top. And that's the case with his. The fraudsters just paint on bigger characters.'

Toby grinned. 'Why does that make me so happy? I'm such a child. So he's busy bigging himself up, but in fact he's probably no better off than I am.'

Eve smiled back. 'Quite possibly.' But as she returned to the table with their drinks, she wondered. Was Horace just an annoying snob who wanted to appear richer than he was? Or was he in need of money, just like Jamie, and trying hard to hide it?

But it didn't fit with an impromptu killing and she couldn't see Nena agreeing to meet him in the woods. Besides, he'd have had to get past Jamie to steal the painting. He couldn't have known he'd conveniently leave his desk for twenty minutes.

At home, before she went to bed, she googled Horace. She remembered him saying he worked in fine tailoring and always selected the best clothes for his customers. She found the upmarket store he worked for in London, but he wasn't the manager or even a head of department. He was listed as a retail assistant. She doubted he did any selecting unless you counted pulling a suit from a clothes rail. His wages couldn't be high.

After that, she spoke to Robin.

'How's the case going?'

'*Slowly.*' He sounded as strained as she'd ever heard him. '*Let's focus on Saltwater Cottages instead. Greg's been in touch. I understand the police are keen on Liam for Nena Field's killing. They're interviewing him and his wife again first thing tomorrow. Greg's worried Palmer will go at them like a bull in a china shop and fail to get the answers he wants.*'

'Figures.' Eve filled him in on everything. 'I've contacted Greg about Nena's missing painting.'

'*He mentioned that. They're checking the ones in her room and looking at her bank account too, for signs of a sale. If they draw a blank, they'll search the cottages again and talk to local fences as a precaution, but Palmer thinks it's unlikely anyone could have got a large artwork out of her room. You've considered her giving it away? Or burning it if she felt it wasn't up to scratch? You said she'd had a fire.*'

Eve repeated the arguments she'd made to Simon.

'*Are you sure she'd have reused the canvas or board? She was phenomenally wealthy.*'

He had a point. 'Okay. Perhaps you're right. But I find it hard to imagine her feeling dissatisfied with her work.'

He laughed. '*Maybe that wasn't it, then. She could have painted someone she hated and destroyed it, just like Tess and her print.*'

That seemed unlikely. 'She was a very different type. I think Tess's actions stemmed from a feeling of powerlessness. I doubt Nena ever experienced that.'

'*I'll keep you posted anyway. Speak soon. I love you.*'

'I love you too.' London felt so far away. 'Take care.' But he'd already rung off.

19

Eve rose early the following morning. She had a mission that might take some time...

After walking Gus round the green, she deposited him at home and made for the village store. Eve wanted Moira the storekeeper's gossip and background knowledge. She'd been in the village for years. She'd have all sorts of information about Nena and the chief suspects for her murder.

The store bell jangled as Eve let herself in, to the sound of humming fridges and the smell of coffee, tea and freshly baked bread.

'Ah, Eve dear!' Moira's face lit up like a lantern at her appearance. 'The very person.' She was on her own in the shop, so probably anyone would have done. 'How is poor dear Simon? He must be so upset at Nena's death.' She heaved a great sigh. 'Such a terrible thing to happen. And so soon after he'd opened too.'

'You know Simon. He's bearing up.' As ever, Eve was determined to keep the information flow one way. She fetched a block of cheese from the fridge and set it on the counter. 'What

about you, Moira? You must know all the key players. You're
Saxford St Peter's mainstay.'

Moira simpered. 'Well, I couldn't possibly make that claim,
but people have been kind enough to say so.'

Eve smiled back innocently as Moira talked about Nena.
Her tales tied in with what Eve had already heard, though the
spa room her father had built for his nine-year-old daughter was
noteworthy.

Moira referred to Liam and Iggy's dad as 'difficult, with a
violent temper', which made Eve think of Liam's description.
Good man, my father.

The storekeeper sighed. 'The boys must be hoping Nena's
murder will be resolved as quickly as possible. I mean, we all do,
obviously, but their circumstances have changed since Simon
took them on. Iggy was living in a most uncomfortable-looking
caravan on some land near his dad's old workshop on Shingle
Lane. Liam got his parents' house, but it's run-down, I'm afraid.
Tiny and damp. He's letting it out, though it's a scandal to make
tenants pay for such a place.' She shook her head. 'I know dear
Tess was uneasy about it.'

'What do you think of the brothers?'

Moira folded her arms. 'I'm afraid Liam's like his father.
You know me, Eve, I don't like to speak out of turn.'

Eve bit her lip.

'But when I heard dear Nena had been killed, I wondered
about Liam. There's something cruel in his look. It's such a
shame that Tess chose him over Iggy.'

'Do you know if Iggy has a girlfriend?' She still doubted he
and Tess were having an affair, but she might be wrong.

Moira appeared to focus on the question intently. 'I don't
have any *definite* knowledge, but he was in here a few days
before Nena's death. He bought a dozen red roses and went off
whistling. I didn't like to ask who they were for, naturally.'

Very hard to believe. She'd probably made arch comments and been bitterly disappointed when Iggy hadn't spilled the beans. Either way, the news was interesting. The roses had to be for a lover, but she didn't think it was Tess. Where would she put them without Liam seeing? She wondered again about Nena. She'd have been delighted by that sort of attention. They could have been keeping their relationship secret if she'd yet to finish with Liam. Perhaps she'd promised Iggy she was about to, and Liam had found out. Jealousy would add to his motive for killing her. Even if he'd wanted to end the relationship, Eve couldn't see him shrugging off the betrayal. He appeared to resent Iggy.

'I imagine Iggy's ended up a lot happier than Tess,' Moira was saying. 'As for Liam, I'm afraid Simon will find him a liability, whether he's guilty or not. Though I can see why he employed him, of course. His dad did all the odd jobs and small building works in this area, and I have to admit he was skilled. Liam learned it all from boyhood and inherited his dad's workshop. Of course, Iggy's very competent too. When Simon was renovating Saltwater Cottages, he took unwanted fixtures and fittings to villagers who could use them. I know he put in a new fireplace at Gwen Harris's place. But he's the right choice for custodian. Liam wouldn't suit a customer-facing role. I'm sure he'd be unreliable with the lady guests.' Her brow drew down in disapproval.

Lady guests. Right. 'Well, it's been very useful to hear your views, Moira.' Eve pushed the cheese towards her, and the storekeeper rang up the price on her old-fashioned till.

After they'd said their goodbyes, it was time to get home and prepare for the day. Eve had had a message from Iggy saying Sadie could see her that afternoon. She wanted to check Jamie's story about Melanie Blomquist and perhaps break his alibi. Hopefully she'd get to the bottom of Sadie's secret connection with Nena too.

She was about to cross Love Lane when Viv ran to join her.

But today there was no bounding, nor breathless requests for news.

Eve looked at her damp eyes. 'What is it?'

'I've just heard from Simon. Someone at his bank's head office is coming to Suffolk to meet with his local manager. Simon's known the manager for years. Family friends. He used to have dinner with our parents. The head office guy's all squeaky and smart. He thinks the manager's cutting Simon too much slack. That he ought to call in his debts now. Something to do with property values falling. Simon's beside himself. Telling Polly is all the more urgent, but the news is so much worse now. I suggested a video call, but he said he couldn't bear it.'

Eve could see his point, but holding back felt worse.

'It feels as though his life's falling apart.' Viv chewed her lip. 'But what can we do?'

Eve hugged Viv. 'We take a deep breath.' She needed to hold things together. 'Robin says the police suspect Liam.' Thoughts of his lies filled her head. If the police searched his suite, they might find something. He'd cut his hand. He could have done it slashing Nena's tyres or swinging the log which killed her. If he was guilty, he might have blood on his clothes.

An idea came to her. For a moment, she batted it away, but the situation was desperate. 'Viv, I'm guessing the police don't have enough evidence to search Liam and Tess's suite, but we could.'

Viv looked at her, wide-eyed.

'Robin told me yesterday that Palmer's interviewing them again first thing this morning.' She glanced at her watch: 8.30. 'What if I slip into their suite while they're out? I'm still working on breaking Jamie's alibi, but it's harder with Liam and Tess. They're vouching for each other and no one will know they left their rooms unless they were seen outside. If I slip in, I might find evidence of their guilt instead. You could keep watch in the lane and alert me if you see them coming back, but I guess they'll be hours.'

Viv bit her lip. 'We'd need a key.'

Eve nodded. 'I know. And we can't bank on pinching one from behind the desk. But Simon has a set. I know what you're thinking. He'd never condone searching the rooms of his staff.'

Viv's cheeks tinged pink. 'I could nip in to see him and pinch the keys. They're on a hook in the kitchen. I doubt he'd notice.'

'What do you think?'

Viv nodded. 'Simon can be too kind for his own good sometimes. I think we should do it.'

20

Eve met Viv at the bottom of Smugglers' Lane, just before the right-hand turn into Saltwater End.

'How did you get on?'

Viv looked pale and solemn. 'I got the keys. I feel like a heel, but Simon's not hard-nosed enough to save himself at a time like this.'

It was true. He'd never do what they were doing. He'd regard it as too selfish. In the current, desperate circumstances, Eve saw it differently. If Liam and Tess had nothing to hide, what she saw in their room would never come out. And if they were keeping secrets relevant to the murder then they were fair game.

Viv handed Eve the keys. 'You're sure you'll be all right?'

'I'll take every care.' She couldn't say more than that. She'd texted Greg to check Liam and Tess were at the station. She hadn't explained why she wanted to know, of course. Just said that she was trying to find them. 'How about watching the lane from the wood? You shouldn't be seen.'

Viv nodded, indicating a track to their left. 'I can cut through via Shingle Lane.'

She wasn't sure that was a good idea. 'Isn't that where Liam's workshop is?'

Viv nodded. 'And Iggy's caravan. But don't worry, I'll leave the track before I get that far.'

'Good. I know Liam's with the police and Iggy's out of it, but he might spread the word if he sees you.'

Eve made her way down Saltwater End using the back route again, behind the cottages, then peered into Curlew Cottage through its rear windows. There was no one in sight. A side window showed reception was deserted too.

She tiptoed in the back way and up the rear stairs, straining to hear any signs of life. Searching the suite next to Gemma's was a risk. The cook had heard an awful lot the night Nena died.

On the landing, everything seemed eerily still. Eve slipped the key into Tess and Liam's lock and turned it gingerly. The click as it released sounded loud to her ears.

Her primary object was to search for anything that might allow her to tip Greg off. Get the police to push even harder to get a confession from Liam or Tess. She might not find a smoking gun. Jamie could be guilty. But it had to be right to take this chance.

Once she was safely inside, the door closed, she made for the couple's wardrobe. It had a main section where their tops, dresses and trousers hung and a set of shelves on either side, one for him, one for her.

She searched the back of the wardrobe first in case of holdalls or plastic bags filled with bloodstained clothing. She'd watched too many TV dramas. Unsurprisingly, there was nothing of that sort.

After that, she focused on the shelves with their underwear, long-sleeved T-shirts and the like, rifling through each section in turn, her hands shaking with adrenaline. If either of them had bloody clothing, she was relying on them acting in haste, stowing the item without noticing it was contaminated.

She found nothing.

She turned her attention to the section with coat hangers next, losing hope. She was taking such a risk, and it would probably be fruitless.

She examined each piece of clothing front and back and in the pockets too. Looking for any clue or hint. A jacket of Liam's was the second to last item she checked. She put her hand in the pocket.

There was a tear.

Hardly significant, but the feeling of something less usual still sparked hope.

She took the jacket from the wardrobe and turned the pocket inside out.

Not just a tear, also a stain. The pocket lining was mid brown, which didn't help, but it looked like blood.

Eve took a tissue from her bag, wetted it under the bathroom tap, then dabbed at the stain. It came back a darkish, brickish red. She stowed the tissue safely.

Liam's cut hand. She needed to think what this meant but not now. Time was too precious.

She stuffed the pocket lining back and replaced the jacket, quivering with urgency.

After that, she re-checked the areas she'd searched the day before but nothing had changed. Tess's diary was still blank.

Then she went from room to room, scanning for anything that felt off-key. She checked the bins. The one in the bedroom contained something shiny amongst tissues and cotton wool. Crouching down, she reached for it.

A silver bracelet. It was inscribed with the words: 'All my love, LN.' Next to it was an engraved heart and a date. This month, this year.

Had Liam bought it for Tess out of guilt? Because deep down, he knew how valuable their relationship was? It would tie in with him wanting to finish with Nena, and a violent row afterwards. Eve didn't imagine Nena would have handled rejection well.

She wasn't surprised Tess had chucked the gift in the bin, given she knew about the affair.

But did Liam know that she knew? When had she binned the bracelet and was he aware of the fact? The bin was on her side of the bed, the bracelet almost covered and the contents looked like Tess's. He could have killed Nena to stop her talking with no idea that his secret was out.

At that moment, Eve's phone vibrated. Viv.

Gemma's in the car park. You'll just miss her but only if you leave now!

Eve stuffed the bracelet back into the nest of rubbish, her breath shortening. Fear had taken hold. She mustn't lose concentration. Viv was right. It would be far better to leave now than risk the cook hearing her creeping about. And her suite was right next door. Time it badly and she'd bump into her on the landing.

Her mouth was bone dry as she let herself out.

Back stairs or front? Which way would Gemma come? There was no time to text Viv to ask. She chose the front stairs.

As she neared the bottom, phone in hand, another text came in.

She's about to come into reception.

Heck. Eve felt blood rush up her neck as she dashed back up the stairs, across the landing and down the rear set. Faintly, she could hear movement in the front of the building. A door closing.

She grappled to find the key to the exit, fumbling and clumsy, then breathed a sigh of relief as she let herself out.

'Thank goodness you got out okay. I've bitten my nails off.' Viv was bouncing again, but Eve could see it was nervous excitement.

'Sorry. I didn't have time to reply. You're a lifesaver.' Though a little more detail, a little earlier wouldn't have gone amiss.

Viv held her head up. 'We make a good team, don't we? How did it go in there?'

As her breathing returned to normal, Eve explained what she'd found. 'I'll get word through to Greg Boles. He won't be able to do anything about it officially and I expect he'll be cross with me for sneaking in, but at least he'll have the information in the back of his mind.'

Viv shuddered. 'Glad you're the one who has to confess.'

'Thanks.'

'Home now?'

'Yes, but via the bins. I want to see if I can find any trace of what Nena burned in her fireplace.'

They used a round-about route again to avoid being seen.

'What do you make of the blood in Liam's pocket?' Viv asked.

'What with the tear, I'd say he was carrying a knife and cut his hand on it. Maybe while he was slashing Nena's tyres. I imagine it's tough work. I didn't notice his injury until Monday, but thinking about it, he had his hands stuffed in his pockets when the police came on Sunday to investigate the tyres. It was in his interests to hide the injury from that point on.'

'So you think it was him, not Jamie?'

'That's what I'm betting, in an attempt to get Nena to leave without breaking things off officially, like I said.'

'Because he worried she'd tell Tess in revenge?'

Eve nodded. 'I suspect he sent the note Iggy mentioned first, but made no headway. Then slashed the tyres, which was more physical and dramatic.'

'But it still didn't work. And the brick?'

'I think Gemma's more likely for that, though I'm not sure who her note referred to and what the secret is. Either way, it's like I thought before. Liam trying to get Nena into trouble with Simon would be a risk. Their affair might come out and Liam could have got the sack.'

'So Liam tried the threatening note and the tyres to no avail. He was getting desperate by then?'

'Quite possibly. He might have decided to end the relationship after all, in person, in the woods. She could have laughed at him. Threatened to tell Tess.'

'So he lashed out and killed her.' Viv shuddered. 'But all the time, Tess already knew.'

'Yes. The print of Liam and Nena makes that clear. It explains her throwing away Liam's bracelet too. And according to Gemma she was crying after Liam left their suite the night Nena died. But Liam won't have heard that, and he probably never saw the bracelet in the bin.'

'And given the sort he is, he might never have noticed she wasn't wearing it. Even Oliver, who loved me dearly, was very vague about that kind of thing.' Viv looked emotional for a moment. She'd lost her husband so young.

Eve squeezed her arm. 'I think it's quite common.'

Viv nodded and Eve saw her swallow. 'So, we have interesting information, but still nothing concrete.'

'I'm afraid not.'

The bins were in sight. Eve looked around, checking for movement. How long would it be before Liam and Tess came back?

If what Nena had burned was relevant to her murder, her

killer might be concerned about the remains of the fire too. They might guess what Eve was looking for.

Snatching one last look around her, she scuttled to the corner of the car park where the bins sat. There was a hedge between her and the downstairs windows in the nearest house. She glanced at the building's upper floor, but it was in darkness. It was one of the cottages for guests, and they'd all gone home.

She explored the general rubbish bin first, but there was no sign of ash. After that, she checked the one for green waste and even recycling.

Nothing.

Any remnants must have been taken away with the previous collection, unless Nena had removed them herself. How desperate had she been to cover her tracks, and why? Eve couldn't begin to imagine.

21

Eve turned to Viv as they left Saltwater Cottages' car park. 'I'm due back here after lunch to interview Sadie, but for now, what do you say to walking along Shingle Lane past Iggy's caravan and Liam's workshop?'

Viv's eyebrows shot up. 'You didn't want me to go there earlier.' She folded her arms. 'It's almost as though you don't trust me!'

'Perish the thought. Safety in numbers, that's all: two of us to keep lookout. It might be the best chance we get. Liam's probably still with the police and I don't suppose Iggy would hang out in his caravan in preference to his suite. I'd like a snoop.'

Viv took a deep breath. 'And there was I thinking we could relax for a bit. But in for a penny, in for a pound. And then I'd better take the keys back to Simon before he notices they're missing.'

They strolled down a pathway to one side of the track, under overhanging trees. The air was heavy and damp. Neither of them spoke. Eve felt tense. For all she'd said, it wasn't impossible that Iggy was at the caravan. He had an alibi, but he'd held back about the note Nena had received. It was as she'd thought, he might have an idea of the killer's identity and be protecting them.

The workshop and caravan were in sight now. The day was gloomy and overcast but there were no lights on.

'I don't think anyone's there,' Viv murmured. She must be nervous to lower her voice.

'Unless they're sleeping,' Eve answered. It suddenly struck her that Iggy might slip back onto home turf to get away from it all.

She moved cautiously, checking underfoot for twigs that might crack and pebbles that could accidentally be kicked. She lurked by the caravan's rear window, out of sight of the workshop, and peered in, holding her breath.

Unless Iggy was in the bathroom, the place was empty. He'd left it tidy. All the cupboards and the wardrobe were neatly closed. There was no sign of a bed. Eve guessed the daytime seating must convert. She could see mould on the inside of the windows, but only tiny traces. Iggy must wipe it away on a regular basis. Living there would involve a lot of effort. It would be horribly uncomfortable in winter too. A job with accommodation would be a huge bonus and Saltwater's rooms were beautifully done out.

It must be galling for Iggy, Liam getting their parents' house when he was the elder brother. And Liam had married his old girlfriend too. She couldn't see Iggy protecting him. He must think Tess or Jamie had sent the anonymous note to Nena. Tess probably. She'd had every reason to, and they were old friends.

Viv was edging towards Liam's workshop. Eve glanced behind them, then scanned the undergrowth and the route ahead to make sure they were still alone.

All was quiet. She followed her friend and peered into the gloomy interior. Liam's lair was very different to Iggy's caravan. Chock full of tools, which were strewn all over the place. And in this case there *was* a bed. Of sorts. A mattress,

complete with thrown-back duvet and pillows abandoned at
odd angles.

Eve had been wondering where he and Nena had met. It
wasn't the most salubrious love nest, but it had to be better than
sneaking past reception to her room, or using the suite he shared
with Tess. She wondered if Tess ever visited the workshop. The
mattress told its own story.

She visualised Nena sneaking into the rickety building with
Liam. Iggy might have spotted them. He might not come to the
caravan often. Just enough to air it and wipe off the mould,
perhaps. But he could still have seen.

'We'd better hurry,' Viv whispered. 'I want to get those keys
back to Simon. It's tying my stomach in knots.'

Eve nodded and they turned towards the end of the track,
which petered out into a narrow pathway. Eve hoped they
didn't meet any Saltwater staff coming the other way. There'd
be no avoiding them. But they made it onto Hidden Lane
without mishap and her heart rate gradually returned to
normal.

Back at home, Eve greeted a pleasingly ecstatic Gus, then called
Greg Boles to fill him in on her various discoveries. She didn't
explain that she and Viv had pinched Simon's keys, implying
she'd taken the chance to snoop when it presented itself. Greg
told her not to do it again but he was relatively nice about it. At
least he knew what she knew now. Meanwhile, he told her the
police had checked and it didn't look as though Nena had sold a
painting recently. There were no large deposits unaccounted
for in her bank statements. Palmer was inclined to think she'd
given it away or more likely destroyed it because everyone said
she was 'mercurial'. But Nena had been perfectly steady in her
self-regard.

Eve shook her head and settled down to research Sadie, in

preparation for their talk after lunch. The exercise was frustrating. She had no social media, which was relatively rare these days. Eve found odd mentions of her though. A contribution to a fundraising effort here, a caption on a post about a community event there. By the time she'd finished, Sadie was still a closed book.

She was about to get herself some lunch when Toby texted.

Fancy coming to the Cross Keys for a sandwich?

She replied:

You are keen to drum up trade!

He responded with a laughing emoji.

Always, but also, I have gossip.

Five minutes later, Eve and Gus entered the bar. Eve ordered a cheese toastie with local ham and a glass of Coke as Gus and Hetty performed their comical rough-and-tumble greeting. 'Can I get you one?' Eve asked.

'Thanks.' Toby grinned and poured himself a Coke too.

'So, what's up?' Eve sat on a bar stool and waited for her food.

He lowered his voice, 'Just a point of interest about horrible Edgar Horace.'

'Ah. What's he been up to?'

'Spending big, by all accounts.'

Eve raised an eyebrow.

'He's been showing off a ruby brooch he bought his wife this morning. Got it on a trip to Blyworth.'

'Real ruby?'

He nodded. 'Rubies. Plural.'

'Heck. But we know he brags. It could be a fake.'

'That's what I thought, but apparently it's not. When he left the bar, several people were gossiping about him. He's already offended half the village. Someone said they doubted the gems were real, but one customer recognised the name of the jewellers he'd mentioned. She's got a friend who works there. She texted and found it was all true. The shop's staff had been gossiping about it ever since. It was their most expensive item.'

'Wow.'

'It's interesting. And vexing. He's incredibly stingy over small things like the cost of our tonic water. Beyond that, I wonder what he's doing with a fake Rolex.'

'Unless he's just come into money.' Eve was back to thinking about Nena's painting. He could have stolen it. But accessing her room would have been tricky. And she doubted he could have sold it already. Unless he had a contact set up...

'It might mean nothing,' Toby said, as one of the casual staff appeared with Eve's sandwich, complete with a colourful salad.

Eve thanked them and frowned. 'All anomalies gratefully noted. Thanks, Toby. I'll keep it in mind.'

When she'd finished, she had time to spare before she was due at Saltwater Cottages. Gus could do with a decent walk so she set off down Heath Lane. They could wander in the far reaches of Blind Eye Wood near the estuary before heading south for the interview.

She was so absorbed by thoughts of Edgar Horace that she didn't immediately notice Gus sniffing a piece of bark.

It was a largeish sheet of it, separated from the log it had come from.

The shape reminded Eve of a map of Scotland.

She stopped dead, pulling Gus away from the bark, to a protesting whine. After that, she photographed it, taking several shots from different angles.

'I know you want to investigate, Gus, but this is important! Nena's branch had a bit of bark missing. And it was exactly the same shape.'

Goosebumps rose all the way up her arms. 'Nena was killed all the way over by the burned oak. So what the heck is the bark from the murder weapon doing here?'

There was no reason for someone to rip the bark off, then carry the log to a different part of the wood.

But if a killer was planning a murder and wanted to make it look impromptu, there would be every reason to search for a suitable log and place it near where they intended to use it. It would mean Nena had definitely been in the wood for an appointment. Eve imagined the bark had come off before the log was moved or been knocked off when the killer picked it up.

She called Greg Boles and explained.

This made all the difference. It looked as though someone had planned Nena's death very precisely.

Eve's head was teeming with thoughts as she cut back towards Saltwater Cottages. Gone were ideas of Jamie chasing after Nena, then losing control. If he was guilty, he'd set out to take a life. Could he possibly have done that?

He'd have to have been consumed by protective anger, but that was possible. He might have felt Nena deserved to die for the trouble she was causing. It was the same for Tess. And it certainly didn't rule out Liam. She could see him planning the killing when the slashed tyres and threatening note didn't get results.

She was nearing Saltwater End when her phone rang.

Robin.

It was unusual to hear from him in the middle of the working day.

She tapped quickly to answer. 'Are you okay?'

'*Yes. I've had a call from Greg. You rang him just now?*'

'That's right.' Eve explained what she'd found.

'He was calling me to check on things this end, but he wanted to slip you some information too. He couldn't when you rang. He wasn't alone. You're interviewing the Saltwater manager today, right?'

'Yes. I'm on my way there now.'

'Well, this is relevant. She inherits a third of Nena Field's fortune. And it's one heck of a lot of money.'

22

Eve was focused on Robin's news as she approached Saltwater End. Nena's other beneficiaries were irrelevant – they'd been nowhere near Saxford at the time of the murder – but Sadie would be a top suspect if it weren't for her alibi. What connection had she had with Nena, and why the heck had the artist left her so much money? Eve thought again of the scene she'd witnessed between the pair. Nena had said she wanted to give Sadie money for her birthday – seemingly an act of generosity – but Sadie had looked tormented. She'd said she didn't want it, but Nena had said she must. The feeling of threat had hung in the air. *I'll never finish paying you back*, Nena had said. But pushing money onto Sadie was a weird form of revenge.

Regardless of the alibi, Eve needed to understand their connection before she left. She still didn't know the meaning behind the message tied to the brick. Was the clock still ticking, or had it stopped with Nena's death? For Simon's sake, she couldn't risk abandoning her enquiries into that, any more than the murder.

She'd check Jamie's story about Melanie Blomquist too. If she could prove he was lying, it meant he'd been away from his desk for a stretch for some secret reason. His boyish face flashed in her mind. She thought of his mum in her nursing home and his dad, making his life a misery, but it was no good. She had to know the truth for the sake of Simon and the other staff.

She met Sadie in the lane, close to Curlew Cottage. Gemma was outdoors too, a little further away, and Iggy off to one side. Eve wasn't surprised they wanted some air. It must be horrible, cooped up in the cottages waiting to hear their fate. They'd be wondering if Tess or Liam were guilty and if they were in danger. It would be hard for Jamie too, stuck with his dad. Out of the loop. Imagining the others discussing his possible guilt.

Sadie glanced quickly at her staff, and Gemma turned as though she'd sensed it. Her look was as cold as the weather. Eve wondered what tensions were playing out under the surface. It was the second time she'd seen Sadie, Gemma and Iggy in close proximity looking strained. She wondered if they'd been arguing before she arrived.

'Please, come on in,' Sadie said. 'We can go to my rooms. I'll make you a coffee.'

Eve thanked her and followed her upstairs.

Her sitting room was decorated in cream and navy. Sadie motioned Eve to a corduroy sofa. 'Simon's done us proud. I love my new home.' She sounded sad. Maybe she was anticipating having to leave.

'It's wonderful,' Eve replied as Sadie went through to her kitchen. 'I could see what a success Saltwater Cottages would be when I arrived. I'm very sorry that something so tragic has happened.'

'Thank you.'

Sadie seemed composed, despite her secret connection with Nena, though Eve felt she was the sort to batten down her feelings.

She handed her a coffee and sat down on the sofa opposite.

Eve thanked her. 'By the way, I gather a friend of my mother's, Melanie Blomquist, has been in touch.' Eve threw caution to the wind and used the same fiction she had for Jamie. She might get found out, but that hardly mattered given the stakes. 'Jamie took her initial call, I gather.' Eve pulled a rueful face. 'He said she seemed a bit tricky, so he didn't prolong the conversation. I'm sorry. I hope she's not difficult if she ends up staying here.'

Sadie raised an eyebrow. 'He said that?'

'We were talking as friends in the pub,' Eve said hastily. 'Having a joke about it. I egged him on.'

Her expression lightened a little. 'I see. I must admit, I didn't realise they'd spoken. She talked as though she'd left a message.'

I'll bet she did.

'Anyway,' Sadie went on, 'I spoke to her this morning and she was very pleasant. She explained her late call the first time. She got the time difference wrong. Of course, she won't be able to join us this time, we won't reopen before she leaves, but she said perhaps she would in the future.'

'Of course.' That had been close. Not knowing the length of her stay in London – or even that she was travelling from abroad. 'I'd love to ask you about Nena now, if I may.'

Sadie frowned. 'Iggy said it was Saltwater Cottages you wanted to talk about, for your other article.'

'I'd like that too. But Nena's obituary is the most urgent. A couple of people mentioned it was you who suggested her as a tutor.' Eve put her cup and saucer on a low coffee table and focused on her host. 'Everyone was surprised she agreed to come.'

Sadie repeated Nena's story: that she remembered Simon from childhood riding lessons.

Eve leaned forward. 'To be honest, Sadie, I know you secretly knew each other better than you let on.' She explained what she'd overheard, and Sadie blanched. 'She was being generous, so I'm guessing you had a close bond.' She wouldn't detail the undercurrents she'd noticed. She'd rather see what explanation Sadie gave. 'You were probably the reason she agreed to come.'

Sadie put her head in her hands, her fine silver hair falling forward, and took a deep, shuddering breath. 'I felt terrible about accepting her birthday gift. She had so much money, of course. I suppose it was an easy way to convey her feelings. She was grateful to me, you see.'

And it was what her parents had done to her: showered her with material gifts.

'Could you explain the background? I understand you were keeping your friendship secret while Nena was alive, and I don't have to make it public if you'd rather I didn't. It will just inform what I write. You were clearly an important part of her life.'

Sadie gave a quick sigh. 'I first met her when I lived in London. I don't want this mentioned in the obituary, but she was falling-down drunk in a bar, surrounded by men who were vying to take her home. I picked her up, dusted her down and got her a cup of black coffee.' Her chest rose and fell. 'My own daughter died when she was five. She and my husband were killed in a traffic accident. I suppose I imagined how I'd have felt if she'd lived, and ended up in a bar in that state. I did what I would have wanted any stranger to do. Took her under my wing. She'd clearly gone off the rails. She didn't want to go to her family. She would have been quite happy to be left to her fate. In the end, I persuaded her to come and stay at my flat. She was there for three months.'

'Hence the gratitude.'

Sadie nodded and lowered her eyes for a moment.

'When was this?'

'Goodness. Years ago.' She frowned. '2010, maybe? And you're right, her coming here was down to me. Ironically, I thought her presence would guarantee success for this place.' She sighed.

Eve was puzzled. She was convinced Sadie had been scared of Nena, so why invite her?

'You might as well know,' Sadie went on, 'Nena's left me a substantial bequest. It's bound to come out.'

The confession confirmed Eve's opinion of Sadie. She was cool and practical. It was smart PR to tackle the news head-on. A third of Nena's fortune would be millions, but if Sadie had turned her life around, Eve guessed it made sense. Perhaps Sadie had become a mother figure: someone less oppressive than her real mum. It would be interesting to meet Ms Lamb if she agreed to an interview.

'The bequest was a bolt from the blue,' Sadie said. 'Of course, I was far more likely to die first.' She shook her head. 'Nena once told me she was the live-fast, die-young type, but I don't think she meant it seriously. She was a tease. It's entirely possible she named me in her will to irritate someone else.'

Eve could imagine that. 'What was she like to live with?'

Sadie stared into her coffee. 'Difficult, back then.' Her eyes were glistening. 'I was naive. I had no idea she was hooked on drugs as well as drink. But I felt sorry for her.' She looked at Eve intently. 'I'm trusting you not to include these details. I looked you up. You don't do gutter journalism.'

'You're right. You can trust me. But why keep your friendship secret?'

Sadie paused. 'When Nena became famous it seemed sensible. News that she had to be scraped off a bar floor by a stranger would still make headlines today.'

Especially in the wake of her death. But what Sadie said made no sense. Nena had embraced publicity, the more outrageous the better. And besides, they didn't have to tell everyone *how* they'd met.

It didn't explain the feeling of threat when Nena had pressed 'a few thousand' on Sadie as a birthday present either.

Sadie's knuckles were white as she clutched her coffee cup. 'I think, if you'll excuse me, I'd like to leave it there. It's been hard to cope with. Maybe we can talk about the courses when all this is over.'

'Of course.' Eve rose from her seat.

As she left Sadie's room, she felt thwarted. What was she hiding? She wondered what the manager would do next. She'd been like a coiled spring, ready to burst with pent-up tension. It was human nature to want to let it go.

If there was anyone she could confide in, she'd probably seek them out. Eve considered the situation. She didn't seem close to the other staff.

In which case she'd call someone.

Eve glanced around her. Listening at the door would leave her horribly exposed if anyone appeared on the landing. She tried hovering just outside, but she couldn't hear anything. What to do? She was potentially missing something this minute. At last, she put her ear to the door.

She'd been right, Sadie *was* making a call. Eve could just hear her. *Please don't let anyone come by.*

It took a moment to make sense of the muffled sounds. When she did, Sadie's words distracted her from her anxiety.

'I wish I could turn back time. If only I hadn't gone out that night. Her gratitude's like a knife, twisting in the wound. I should never have lied.' There was a long pause, then Sadie added: 'No, no. The police think she died sometime after eleven thirty-five. It's just as well. I'd be suspect number one if the truth came out.'

23

Eve was still focused on Sadie's words as she crept along the landing, but she needed to re-focus. It was time to talk to Tess again. She'd never tackled her directly about Liam's affair, and her softly, softly approach wasn't working. She was running out of options. If she forced the issue, Tess might let something slip.

She steeled herself and went to her suite, which was round the corner from Sadie's. If Liam was in, she'd make an excuse to talk to Tess in private. She knocked.

No reply. But faintly now, she could hear sobbing. 'Tess? It's Eve Mallow. Please, can I do something?'

If she knew why Eve was knocking, she'd never let her in. Eve took a deep breath and tapped again, softly.

At last, Tess opened up. She looked terrible, white-faced and red-eyed.

'I'm so sorry. You must be having such an awful time.' Whatever the truth, that would be the case.

Tess pressed her fingers to her eyes, as though she was trying to keep the tears in. 'The police are all over us. I'm sure they think Liam or I are guilty. They're digging up every little detail from our past.'

She gulped and Eve wondered if they were uncovering things about Liam that she hadn't heard before.

'They're questioning everyone. Making judgements about my dad, and me because I'm his daughter. They even tried to talk to Mum, who barely knows who I am. I don't think I can stand it much longer. You don't think I did it, do you?'

What the heck to say? Tess seemed far less likely to commit premeditated murder, but she couldn't rule her out. 'It doesn't matter what I or anyone else thinks. I just wish you weren't suffering.' What on earth did Palmer imagine he could get out of Jamie and Tess's mum? It seemed horribly cruel to question her.

It didn't look as though Tess was going to invite her in, so Eve lowered her voice. 'I suppose they're focused on you and Jamie because of Nena and Liam.' She'd never have said it if she wasn't sure Tess knew. 'I'm sorry. I caught sight of them. I'm pretty sure Liam wanted to end it.'

Tess was crying again. When she spoke, it was in an urgent whisper. 'It's true. I hated Nena. The affair was like sport for her. She didn't care. But she's not the first and I doubt she'll be the last. If I went about killing Liam's lovers, Saxford would be strewn with bodies, I promise you.'

Her eyes were wide and bleak.

'I believe you.' But Eve meant about Liam's conquests. She still wasn't sure about the murder, because Nena was manipulative. She'd seen her in action. If she wanted to make you feel worthless and desperate, she could do it, Eve was sure. And Tess had had to put up with her mind games day in, day out.

'Where did you go when you left your room that night, Tess? I know you weren't sleeping, like you said, or showering, as Liam claimed.'

She shook her head. 'I just went for a walk, because I was so miserable. But I didn't want anyone to know about Liam's betrayal or how upset I was.'

She sounded honest, and it made sense. Liam might have lied about it for related reasons: to hide the misery he'd caused Tess and the complexity of their relationship with the victim. Except Eve suspected he'd no idea Tess knew about the affair. He'd certainly been scared of discovery when he'd kissed Nena in the foyer.

So the question remained, why would he lie about Tess's movements?

'Did you know someone sent Nena a poison pen letter before she died?'

Eve watched Tess's response carefully. Confusion, followed by fear.

'What? No, I had no idea.'

'It might have been from the same person who slashed her tyres. Can you guess who that might be?'

Tess shook her head, but she wasn't meeting Eve's eye any more. That would fit if she suspected someone dear to her: Liam or Jamie.

'It could have been Liam, I guess.' If there was any chance Tess hadn't thought of it, Eve needed to raise it now. It might keep her safe.

She shook her head. 'Whatever he's done, he's not a killer. Fundamentally, he's still a little boy. He gets scared. He wouldn't risk our future.'

Eve opened her mouth to say more, but Tess had withdrawn inside her suite and was closing the door. 'Thanks for trusting me,' she said, just before she disappeared out of sight.

Eve was filled with a mix of guilt and anxiety as she walked home. She wanted to trust Tess, but she didn't. Not one hundred per cent. The emotions involved were too intense. And was Tess right to trust Liam? She must solve this.

She almost marched into Iggy, who was coming the other way down Dark Lane.

She rallied her thoughts. He might have useful information. He appeared to have searched Gemma's room and she wanted to know why. If she could prove Gemma had thrown the brick, she could tackle her again. If Nena was her target, she and the killer might share a grievance. It could put a new slant on things. The affair didn't have to be the motive.

She greeted Iggy.

'I've just seen Tess. She's so upset. I know the police are bound to go in hard and push everyone but the pressure must be immense. You're still friends, I guess?' Tess could use one right now.

Iggy looked pained. 'For sure. Thanks for letting me know. I'll have a quiet word with Sadie and Gemma too. We'll rally round.'

'That sounds good. I've been gathering information for my article about Saltwater. How's Gemma working out as cook?'

He looked surprised. 'Brilliantly, I think. Her food's amazing. It'll be odd for her when the head chef arrives.'

Eve agreed. She seemed perfectly capable of running the kitchens. 'Yes, her cooking's superb. She just seemed a bit,' she searched for the right word, 'withdrawn, when we spoke. Not that it's surprising after everything that's happened. You haven't got any worries about her?'

'Just the opposite.' He was smiling.

'I wondered if someone had. I saw a silhouette behind her curtains recently. It looked as though they were searching the place. I knew Gemma was out. To be honest, I thought it might have been you.'

He flushed. 'No. Definitely not me.' He had the grace to look down. 'That's worrying. I'll keep an eye out.'

She wondered whether to push further, but she wanted to

keep him onside. As she continued her walk home, she was more perplexed than ever. She sensed Iggy was genuinely pleased to have Gemma onboard. Did that mean he'd had worries but been reassured? She sighed. Either way, it was time to catch up with the gang and focus on the killer.

24

Eve invited Simon, Viv, Sylvia and Daphne to Elizabeth's Cottage for updates. As she waited for them, she checked her email and found Nena's mother had agreed to see her on Friday. She replied to confirm.

When her friends were seated in her sitting room, a fire blazing at one end and Gus lounging luxuriously on the rug, she gave them her news, beginning with Sadie. Their faces changed with shock as she told them about Nena's bequest, and again as she relayed their interview and the phone call.

'I don't think Sadie was after Nena's wealth. She said her gratitude was like a knife in the wound, and that fits with her reaction when Nena pressed money on her before she died.'

'Weird,' Viv said. 'Who wouldn't want a small fortune?'

Who indeed? Eve couldn't imagine why Nena's generosity was so painful, but she was sure that Nena had relished the fact. 'Sadie strikes me as a careful, private woman who likes to live quietly. I appreciate she wouldn't want fuss and publicity, but I'm sure there's more to her reticence than that. What she said on the phone sent chills down my spine.' She read from her notebook: *'The police think she died sometime after eleven thirty-five. It's just as well. I'd be suspect number one if the truth came out.* I suppose she meant the truth about her and Nena's past, not the time of death, because there are multiple witnesses who prove Nena didn't die earlier.' Unless everyone was lying, including three random Saltwater guests, which was way too far-fetched. She took a deep breath. 'Sadie's not a suspect, but I need to find out more. Any history that explosive might feed into what's happened.'

Viv nodded. 'It sounds pretty shady.'

Simon's floppy dark-brown hair fell forwards. His head was in his hands. He wouldn't want fresh questions. She needed to home in on the people who could actually be guilty.

'Let's look at the suspects again. I've got an update and it makes a difference. I believe Nena's murder was premeditated after all.' She explained about the bark.

Daphne put her hand to her forehead. 'How dreadful to plan it, and with such cunning.'

'I know.' It had made Eve shiver. 'We need to fit it with what we know. Let's start with Liam. He was having an affair with Nena and I now believe it was he who slashed her tyres.'

Viv went pink.

'What makes you so sure?' Simon asked.

Eve and Viv's eyes met before Eve leaped in. 'I managed to sneak a look inside his jacket pocket.' She explained the blood and the tear.

Simon's eyes widened. 'But how did you manage to look?'

Sylvia leaned forward and patted his arm. 'Them that asks no questions...'

Simon closed his eyes and shook his head.

Eve carried on before he pushed further. 'My theory still stands: he was trying to frighten Nena with the tyres and the threatening note. I think he realised he was in too deep and wanted her to leave. He probably worried she'd tell Tess if he offended her. We know his efforts failed. He could have planned the killing as a last resort. I'd say he's brutal and selfish enough. And there's a chance jealousy came into it.' She explained her thoughts about Iggy and Nena's possible involvement. 'Even if he wanted Nena out of his life, I'm sure it would have made him angry. It's clear he's despised Iggy for years.'

'Tess would have to be lying for Liam, of course,' Daphne said.

Eve nodded. 'Yes, but I think that's possible. She must have hated Nena. Liam's hurt her badly too, but she seems fatalistic about it. She says he's like a little boy.'

'If only we had some proof,' Simon said.

'I know. At least the police are focused on Liam too. The weird thing remains: if he or Tess are guilty, they must have left their suite to kill Nena after they talked to Sadie at eleven fifteen. The key time is eleven thirty-five onwards. We know Nena didn't reach the woods before then. Yet they both lied about their movements earlier in the evening: Liam about his rounds and both of them about Tess not leaving their suite. Tess admits she went out for some air now. But who cares where they were then? I'm still mystified by it.'

They looked at each other, then Eve glanced at her notes.

'Let's move on to Tess. She admitted she knew about the affair when we talked today. That photo of Iggy in her drawer was interesting too. I didn't let on I'd searched her things.'

Simon shook his head. 'But you don't think Iggy's red roses were for her?'

'No, because she'd have nowhere to keep them without Liam seeing. I suspect the photo's just a sign that she was thinking of the old days. She probably wishes she was in love with Iggy, not his brother.'

'You'd think her patience with Liam would have run out,' Viv said.

'Absolutely, and perhaps it has. She chucked his bracelet in the bin after all. She could still love him but be determined to leave. She certainly cares. Gemma heard her crying after Liam left her room, the night of the murder. She had good reason to want Nena dead and we all know how successfully Nena wound people up. It's a lot harder to see her killing from passion now the murder looks premeditated, but it's not impossible. And passion's not the only motive.'

'It isn't?' Viv asked.

'I'll come to that.'

'And Jamie?' Daphne put in, taking a sip of her tea. Her eyes were anxious.

'After talking to Sadie, it looks as though Melanie Blomquist's call went to voicemail, which suggests Jamie was absent from his desk and is lying about it. It would have been risky to go to the woods, but I could see him being angry enough to do it. But again, a spur-of-the-moment killing seems more likely.'

'So it's Liam for killer then.' Viv raised her mug. 'I approve. He's a nasty piece of work.'

Eve considered her rival theory and wanted to wish it away. 'I agree. But I'm still curious about Nena's artwork. Did you find anything useful about the pieces on her wall, Daphne?'

Her friend nodded. 'We were going to update you. I showed a friend of mine the photos you took. She's a Nena Field expert. Both the paintings were shown at an exhibition last year. She remembered because they were on board, not canvas.'

'Top sleuthing!' Viv said.

'Yes, that's invaluable. Thank you.' Eve considered the implications. 'So there could be a missing painting to account for.' She texted Greg to update him. 'It's not impossible Nena gave it away or destroyed it, but a sale looks unlikely, with no unexplained deposits in her account.

'So I think we have to bear theft in mind as a possible extra motive. And I'm afraid Jamie had the best opportunity to take something. He might not have killed Nena. He could have watched her leave and taken his chance. But I'd say he must have known two things: one, that no one else knew what she was working on, and two, that she wouldn't be coming back. It's possible he and Tess worked together. They hated Nena and if killing her would support their mother and bail out their dad, I could imagine them planning it. In that scenario, Liam would have to be lying for Tess, but again, I could see it. I'm sure he wanted to end his relationship with Nena and lying could save his job and the status quo. And that's without the added temptation of the proceeds from the painting, if it was stolen.'

Daphne put her head in her hands. 'It's so awful.'

'I know. I'm sorry. I still don't know what Nena was using her ink for either. Perhaps there are two artworks missing.'

'Couldn't someone else have pinched them?' Simon asked.

Eve frowned. 'It would have been difficult, I think. Someone predisposed to steal would have to have seen Nena leave, then waited on the off-chance that Jamie would disappear too, with no idea of how long he'd be gone. There'd be plenty of potential for him to catch them at it. And they'd have needed a key to Nena's room. Even if they pinched one from behind the desk it would have taken time.'

Viv huffed. 'Put like that, it sounds nigh-on impossible.'

Eve nodded. 'Perhaps I'm rushing down a rabbit hole. The missing painting might be totally innocent.' But she still couldn't quite believe it. 'If there *was* a theft, the other question mark is grumpy Mr Horace. There's something odd about him. He portrays himself as wealthy and successful, but his watch is a fake and his job's lowly. Yet since Nena's death, he's spent a fortune on a ruby brooch, according to Toby. I could imagine him fuming over Nena's insults. I'd say his skin's wafer thin. Anger and greed combined might work as a motive, but I don't see how he'd have stolen and sold the artworks.'

Eve's phone went. Robin. She took the call upstairs.

'How's the investigation going?'

'It's a rollercoaster. There are multiple potential witnesses but they're too scared to talk.'

'If anyone can convince them, it'll be you.'

'I really hope you're right.' There was a long pause. 'I've got news for you, for what it's worth. Greg's been in touch. He's been sitting on a detail since Monday for operational reasons.' Eve knew the police sometimes withheld information if they thought they could use it to trip up the killer. 'The news has been officially released now. Nena's pillows had been slashed.'

'That's interesting.' It went with the tyres and the poison pen. 'By the way, do you have a list of the guests' alibis?' She was thinking of horrible Horace.

'No, but Greg said none of them rang alarm bells.'

She imagined Horace's wife alibied him, but that didn't count for much.

After they'd said goodbye, Eve passed the news on to the others. 'The pillows sound like part of the campaign I think Liam was waging. He could have sneaked into Nena's rooms during Jamie's mysterious absence.'

When she was alone with Gus, everything she knew swirled in her head, thoughts mingling as she made supper.

It was only as she sat down to eat that she realised what the news of the slashed pillows meant.

25

Eve needed to see Liam. With a murderer on the loose, and Simon in imminent danger of losing everything, it wouldn't wait.

She called his mobile and told him she knew what he'd got up to, the night of the murder. He agreed to meet her at the Cross Keys, though he didn't sound happy about it. She wasn't ecstatic either. What if she was wrong? But logic told her she wasn't.

Forty minutes later, she was sitting opposite him in the pub. She wished Gus hadn't left her to it. He was communing with Hetty as usual.

Liam's handsome face and cruel eyes showed mixed emotions: irritation, anger, wariness, and a hint of fear. She cleared her throat. Why was she so nervous? She was surrounded by friends and neighbours. But she couldn't stay in the Cross Keys forever.

Liam sipped his pint of Adnams. 'So tell me, what was I "up to" the night Nena died?' His voice was heavy with sarcasm.

'I'd like to start further back. The day I arrived at Saltwater Cottages I saw you and Nena kissing just outside her doorway. I know you were having an affair. I had a feeling you wished you could break it off.'

Liam's eyes were fiery. He said nothing.

'That night – Saturday – someone slashed Nena's tyres. When I bumped into you on Monday morning, you'd injured your hand. You told me you'd cut it on your axe, but that made no sense to me. It's not as though you'd accidentally grab the wrong end.'

Still, Liam was silent.

'I heard a rumour that you'd told the police a different story. It was clear you were lying. I guessed you'd cut yourself slashing Nena's tyres.'

'And why would I do that?'

'Because you wanted to scare her off. Get her to leave without crossing her.'

He scoffed. 'Why wouldn't I just finish with her?'

'Because she might tell Tess. I think you sent her a threatening note too. I heard she'd received one.'

Liam's gaze flicked from side to side, like an animal looking for an escape route.

She was sure she was right. 'I believe you wanted her to feel sufficiently threatened that she'd pull out of her contract at Saltwater and leave you alone. But it didn't work. And then someone killed Nena.'

'It wasn't me!' Liam grated the words out. He was partway through destroying a beer mat. 'The police haven't pinned it on me, and you won't either.'

She ignored him. 'I think you already knew about the latest news to come out.' She showed him a report online about Nena's pillows. 'You slashed the tyres, wrote the note and destroyed her pillows.'

'All right!' He threw his hands up. 'So what if I did? She wouldn't leave me alone!'

He hadn't been willing to face the consequences of his

actions. Come clean to Tess. Like the weasel he was, he'd decided to terrorise his lover instead. But Nena hadn't scared easily.

'Killing her would have solved your problem.' Eve said it lightly. She wanted to see his response. Partly just for the satisfaction.

'It would.' Liam's knuckles were white on his glass. 'But although I was getting to hate her, it never crossed my mind. I was hoping the pillows on top of everything else would do it.'

'How did you get into her room?'

'I've got keys. I waited for Jamie to leave his desk so I wasn't seen.'

'What time was this?'

Liam drew himself up. Shifty. Cagy. 'I can't remember. Why should I tell you anyway?'

'You knew she was out.'

He sighed. 'All right, yes. I'd seen her leave and Jamie wasn't on the desk.'

It must have been during his absence in the run-up to midnight. On one level, Liam's admission was damning, but in fact, Eve was now convinced he was innocent.

It came down to the killing being premeditated. Why would Liam slash Nena's pillows if he knew she'd be dead before she got to see them?

He could have stolen her artwork though. She went for shock tactics. 'What did you do with her painting?' She scrutinised Liam as she spoke.

Total confusion.

'What do you mean?' He was too perplexed to answer aggressively. She was convinced he hadn't taken anything.

'She was working on an oil painting. No one knows where it went.'

'Well, I'm in the same boat.' His brow was furrowed.

'You have to tell the police about slashing the pillows.'

'You've got to be kidding me.'

'It makes it clear you're innocent.'

He looked incredulous. 'How do you work that out?'

She explained.

'I think you're crediting me with more rationality than the police will.'

He might be right, but if he didn't tell them, she would.

'What were you really up to when you told me you were doing your rounds, earlier on Sunday evening?'

He opened his mouth but she cut across him. 'I know you fed me a line. You got your story muddled.'

He frowned. 'I don't know what I said, but I was out checking the cottages. I vary my route. It gets boring otherwise.'

He folded his arms and she knew she'd get no more out of him.

Later that night she updated the WhatsApp group. She was convinced Liam was innocent but his lies still bothered her. What the heck had he been up to, earlier on Sunday evening? It had to be something serious for him to keep lying. If he wasn't the killer, perhaps he was an accessory. He could have gone to fetch a suitable murder weapon and place it where Nena had died. But if so, why slash her pillows when he knew she'd soon be dead?

Eve slept uneasily that night. She dreamed of thudding feet, running down Haunted Lane.

26

Over breakfast the following morning, Eve tried to put her nightmare out of her head. Hearing the footfalls was said to signify danger, but anyone might conjure them up at a time like this.

She sat in her dining room, facing facts. The idea of Jamie or Tess committing cold-blooded murder was horrific. But Nena had cared nothing for Tess's feelings. Meanwhile, Jamie was the sort to feel his sister's pain. The prize could have been an enemy removed and a valuable painting to sell. The money would seriously ease their situation.

She put her toast down. Didn't feel hungry. 'I can see it, Gus. It would be a terrible, desperate plot, but it's possible.'

Eve followed the train of thought. She was already sure Jamie had been away from his desk long enough to steal and stow Nena's painting. It would have been risky, but less so than sneaking off for forty minutes to commit murder. Meanwhile, Tess could have left any time after 11.15, when she and Liam had talked to Sadie. She could have told Nena she wanted to meet and used the back stairs and the dining-room exit to sneak out. Eve doubted Nena would have seen the danger, least of all from kind, gentle Tess.

All Tess needed was for Liam to alibi her. Either he was in on it, or more likely – given he wouldn't slash pillows for a dead woman – he'd been presented with a fait accompli. In that case, it would have been in his interests to agree. If he gave her away, he'd lose out too. And besides, he'd wanted to get rid of Nena.

Eve drained her coffee. 'I don't like any of this,' she said, giving Gus a pat, 'but however awful it is, it has to be resolved.'

Gus got up and shook himself as Eve grabbed her mobile. She needed to tell the police what she'd discovered.

She spoke to Greg Boles and explained why she thought Liam was innocent.

'Don't get me wrong, he's a nasty piece of work, but slashing the pillows makes no sense if he knew Nena would never see them. And the murder looks premeditated now.'

'*True...*' Greg didn't sound convinced. He lowered his voice. '*I'm not sure the DI will believe it.*'

Eve had to admit it wasn't proof, but she was sure in her own mind.

At that moment, a hubbub started in Greg's office. It increased in volume. Urgent comments. A voice raised in command.

'*I'm sorry, Eve.*' Greg sounded breathless. '*I've got to go. There's been a development.*'

She was left wondering, a chill trickle of fear snaking down her spine. Echoes of last night's footfalls played in her head. *Ridiculous.*

'C'mon, Gus.' She fetched his leash, half wanting to stay inside and close her eyes to reality. It wouldn't do. 'We need to find out what's going on.'

As they walked up Haunted Lane towards the village green, hope did battle with fear. Greg's office had gone from being calm and quiet to a hive of urgent activity. That could mean one of two things.

Please let them have made an arrest. She closed her eyes for a moment as though concentrating could make it happen. An arrest now could save Simon's future. The alternative didn't bear thinking about.

She saw a patrol car drive by.

Please.

Then another.

And then an ambulance went past.

Eve felt cold all over. *No, no, no.*

Viv must have seen her from Monty's window. She was by Eve's side in a moment. Gus whined and pressed himself close to Eve's legs.

'What's going on?' Viv's eyes were wide, her face pale. 'I saw the police. And an ambulance. Someone's been hurt?'

Eve only hoped it wasn't worse. 'I don't know.'

'I can't bear it if someone else has died.' Viv's eyes filled with tears. 'I hope to goodness Simon's safe.'

Jonah strode over from the teashop, solid and reassuring, with his kind brown eyes and bushy beard. 'Come here, Mum.' He pulled her into a bear hug which Eve felt was the best comfort on offer right now. Thank goodness he was there.

'I'm going to see what I can discover. I'll let you know as soon as I find out more.'

She walked Gus down Love Lane, following the route the emergency vehicles had taken. A scientific support van passed her. This was just the worst.

The wind was thrashing the trees, blowing Gus's ears back. Delicate work in this weather would be almost impossible.

As she reached Heath Lane, she saw cordons up in Blind Eye Wood. Already, figures in protective suits were combing the area. Palmer was gesticulating, Greg Boles talking to a colleague.

It had to be a second death, but who?

Eve was shaking. As the rain started, she took Gus home, then walked to the village store. If a neighbour had discovered a body, Moira was sure to know.

Inside, the storekeeper was in full flow, but her appearance stopped Eve in her tracks. She was in tears, mascara streaked down her cheeks. Never, in the four years Eve had known her, had she seen her with a hair out of place. The shivery feeling intensified.

And then she heard the name.

'Tess. Yes, I'm afraid so. So very shocking. Struck over the head, just like Nena was.'

27

Eve felt winded. Poor, poor Tess. She texted Viv to tell her the victim wasn't Simon and promised more news soon. It was too brutal to pass her dreadful knowledge on in such an impersonal way. When she reached the head of the queue at the store, Moira leaned over the counter and hugged her. Another rarity.

'Dear Eve. It's so very awful, isn't it? Tess was such a sweet-natured person.'

'She seemed lovely.' Even as Eve had suspected her, she'd still thought of her as a good person who'd gone catastrophically off the rails. 'Do you know who found her body?'

Moira named one of the dog-walking fraternity, a man Eve knew by sight. 'It must have been around eight or so.'

Shortly before Greg had cut her short.

'I know you'll need all the details,' Moira went on, 'but the poor man was so shocked he hardly had any, according to those I've spoken to. Just that she'd been knocked to the ground like Nena. I suppose we must assume it's the same killer.'

Or someone trying to make it look that way.

'I keep thinking about poor dear Jamie,' Moira said. 'What must he be going through?'

. . .

As Eve left the store, her mind was on Jamie too. Because if Liam hadn't killed Nena and the other key players had alibis then she had to ask the unthinkable. Could he have killed his sister? It seemed impossible, but she forced herself to invent scenarios.

Perhaps Tess had murdered Nena and instigated the plan for Jamie to steal her painting. It could have led to crippling remorse that she couldn't conquer. She might have told Jamie they'd have to come clean after all, because she couldn't bear it.

Jamie could have killed Tess to stop her talking, thinking of the effect it would have on his mother. They could have argued in the woods. Jamie might have remonstrated with her then lashed out in misery and fear.

It was a horrible thought. Maybe she was wrong about Liam. Perhaps he could have slashed the pillows, despite planning to kill Nena shortly afterwards. A double bluff.

But a small voice told her it made no sense. It would be too much risk for too little reward.

In the back of her mind, Edgar Horace floated, with his fake watch and the sudden purchase of a ruby brooch. But him accessing Nena's room still seemed like a stretch, let alone stealing a painting and selling it in such a short space of time.

Perhaps Nena and Tess had been killed by two different people.

Back at Elizabeth's Cottage, Eve called round the WhatsApp group to pass on the news. Daphne seemed too stunned to react. Eventually, she promised to tell Sylvia in a voice that was mechanical with shock. Viv and Simon were both in tears. This was a much harder blow than Nena's death. Tess had been in the village since childhood and they'd both known and liked her.

After she'd given Simon a moment to take it in, she gently steered him back to the investigation.

'It's horrible to think clinically at a time like this, but Jamie and Tess were looking most likely for Nena's murder, just by process of elimination. And now Tess is dead...' She let the sentence hang.

'*I can't believe it of him,*' Simon said.

'My gut instinct is the same, but I'm all but certain Liam's out of it and although Edgar Horace's spending is suspicious, he doesn't seem likely.' And Jamie had been under pressure. Sleep deprived. Full of worry. 'There's only one way forward: to work like crazy to find out the truth. Even if Jamie and Tess killed Nena, Jamie might not be guilty this time.' Her mind ran over the possibilities. 'Perhaps it was Liam. He could have lashed out if Tess told him she was leaving.' Either way, it was devastating. Nothing could bring Tess back, but Eve was determined to get justice for her. 'The police will be interviewing everyone at Saltwater today, of course. It'll be hard to progress things, but could I have a list of the centre's guests when Nena was killed? I'd like to call them. I can say I'm collecting material for her obituary and work other questions into conversation. I want to know what anyone passing reception saw. I know the police have asked, but people panic when they talk to the authorities. They might have missed things out.'

Simon took an unsteady breath. '*I'll get you the information. Thanks, Eve. It's got to be worth a try. Poor, poor Tess.*'

After keeping a stiff upper lip, Eve went to the bathroom and had a good cry. It seemed impossible that a woman she'd spoken to just yesterday was dead. She'd been wronged. Unhappy. If she'd killed Nena, then it was the most despicable crime, but Eve couldn't help feeling sorry for her.

She was glad to have a focus when Simon's list came through. She worked methodically down the names, taking detailed notes of each call she made, pausing to air Gus at lunchtime. She met Viv on the village green, under lowering skies that promised more rain.

'I'm thanking my lucky stars for Jonah. He's keeping the show on the road. The news is only just sinking in. Jim dropped in, by the way.'

He was Saxford St Peter's vicar. The most informal, jovial and perceptive one Eve had ever met. Eve wasn't strictly a believer, but she believed in Jim all right.

'He's inviting the villagers and everyone at Saltwater Cottages to share memories of Nena and Tess at the church tomorrow.'

It sounded like a good move. The villagers would need solace, and company would help. The occasion might be informative for Eve too.

'I promised I'd tell you and spread the word.'

'Thanks.'

'Simon told me you're ringing round the guests. Anything yet?'

Eve longed to provide good news. 'Lots, but nothing helpful I'm afraid.' As Viv's face fell, she gave her arm a squeeze. 'I've got more to go. I'll keep you posted.'

Back at home, Eve ate lunch, then Gus settled at her feet as the sky outside darkened and the rain began to fall. She spent all afternoon calling.

By the time she'd finished she'd spoken to the witness who'd noticed Jamie was away from his desk at 11.45 p.m. No one else had information on his movements. Most people had left Curlew Cottage by ten, when the bar closed and he'd come on duty.

She got a few interesting snippets, though. Someone had seen Sadie striding along Saltwater End at around twenty to eleven. She was moving so purposefully that she'd blanked them, which the guest thought was odd, because she'd been scrupulously polite in general.

There was another who'd seen Tess dashing through the grounds sometime after ten thirty, head down, in floods of tears. That must have been after Gemma had heard her crying in her suite. It proved she'd gone out.

And then there was the chatty woman who'd talked about Iggy strolling along Saltwater End in a dream, whistling a love song. She'd clearly fancied him and wanted to know if he was in a relationship. That had been earlier in the evening. It had only struck Eve because it reminded her of the roses he'd bought from Moira.

She thought again of Iggy's cheerful reaction to Nena's spilled ink, and of her telling him about the poison-pen letter. If the roses hadn't been for her, she couldn't guess the recipient. Moira would have done her level best to find out. The fact that she'd failed probably meant the relationship was secret, which would fit. Nena would have been two-timing Liam.

Eve carried on reviewing the guest responses and came to the man who'd seen Nena reading in her room at 11.20, a little after Sadie had spotted her. There were a couple of others who'd glimpsed her similarly occupied too, but this last man had commented on her expression.

'I caught sight of her smile, just briefly. It's funny, I thought at the time she looked as though she was planning some kind of mischief. But I never thought it would lead her into danger. If only I'd known.'

Eve visualised her in the wing-backed armchair that stood by her mirror, anticipating an adventure, perhaps. It had all been cut short so quickly.

It was later that evening that Eve realised she'd had a visitor. There was a bit of paper on the doormat, folded in half.

Inside was typed:

NONE OF KEY PLAYERS HAVE ALIBIS. EARLY DOG WALKER SAW SADIE IN THE WOODS AT 6.30 A.M. CLOSE TO WHERE

T ESS N ORLAND WAS FOUND . D OC ESTIMATES TIME OF DEATH BETWEEN MIDNIGHT AND 3 A.M.

Greg. He didn't usually contact her directly. The thought filled her with worry about Robin. Perhaps he hadn't responded when Greg called. She texted him.

Hope you're okay. I love you.

His reply came within seconds, flooding her with relief.

Hanging in there. Love you too. Please take care.

She wasn't sure if Greg had told him about Tess. He had enough on his plate at the moment. She'd wait to fill him in.

As she went to bed, she turned her mind to Greg's note. Sadie had been in the vicinity of Tess's body the morning after her death, just as she'd been with Nena. Yet her alibi for Nena held firm. It couldn't mean anything, but as Eve slept, she dreamed of it.

28

The following day, Eve went to St Peter's with Gus for Jim Thackeray's gathering in memory of Nena and Tess. The church was a comforting place with its soft lighting, white walls and angel roof. Jim stood near the door welcoming people. Quietly kind and grave today, yet informal as always. Speaking from the heart.

Eve's neighbours were dotted about the church, some kneeling in pews, praying, some standing in small groups, crying or talking in hushed tones. Small children were less quiet, with no real idea of what was going on. Their chatter and running feet helped. It was a touch of normality. Gus was adding to that, spotting his favourite villagers in turn and pottering off to see them with a tentative wag of his tail.

Eve couldn't see anyone from Saltwater Cottages yet. She went to join Viv and the gang from the Cross Keys.

Jo's eyes were teary. 'A terrible business, this.' She shook her head and turned to Eve. 'Are you making any headway?'

Eve kept her voice as low as Jo's. 'Some, but no break-through yet.'

'A lot of people suspect Liam, of course,' Jo said, checking over her shoulder before she spoke. 'There's been all sorts of mutterings about him and Nena, so it doesn't surprise me.'

Eve thought of Tess's discarded silver bracelet. Liam lashing out in selfish panic was definitely believable if Tess had decided to end the marriage. Jo carried on talking quietly about the Norland brothers until a hush fell over the room. Simon had arrived. His eyes were red-rimmed. Viv rushed over to pull him into a hug.

Ten minutes after that, the party from Saltwater Cottages appeared in dribs and drabs. First Sadie, looking pale, her eyes bloodshot. Then Gemma, stiff and tight-lipped. Her hard gaze drilled into the back of Sadie's head. It made Eve think of the time she'd seen her, Sadie and Iggy outside Saltwater Cottages, each of them tense and watchful.

Liam and Iggy walked in, wearing dark suits. Liam looked at the floor. Iggy was in tears. Eve thought of his and Tess's youthful romance and Tess's photo of him in her drawer. It was so tragic.

Last of all came Jamie. She could hardly watch. Like Iggy, he was in tears, collapsing in on himself. Poor Jim; he was moving from one group to another, there were so many people to comfort. Ultimately, he stuck with Jamie, who looked the most devastated. Iggy and Liam were quickly surrounded by villagers.

'Moira's right in there, I see,' Viv said, taking a biscuit from the selection Jim had provided. 'I'd swear I just saw her elbow Deidre Lennox out of the way.'

They talked about Tess and the case, endlessly chewing over ideas in hushed tones. Half an hour later, they were disturbed by raised voices.

Liam and Jamie.

'What were you thinking of, letting Tess go out alone so late at night? When there'd just been a murder?' Jamie was leaning in close to Liam's face, his fist bunched, his gaze boring into his brother-in-law's. 'It's not the action of a caring husband! But of course, we all know who you cared for!'

Liam thrust his face still closer to Jamie's, as Jim hurried towards them. Jim said something, his hands raised placatingly, but his words were drowned out.

'What are you implying?'

'That you weren't bothered about my sister. You take more care of your tools than you took of her. Didn't you think it might be dangerous to let her wander off like that?'

Eve saw Jo catch Toby and Matt's eyes and tip her head towards the quarrel, but she needn't have intervened. They were already on the move.

'She was upset, you halfwit! She wanted to be alone! What do you imagine I could do? I wasn't her keeper!'

'You could have followed her. And perhaps you did. Someone must have. I know what you've been saying about her. That she was a pain. Impossible to live with. Word gets back, you know?'

Liam lunged at Jamie. It could have been far worse if Matt and Toby hadn't pulled them apart.

'I don't think Jamie killed Tess,' Viv said. She, Eve and Simon were walking along the beach.

'You're probably right.' Eve had baulked at the idea instinctively. Besides, his misery and distrust of Liam had sounded genuine. 'He or Tess could still have killed Nena, though. And taken the painting, if it was stolen. Then maybe Liam killed Tess, just as Jamie suspects.'

Simon put his hand to his forehead. 'It's possible. How on earth can we prove it?'

'The police were already keen on Liam for Nena's murder

and I doubt they'll take much notice of my theories. Perhaps they'll arrest him for both.'

'I want justice,' Simon blinked in the fierce wind, 'not just a resolution. But I can believe Liam's guilty.'

Eve wished she wasn't so convinced he hadn't killed Nena.

'What now?' Viv asked.

'It's a small thing, but I'd like to go to the doctors to ask about dog bites.'

They looked at her questioningly.

'Gemma claims she got hers walking in the fields. If I can find something that suggests otherwise, I've got a reason to push her on it. She could be your brick thrower, Simon, and her note might refer to anyone. Maybe she found out something about Liam or Jamie that could help us. I can't see why she'd push you to investigate, but I'd like to get it out of her.'

'Good thought,' Viv said, 'though how you'll get a doctors' receptionist to give out personal information is beyond me.'

'I won't have to. I've got a plan.'

'All right, Sherlock. Want me to watch Gus while you go in?'

'Sounds good.'

'I'd better get back,' Simon said. 'The guy from the bank's head office has given me piles of forms to complete. I've got a call with Polly in a bit too. And soon she'll be home so we can talk properly. How on earth will I explain?' He looked as uneasy as Eve had ever seen him. 'I'm scared about what she'll say.' His voice had lowered to a whisper.

As they watched Simon leave, Viv said, 'If Polly lets him down, I will sneak into their house and swap her shampoo for chilli oil.'

'I know it'll be a shock, but it's like you said before. She loves him to bits.'

Viv took a deep breath. 'Yes, you're right. His fear's getting to me.' She turned to Eve. 'Do you think *we* should tell her? Put Simon out of his misery?'

'Definitely not.'

'Your certainty is slightly intimidating.'

'It's the only thing I am certain about, if that makes it any better.'

They walked up Heath Lane in silence, then up Love Lane and over the bridge to the surgery. Viv waited outside, crouching down to fuss Gus. Eve suspected it was dog comforting human, not the other way about.

She pushed on the surgery door. For all her confident talk, she wasn't looking forward to play-acting.

At the counter, the receptionist pushed her glasses up her nose and looked at Eve, her eyes narrowing. 'You don't have an appointment today, do you, Eve?'

'It's all right. This is about something different. I know you can't discuss cases, but I wondered, in a general way, if any patients have been in with dog bites recently.' She lowered her voice. 'Only I'm a bit worried about a badly controlled animal near the stables. I'm trying to find out if it's as dangerous as I think it is. I was hoping to get a sense of whether it's actually bitten anyone. It scared me, but if it's harmless, I don't want to cause trouble.'

The receptionist's brow furrowed in concentration. 'I've heard rumours about that dog, but like you, nothing concrete. I blame the owner.'

'I'm sure you're right.'

She took her glasses off and polished them. 'We did have a dog bite case in recently, but as far as I know it was a different animal. A loose one, out in the fields.' That sounded like Gemma's story. 'Shocking, letting an animal run wild like that. You'd think people would be more careful.'

'It sounds like a frightening encounter. I hope they reported it.'

The woman nodded. 'I suggested she should, but she didn't sound keen. She thought it would be pointless when she couldn't identify the owner. When I pressed her she got quite shirty. Some people have no sense. She'd tried to clean it up herself too. Clearly left it a while before letting us have a look.'

She tutted and Eve pulled a sympathetic face and thanked her for her time.

Outside, Eve told Viv what she'd heard. 'It's suggestive. The delay and the reluctance to involve the authorities both look suspicious.'

'They certainly do! What the heck does Gemma mean by vandalising my brother's house?'

'I don't know, but I hope I can use what I've discovered to push her into telling me. I can pretend to know more than I do.'

At home, over lunch, Eve googled Gemma and found the restaurant where she'd worked previously. A highly rated establishment in a place called Porthruan in the West Country. According to the restaurant's 'About us' page, they'd won countless awards and had featured in the national papers with glowing reviews.

Eve had assumed Gemma had been an underling, but it was like Edgar Horace in reverse. She'd been Chef de Cuisine, leading a team.

Yet now she was a sous chef, and at a venue where food wasn't the primary attraction. It was a definite step down.

She called Simon to ask about it.

'*The demotion crossed my mind,*' Simon said, '*but she said she didn't see it that way. She claimed she'd love to help put Saltwater on the map for its cuisine as well as its classes, and it meant the world to be near her mum. She's frail, apparently.*'

'And her references were fine, obviously?'

'*Glowing.*'

Eve was thoughtful after she'd rung off. She looked down at Gus. 'I'd want to be near my parents if one of them was ailing.'

She hated being so far away, despite their good health. 'It could all be true.' But it was as she'd thought before: it seemed odd that Gemma's mum had moved recently if she was ill. Perhaps Gemma had come to Suffolk for other reasons. To get close to someone she despised? She'd admitted she hadn't liked Nena. It was like Sadie: if it weren't for her alibi, Eve would be looking at her very closely indeed.

29

Over lunch, thoughts of Gemma fizzed in Eve's head, but it was time to shift focus. She was due at her appointment with Nena Field's mother. Her information would be vital for the obituary but potentially for the case too. Eve still clung to the hope that Tess hadn't killed Nena before being killed herself.

Nena's mother looked fragile. Her fine silvery hair hung lankly, and her blue eyes watered as she greeted Eve.

Eve went from being lost in the puzzle of her daughter's death, to being right back in the storm. 'Eve Mallow. I'm so very sorry for your loss, Ms Lamb.'

A tear slipped down Nena's mother's cheek and Eve took her hand and held it.

'Thank you.' The grip in return was tight, as though Eve was a life raft. 'Please, call me Delilah. Do come through.'

They entered an elegant sitting room with Regency furniture and floor-to-ceiling windows. The gathering dusk was shut out by long silk curtains.

A second woman appeared, similar to Delilah in age but with more vitality. 'Elsa,' Delilah said vaguely. Eve wondered if she'd been given sedatives. 'A very old friend.'

Elsa's eyes were bright and birdlike as she nodded to Eve. 'I'll make tea.'

'Please.' Delilah motioned Eve to a chair by a coffee table. 'So you're writing about Nena.'

Eve nodded. 'For *Icon*. Obituary writing's my profession. I was staying at Saltwater Cottages when Nena died. I'd started to get to know her, so the job feels personal.'

There was quiet desperation in Delilah's eyes. 'I'm glad you knew her. Nena was everything to me. She was forever travelling after she got famous. I felt as though I hardly saw her. I was excited when I heard she'd be in Suffolk for a while.'

Heard? Eve hesitated. Delilah must be in enough pain already. 'She didn't tell you herself?'

The woman gave a faltering smile. 'Someone got there first.'

'It must have been lovely to see her.'

She hesitated. 'We hadn't actually met up yet. We had a date pencilled in.' She twisted her hands. 'I wanted to visit her at the centre, but she said she was busy. It was understandable, of course.' Her voice cracked. 'I can't believe it's too late.'

'It's terrible. So sudden and unpredictable. I can imagine Nena was rushed off her feet. Planning lessons and dealing with guests all day.'

And sleeping with Liam in his grotty workshop, of course. She guessed Nena hadn't been sentimental about her mother. Or they hadn't got on.

Elsa reappeared with tea, then faded into the background.

'Were you and Nena close when she was a child?' Eve asked gently. 'I know I was a horror when I was growing up. I don't know how my parents put up with me.' In reality, she'd been boringly conformist. Worked hard at school. Never got into trouble unless there'd been a miscarriage of justice. Those had always cut her to the quick.

'We were very close,' Delilah said. 'Of course, it was a difficult time when her father and I separated, but it was for the best. Pointless to make a child endure our rows.'

That made sense.

'I did my utmost to let her know she was loved.' Delilah's voice was tight. 'I found it difficult. She would spend the school year with me, the summer holidays with her father. The fun bit.' Her tone was momentarily bitter. 'It was emotionally confusing for us all.'

'You missed her when she was with her dad, I guess?'

'Desperately.' Her voice was almost inaudible. 'I was always scared in case she didn't want to come back. The treats her dad gave her and the freedom of the long summer holidays were a heady mix. I tried to make life here as appealing as possible.'

The fear was still there in Delilah's voice, despite the deaths of both her daughter and her ex-husband. Eve felt desperately sorry for her. All that time spent in high anxiety in case she put a foot wrong. Eve could totally see it. If she and her ex had split when the twins were children she'd have been in the same boat. Thank goodness she'd never needed to work out how to handle it. The long stretches Nena had spent with each parent sounded unusual. She must have felt uprooted each time she'd moved. Eve guessed switching parents every other weekend, or midweek, would have allowed for more of a routine. Though from Nena's point of view, each move might have been exciting, and Eve knew how adaptable kids were. 'Was Nena's dad keen to have her?'

'Oh yes, he was always desperate to take her away from me.'

Eve thought of the spa room he'd reportedly had built for her. Had he felt the exact same pressure Delilah had? Nena had spent a much larger chunk of each year with her mum. Maybe he'd wanted to go big each time she visited, to ensure she never forgot him or stopped wanting to come.

'I read an article that mentioned Nena spending six months

with a friend of yours, when you couldn't look after her. Her father didn't want to have her then?'

'It wouldn't have worked. He was so busy.' Delilah spoke quickly, her tone defensive. 'He wouldn't have paid her any attention. It was better for Celia to have her.'

'Could I get in touch with Celia? It would be lovely to get her memories too.'

But Delilah shook her head. 'I got a letter telling me she'd died.' She sighed. 'It was such a shock.' She wandered over to a bookcase and took out an album to show Eve. It was full of pictures of Nena growing up. Swimming in the sea, preparing to dive off a boat backwards, looking drunk at a party. Laughing, her eyes sparkling.

'Could I include some of these?' Eve said. 'I could get someone from *Icon* to digitise them. They're wonderful for showing the sort of person Nena was.'

Delilah nodded as she blinked away tears.

They carried on talking for another half hour, then Delilah put her head on the table and wept. It was without warning and Eve was horrified that she'd pushed the woman too far. She whispered that she would go.

It was the companion, Elsa, who saw her out.

'I'm sorry,' Eve said. 'It's such a terrible time.'

Elsa nodded. 'She and her former husband both doted on Nena.'

'It sounds as though Delilah was very anxious about their relationship after the divorce. Was her husband trying to get sole custody?'

But Elsa shook her head. 'I was friends with them both, and Alfred wasn't a bad man. He was panicked about losing Nena, just as Delilah was.' She shook her head. 'I put it down to their background. They were each bullied for years at school. They bonded over it, but it damaged them. Neither of them had any sense of self-worth. Delilah's the best friend I could wish for, but she can't see it herself. I don't think she could imagine why Nena might want to stay with her.'

That explained a lot. And because of Delilah's desperation, Nena appeared to have lost all respect for her. Perhaps for her father too.

It was achingly sad. 'Thank you for being so frank. I certainly won't put it in print, but it goes a long way to explaining some of the things Nena did.'

Elsa shook her head. 'She was extraordinarily difficult by the time she was a teenager. I always worried about how her life would pan out.'

Thoughts of Nena and her parents filled Eve's head on her journey home. Memories of Delilah sobbing plagued her. Thank goodness she'd got Elsa.

Halfway back to Saxford, her phone rang. Robin. She answered hands free.

'How are things?'

'*A bit of progress today.*' She could hear the smile in his voice. '*One person's talking. His evidence won't do on its own, but it's a start.*'

'That's great news.'

'*But I was calling about Tess.*'

'The police are going hard after Liam, I guess.'

'*That's right. They've seized the jacket you found with the bloodstain. He's admitted to the tyre and pillow slashing, but he's making the same argument against Nena's murder that you did. Palmer's convinced it's him for both killings, but they haven't got enough to tie him to either yet. They're taking his suite apart and searching the woods with a fine-toothed comb. Greg says Palmer's not looking at anyone else. There's not much more, but Tess was wearing that silver bracelet you told me about when she was found.*'

The present from Liam.

'That's interesting. Thank you.'

As they said their goodbyes, the implications sank in. Tess had been in emotional turmoil. She'd known Liam was a louse, and it had cut deep. If she hadn't cared, she'd have put the bracelet to one side. Chucking it in the bin showed her hurt, just as slashing the print had. Yet by the time she was killed, she'd been wearing it again. Unless he'd put it on her dead body, she'd still loved him. And assuming that was true, Eve doubted she'd threatened to end their marriage. Her image of Liam lashing out in fear of losing her faded. Of course, he could have killed her if she'd known he'd killed Nena, but Eve was still sure he hadn't.

So if Liam hadn't killed Tess, who had? Jamie, to protect himself because she knew he was guilty? Because they'd been in it together, or she'd discovered his plans? Eve's chest ached at the thought. Surely he wouldn't have?

As her headlights played over the grass verges, she reviewed her previous thoughts. The possibility that Jamie had stolen Nena's painting. The fact that he was short of money and had every reason to be furious with Nena. The knowledge that he had left his desk for longer than he'd admitted.

She could still envisage him and his sister working together, with him as thief, and her as murderer. Vice versa was also possible, but the longer Jamie was away from reception, the greater the risk.

But for Jamie to kill Tess as well? She was with Simon and Viv. She couldn't accept it.

The problem was, if Liam hadn't killed Tess in a crime of passion, it seemed likely that Nena's killer had taken her life because of what she knew.

It was all very well to dismiss Jamie, but if Eve was right, and Liam was innocent of that crime, then Jamie was the last suspect standing. Unless you counted Edgar Horace, who was probably only alibied by his wife.

As she tossed and turned that night, she kept coming up against a mixture of circumstantial evidence and gut instinct that refused to be denied.

But if neither Jamie nor Liam had killed Tess, then it was unlikely they'd murdered Nena. So who was guilty? What was she missing?

As the hours crept on, Eve's mind was full of muddled thoughts and images. The photos she'd taken of Jamie's notebook. Melanie Blomquist's call. The indented numbers. Jamie's breathlessness. His personal situation. Then everything else she knew. Facts and observations tumbling like leaves in an eddy.

At around three in the morning, several disparate thoughts mingled.

She sat up in bed, shivering. *Heck.* Disparate they might be, but they could be related... What if that was the answer?

She needed to talk to Simon and someone who knew Edgar Horace.

30

On Saturday morning, Eve dug out the details of the gentlemen's outfitters where Edgar Horace worked and dialled their number. Gus sat by her side, his eyes fixed on hers each time she looked down. She'd swear he looked judgemental.

As the ring tone sounded, she went over her lines again.

'*Simpkins Outfitters. How may I help you?*'

'Oh yes, I'm sorry to bother you. I'm calling from the Cherry Tree. We're a restaurant. I have a booking and the guest has given us this number. But I'm afraid we've got a problem. The name's not clear. It looks like Edward something? And the surname – I'm not sure. It begins with H. It might be Horace.'

The voice at the other end became sniffy. '*That sounds like Edgar. Edgar Horace. Though what he was doing giving you our number I don't know. We're not his secretarial service.*' They paused and apologised, as though they realised they were shooting the messenger.

'Edgar,' Eve hesitated deliberately. 'You're sure? Is Mr Horace the manager there?' She knew he wasn't, of course.

The voice scoffed now. '*Hardly. Though you might imagine so, talking to him.*'

Staggeringly unprofessional! But if Horace behaved at work as he had at Saltwater Cottages then she could understand it. 'Um...' Eve did the hesitation thing again and tried to ignore Gus, whose stare had intensified. 'Well, I don't want to be indiscreet, but the Cherry Tree is... well, it's high-end. Our customers normally spend at least four hundred pounds a head with us. I'm sorry to ask, but would that be consistent with Mr Horace's lifestyle? Or do you think I've got the wrong person?'

The man on the phone heaved a sigh. '*Oh no, that's perfectly consistent. He has family money, as he frequently reminds us. Working here is part of the deal. His grandfather founded the place and so long as he shows up and smiles at the occasional customer, his allowance is secure. He's been in the same role since he was eighteen. He—*'

The man was interrupted by a voice in the background. Eve missed the words but the tone was sharp. A second later a woman came on the line.

'*I do apologise. Now, how may I help you?*'

Eve told the woman she'd already got the information she needed and got off the phone as soon as possible.

Gus followed Eve to the kitchen as she went to make a coffee.

'A useful call. I'm lucky I got the indiscreet guy first, not the professional woman. So Edgar Horace is wealthy, despite not being a high-flyer. It's the fake Rolex that's inconsistent.' It fitted with her theory. One step forward.

Her dachshund put his head on one side, as though he was giving her points serious thought. She bent to give him a hug.

She called Simon next. He sounded listless when he answered. '*The house feels empty without Polly. Our conversation yesterday was so stilted, and the atmosphere at the stables is odd. Officially, no one knows how precarious my situation is, but everyone's tense. I can feel it. I suppose it's the disaster that's unfolding at Saltwater. If I'm failing at that business, they prob-*'

ably wonder if the stables will be next.' He sounded slightly brighter when she asked her question. *'I'll get onto it straight away.'*

His hopeful tone made her shrink inside. Solving any part of this case would be useful, but she was nowhere near identifying the killer.

It took him a while to call back. Eve doodled nervously in her notepad as she waited, then paced, which seemed to disconcert Gus.

At last, Simon produced the news she'd tentatively expected.

'Thank you. I think this might mean something. We haven't found our murderer, but I suspect the view will be clearer soon. I'll let you know as soon as I confirm anything.'

He didn't push her to tell him now, as Viv would have. Perhaps he felt it would be tempting fate.

Eve texted Jamie next. She could barely imagine how badly he was suffering, but she needed to talk to him. She explained it was relevant to the case, which felt wrong too. It wasn't going to solve the murders, but it might rule him out.

He agreed to meet her at Saltwater Cottages and Eve messaged her plans to the WhatsApp group before heading off.

Forty minutes later, Jamie sat opposite Eve, his pale face dragged down with misery.

They were in a room in the admin area in Curlew Cottage. Eve had seen none of the other staff but she wasn't worried to be alone with Jamie. She felt sure of her ground now she'd done her checks.

She leaned forward. 'I'm so very sorry for what you're going through. And for approaching you at a time like this. Poor Tess's death makes everything all the more urgent. I wish to goodness she hadn't died.'

He nodded, his hair falling forward over his pale, red-eyed face.

'Cards on the table, I was so anxious for Simon that I did some snooping in the aftermath of Nena's death.'

He contracted slightly in his chair. His eyes down.

She waited for him to think about what she'd said, then continued. 'It always seemed odd that you were so breathless and anxious when I came to you for aspirin, the night Nena died. Your explanation, that you'd been worried about a double booking, didn't fit. The software here would stop you offering the same place twice.'

His head was in his hands now.

She went on. 'I'm afraid I peeked at your notes while you were away from your desk. I saw the message you took from Melanie Blomquist. She's not really a friend of my mother's. If you'd talked to her, you'd have confirmed her name, not written it down with a couple of question marks. So I concluded the call went to voicemail. Yet word has it you were also away from your desk ten minutes later. And then I found you, red in the face and breathless, later still. I was scared in case you'd followed Nena into the woods. Got so furious with her that you'd lost control.'

He looked at her now, eyes teary, expression exhausted. 'I didn't.' She had the impression he wouldn't care if he was arrested. Everything was so awful, it couldn't get any worse. 'It's true that I hated her. I saw her making out with Liam. I wasn't sorry when I heard what had happened. But I didn't follow her. I tried to see what she and Iggy were up to on Saturday night when you saw me by the car park. If she was sleeping with him too, I thought I could use it to drive a wedge between her and Liam. But I never went to the woods on Sunday. And you know I'd never kill Tess.'

Eve nodded and took a deep breath. 'I believe you. But you lied to the police. You were gone from your desk for a stretch in the run-up to midnight.' She watched him closely. 'I found a couple of numbers in your logbook. A four and a six. Just the indents of them, as though you or someone else had pressed on that page when you wrote them. And now Simon's confirmed the number of the safe here is 7046.'

Jamie's jaw went slack.

'Why did you write it down?'

He was silent.

'Was Tess going to access the safe originally?'

At last, he nodded. 'She couldn't bring herself to, in the end. She knew it was wrong. But I was desperate, so I went myself.'

'And switched the Rolex that was in there, belonging to Mr Horace, with a fake.'

He slumped in his chair. 'Yes. He was behaving like such an entitled idiot in the bar on Saturday evening. He seemed like the most undeserving man I'd ever met, yet there he was with his expensive watch.'

Eve remembered how Tess had tried to soothe Mr Horace and how Sadie had escorted him to the safe, to stow his watch. He hadn't wanted to go to and fro with it, so she'd suggested he leave it there for the duration of his stay. Then later, she'd seen Tess and Jamie talking, their heads close together. She'd thought they looked shifty at the time.

'How long were you away from your desk? And do you know roughly what time?'

Jamie's brow furrowed. 'I guess I left at around eleven thirty and I was back sometime before midnight. Around five to, maybe? I would have been quicker but I heard Gemma next door in the staffroom, taking a call. It was her mum. She seemed worried about something. Gemma had to keep soothing her. It took a while.'

The call tied in with Gemma's testimony, but the subject matter sounded interesting. 'You don't know why Gemma's mum was worried?'

He frowned and shook his head. 'Gemma just kept saying, "Don't worry, Mum, I *am* taking care."'

Eve was increasingly sure Gemma had thrown the brick. What was she up to? It sounded as though her mum might know about it. She filed the details away for later.

The timing of Jamie's trip to the safe fitted. He'd have got back to reception just before she arrived. 'How did you find a fake for that specific model so quickly?'

Jamie shook his head slowly. 'It was the other way round. I'd seen one, a week or so earlier, and that sparked the idea. Tess and I had been to London to call on my grandfather. My dad's dad.' He heaved out a sigh. 'We've been estranged for years; he's in his nineties now. I'd reached desperation point. I wanted to explain the debt Dad was in. See if he'd be willing to help. I thought he might have softened in his old age. But he told us he'd washed his hands of Dad, and that we should too.' A tear ran down his cheek. 'But I can't just throw him out, can I?' His eyes were pleading.

'I understand. It's a terribly difficult situation. Go on.'

'On the way home, we passed someone selling fake watches. He rushed up to me with one and tried to put it on me. He said everyone would look up to me with a vintage Rolex Submariner on my wrist. It sounded so ridiculous. I was like, what are you even talking about? A vintage what? I could have cried at the idea of spending money on a fake watch. I was already furious at shelling out the train fare for nothing.'

'But when Mr Horace let rip about his Rolex, you wondered if the journey hadn't been wasted after all?'

He nodded. 'I didn't know if the seller would be in the same spot. They must move all the time to avoid the police. But it seemed almost like a sign. I went back on the Sunday instead of sleeping between shifts. I was dead on my feet, but I was desperate. Anyway, I asked around and found him. I sent Tess a photo of the fake to check it was the same. She'd seen it up close and reckoned it was a match. I used money I'd borrowed from a mate to buy it. It was stupid. Stupid.'

Eve's heart went out to him. Stealing was an awful thing to do, but she could understand the temptation. And she agreed: Mr Horace was undeserving.

'When it came to the crunch, Tess was in tears. She said we'd got caught up in a dream. Swapping the watches would be crazy. But I'd seen one selling online for seventy grand. And things have been so difficult...'

She put a hand on his sleeve for a moment. 'So you went ahead?'

He nodded. 'I'd just got back from doing the switch when you turned up. It's normally quiet at night. And now I've lied to the police about where I was and I don't know what to do. And after all that, I realised Tess was right. I couldn't possibly sell the watch. I've been carrying it around. I thought things couldn't get any worse. But now I've lost Tess...'

It was at that moment that the door opened and Sadie came in. Jamie looked at her and burst into tears.

31

Sadie sat down at the table with Jamie and Eve. 'I heard most of that. I wanted a word with Simon and we were next door.'

Jamie's mouth fell open. 'Simon heard too?'

He must have come on the back of Eve's WhatsApp message. He'd be desperate to know what was happening. As for Jamie, he'd be anticipating the sack now, on top of everything else. Eve's heart bled for him. What a mess.

Sadie leaned forward. 'We've all done stupid things in our lives, Jamie.' She closed her eyes for a moment. 'I know I have. Sometimes we face a dire situation, and we make the wrong choice. If we're lucky, we realise and act on it. You've realised, and now we need to work out how to rectify things.'

Eve could have hugged her for being so understanding. But just below the gratitude other thoughts played. What mistake had Sadie made? And what had she done to rectify it? She thought again of the conversation she'd overheard outside Sadie's suite. She'd said she'd be the police's top suspect if they knew the truth. And if she didn't have an alibi. An alibi that could only be broken if she, Gemma and Iggy were all lying.

'I want to do something,' Jamie was saying. 'I'm desperate to. But my mind's blank. I'm so sorry.'

Eve focused on the problem. 'Mr Horace is staying at the Cross Keys. That's a bonus. At least we've still got access to him. And I'd imagine he's easily flattered.' Possibilities played in her mind.

'You've got an idea?' Sadie said.

'I don't know if it'll work.' Just the thought of it was putting her stomach in knots but she told them anyway.

Jamie's eyes widened. 'You're sure?'

Eve nodded.

'Thank you.'

Sadie turned to him. 'And I can help financially. Heaven knows I don't want the money Nena left me.'

'I can't let you do that.' There was pain in Jamie's voice.

'You honestly can. What I did for her doesn't deserve a reward. I'd be delighted to see you make use of it.'

Eve wondered at the meaning behind the words. She had the distinct feeling Sadie would be glad to get shot of the bequest.

Half an hour later, Eve was sitting with Simon and Viv in Simon's office at Saltwater.

'It's a bit of a shocker about Jamie,' Simon said.

'I know. I'm sorry. But he was going through a terrible time, even before Tess was killed.'

'And it's not as though he sold the watch,' Viv said earnestly. 'He knows right from wrong really.'

'Will you keep him on?' Eve could see it was a knotty problem.

Simon put his head in his hands. 'If it ever got out it would be a disaster, but I'd rather give him a second chance.'

Poor Simon. He'd be sticking his neck out when things were already teetering on the brink.

'So, where does this leave us?' he said.

'I think it's unlikely that Jamie killed Nena. It never did sit right with his character and it's hard to imagine him committing a murder as well as an unrelated theft.'

'But you don't think Liam's guilty either?'

The mystery seemed insurmountable. 'Logic says not. Edgar Horace seems unlikely now too. He's genuinely rolling in it, so stealing a painting becomes less of a motive. And although I'm sure he was furious at Nena for making fun of him, I can't see him killing over it, especially not with it being premeditated.'

Viv nodded.

'So we're left with no suspects?' Simon clutched at his hair.

'I'm not so sure. There's something odd going on.' She lowered her voice. 'Gemma, Sadie and Iggy all have possible motives, just as Liam, Jamie and Tess did.' And Eve had seen them together, more than once. Tense, yet often in a group. She shared the thought. 'It's almost as though something's binding them together, but not a natural link. I'm starting to wonder if it's the fact that they alibi each other.'

'You think they could be in cahoots?'

'I certainly think it's possible they disliked Nena and had an interest in getting her out of the way.'

For a second, Eve wondered about Liam and Tess too. Their activities the night Nena died were still unexplained. Had they been laying the ground? But a conspiracy involving five people seemed too ludicrous for words. She turned her mind back to Gemma, Sadie and Iggy.

'Gemma's motive's unclear, but I'm increasingly convinced she threw the brick. If Nena was the object of her anger, she could have killed her. She's a cool customer. Then Sadie inherits Nena's money. I don't think she wants it, but she and

Nena had a secret. She could have killed over that. As for Iggy, he bought a dozen red roses from Moira. Perhaps they were for Nena. He was very cheerful and forgiving when she told him about the spilled ink. Most people would have been irritated at least. She'd made a right mess. The pot was empty and still on its side when Liam fetched the rug. She hadn't even bothered to pick it up or call anyone before the ink dried.

'Iggy and Liam are very alike in looks. Perhaps Iggy was poised to take over from his brother but Nena changed her mind. Liam's been a thorn in his side all his life. He's the younger son, yet he inherited the family home. He's got his dad's ring and his workshop. To cap it all, Tess finished with Iggy and went out with Liam. You could imagine all that building up, with rivalry over Nena being the final straw.'

'And whoever's guilty killed Tess because she'd found them out?' Viv said.

'I'd guess so. Iggy still sounds fond of Tess, but if his freedom was at stake, even he might do it.'

There was a flicker of hope in Simon's eyes. 'A conspiracy sounds possible. It has to be worth exploring.'

'I agree.' She felt a burst of energy. 'I'll expand my focus to include the three of them. I'm going to start with Sadie. Nena left her so much money. There must be something highly significant in their past. I don't believe it's as simple as Sadie made out.

'We ought to keep the artworks in mind too. What happened to them? And if there never was a pen-and-ink drawing, then maybe we're missing some letters. Nena was using the ink for something. We now know that Jamie was away from his desk from around eleven thirty until five to midnight. I'd guess Nena left her room shortly after Jamie left the desk. He says he didn't see her go. Then we've got Liam sneaking in to slash her pillows and – possibly – a thief going in to steal a painting. It was a risk. They had no way of knowing when Jamie would be back.'

'And you're sure it wasn't Liam who stole the artwork?' Viv asked.

'He looked totally confused when I quizzed him about it. I don't think anyone could fake it to that extent.'

Simon leaned forward. 'And Jamie couldn't have taken the painting *and* switched the watches?'

Eve tried to make it fit but facts and hunches blocked her way. 'I can't see it. He felt too guilty to sell the watch. I doubt he's got that on his conscience as well. And how would he know Nena wasn't coming back to report the theft, unless he knew someone had killed her? And I can't believe Gemma, Sadie and Iggy would enlist him into their conspiracy as well.'

'So we're down to Iggy, Gemma or Sadie.' Simon's brow furrowed. 'They could have taken the painting, then followed Nena to kill her as they'd planned, to ensure they were never found out.'

'It's possible. If anyone stole it, it was probably then, as you say. Waiting until after they'd killed would have been too late. Jamie would have been back on reception, and he stayed there until after Nena's body was found. It's odd, though. Unless they knew Jamie would be gone for a while, the theft must have been impromptu. Yet the killing looks planned.' It was more logical to think the painting was missing for an innocent reason as Robin had suggested. She just couldn't quite accept that.

'It feels like we're back to square one, with three new suspects and no clue which might be guilty.' Simon's face was pinched.

And the conspiracy idea was based on thin evidence. Eve kept that thought to herself. A despairing Simon was hard to bear, and Sadie, Gemma and Iggy *had* been acting oddly. She had the distinct impression Sadie and Gemma disliked each other, yet they'd spent hours in the bar together. She turned to Simon. 'Wait until I get back from London. I'm due to see an

old art-school friend of Nena's but I'll look into Sadie's background too. It ought to help.' Eve crossed her fingers inside her
pocket.

'Good luck.' Viv gave her a hug. 'We'll walk Gus for you.
Thank goodness for Jonah. I can't settle to anything at Monty's
right now.'

Before Eve left for London, she did some background research.
Work would mop up some of her tension.

She took a deep breath and forced herself to home in on
Sadie and Nena. She wanted to know about Nena's life when
Sadie had come to the rescue.

Social media might give something away. She opened a web
browser and began scrolling through timelines. Nena had a
Facebook page and there was plenty of accessible stuff on her
personal account too. Publicity must have been crucial to her of
course, especially earlier in her career. She'd only been twenty-
five in 2010, when Sadie said she'd found her in that bar.

Eve scrolled back and back. Eventually, she found the relevant year. It had started off well enough. Nena had been travelling: exhibiting in the States and London, Paris and Berlin.
She'd been so young. The page trumpeted a huge success story,
but perhaps the pressure had been too much. Eve skimmed past
July and August. She'd still been busy. There'd been parties and
receptions in September and October. There were links to
interviews where she'd looked well and sounded coherent.

And then, in November, she found a post that talked about
alcohol. And how Nena had been sober for eighteen months.

Eve checked her December posts, just to be sure, but there
was no sign she'd fallen off the wagon. Just the opposite.

Sadie must have got the year wrong.

Eve went back in time. She started in May 2009. Before
Nena had gone teetotal. The posts were sporadic but when they

came, they were professional-looking. They were mainly about work in progress. Nothing about exhibitions or trips abroad.

When Eve trawled back further, to 2008, there was a gap. The only posts that year were in January. She recorded the gap in her notebook. Perhaps Sadie had put her up then. But what had their relationship really been like? Why did Sadie think the police might suspect her if they knew the truth? They already knew about the inheritance, so 'the truth' had to relate to some secret detail about her and Nena's past. Why had she been scared of Nena?

Eve took a deep breath. She needed to get down to London. Talk to Sadie's former neighbours. People at the local shops and businesses.

Unlike Nena, Sadie had almost no online presence. Different generation and different profession. But few people were completely anonymous in this digital age. Eve remembered finding brief mentions of her on a fundraising page and a post about a community event.

She went back to the links she'd saved and checked them again.

The fundraiser was for a hostel in the Chalk Farm area of London. And the community event was in that district too. It had been held two streets away from the hostel.

It was a good start.

32

Eve questioned her theories about Sadie all the way down to London. She and Nena had shared a secret Eve couldn't fathom and it must be highly significant. Nothing else would explain the vast amount Nena had left Sadie, nor the odd dynamic between them.

And yes, Sadie could be in cahoots with Gemma and Iggy. But it didn't seem likely she'd steal Nena's painting. She'd had the opportunity all right; she'd arrived in the bar later than her colleagues. But if she didn't want Nena's money, why would she take it?

Eve shouldn't get hung up on it. Perhaps it really had been gifted or destroyed. But something told her the latter didn't fit, and if Nena had given it away, surely someone would have seen a guest leaving with a large canvas? People would have gossiped about it.

She put it to the back of her mind. The key thing was the killings and Sadie's relationship with Nena. If she tracked down her former neighbours, she might hear more about the time she'd taken her in.

Eve took out her notebook and reminded herself of the conversation she'd overheard.

I wish I could turn back time. If only I hadn't gone out that night. Her gratitude's like a knife, twisting in the wound. I should never have lied.

Sadie's secret had been eating away at her and Nena had known it. When Sadie had tried to turn down Nena's money, Nena had said she *must* have it. How was she able to use generosity as a weapon? And what had Sadie lied about?

Eve's plan was to go to the network of streets around the area she'd pinpointed. There was a good chance Sadie had lived nearby. A local storekeeper might remember her. If she could find her address, she'd knock on a neighbour's door. It shouldn't be too hard to get them talking. It wasn't as though she'd be asking for Sadie's current whereabouts or anything with implications for her security. It was good that it was the weekend; people were more likely to be in.

Then, later on, she'd meet with Nena's art-school friend. A fresh perspective might help.

From Liverpool Street, Eve travelled to Chalk Farm by tube. It was raining when she arrived. Umbrella up, she made a beeline for her target area and assessed the shops, pubs and cafés. In the end, she opted for an eight-till-late grocer's with 'established 1986' written under its name.

She was glad to close the door on the weather and lowered her umbrella, trying not to make puddles on the floor. She picked up a chocolate bar and a drink and made for the counter.

The balding man who was serving had an impressive greying moustache which quivered as he greeted her.

'I wonder if you can help me?' Eve guessed she'd sound like a tourist, with her American accent. It might help. 'I'm visiting London for a few days and I was trying to track down an old friend. Sadie Thornton. I visited her here in Chalk Farm last time I was in the UK. It's a while back now, though. She might have moved.'

Eve showed him a photo of Sadie that she'd printed from the Saltwater Cottages website.

The man's moustache quivered some more as he looked at it. His brows drew down. 'She looks familiar, but' – he shook his head – 'no. I can't exactly remember.' He shrugged helplessly. 'I'm sorry.'

Eve wasn't surprised. The whole visit was a long shot. She smiled. 'Not to worry. I'm sure her apartment was hereabouts. I'll keep trying.' She handed over her money.

The man gave her the change and wished her luck.

She bought herself a coffee at one of the pubs next, and showed the photo with similar results. After that, she visited a newsagent, a café and a hairdresser.

The hairdresser came closest to a breakthrough. She stood for a full minute with Sadie's photo in her hand, waving it to and fro as she frowned furiously. 'When did you last visit her?'

'It was over a decade ago, I'm afraid. I kicked myself when I lost my phone. My kids were like d'oh, because I hadn't backed up my contacts, but I figured I'd try to look her up in person now I'm here. I thought I'd recognise the streets better.' Eve hoped she wasn't overacting.

The hairdresser gave a sympathetic smile. 'The shops change all the time and there are new builds springing up. I just know she used to come in. Though I don't think she was here long and our records don't stretch back that far.'

At that moment, the door burst open and the man from the grocer's bounded in, a look of triumph on his face.

'I've found someone who remembers!' he said to Eve.

A small woman stood behind him with mouse-brown hair and sparkling dark eyes. She bustled forward. 'Raj mentioned Sadie's name when I came in. He was still trying to place her.'

The man called Raj excused himself and dashed out of the salon again.

'You're quite right,' the small woman said, 'she used to live here. In Beaumont House. The block's just a street away, so you were on the right track.'

The hairdresser looked disappointed at not having got there first.

Eve thanked her and followed her new helper out of the salon. 'Used to? She's moved?' She put her umbrella up again.

The woman nodded as she followed suit. 'I'm afraid so. She must have left soon after you last visited. A decade ago, perhaps?'

'You don't know which number Sadie lived at, do you? I suppose the current occupants might have a forwarding address.'

The woman frowned. 'I do, and you can try, but it's a while back now. People come and go, you know?'

As a former Londoner, Eve did. 'Sadie had a house guest when I was last in touch. A young woman called Nena. She was staying with her for a few months.'

'A few months?' The woman looked confused. 'Are you sure? That doesn't sound right.'

It was Eve's turn to frown. 'How do you mean?'

At that moment, the woman's umbrella blew inside out. She laughed as she tried to right it. Then Eve's umbrella did the exact same thing. By the time they'd got themselves sorted, a layer of formality had fallen away.

'Look,' the woman said, 'why don't we go for a coffee? I can tell you what I know. My name's Bridget, by the way.'

'Eve.' She held out a hand. 'That sounds great, if you've got time. It would be good to get out of the rain.'

'Wouldn't it just?'

Five minutes later, they were sitting in a coffee shop Bridget

had recommended. Everything was steamy, from the windows
to their drinks, and there was a glorious smell of sweet pastries.

'Truth to tell, I'm probably just as keen to ask you about
Sadie as you are to find out where she's gone,' Bridget said.

'Oh?' A quiver of excitement sparked inside her. Anything
non-standard about Sadie could be relevant, and it was non-
standard to leave neighbours with questions. 'Why's that?'

'Sadie kept herself to herself,' Bridget said, 'but I think I
knew her best out of the locals here. We'd have coffee occasion-
ally. That was as far as it went. I live in Beaumont House myself
and I used to leave at the same time as her each morning. I
suppose I felt we were friends, though she was always reserved.'

Eve nodded. Sadie struck her that way too. Maybe it wasn't
her nature but some kind of defence.

'She didn't tell me she was planning to leave. She was rent-
ing, but I never saw a "To Let" sign go up. One day she was
there, the next time I knocked, she was gone. That's why I
doubt anyone will have a forwarding address.'

'I'm sorry. That must have been disconcerting.' Eve would
have been hurt. 'You got no hint of why she'd disappeared like
that?'

Bridget shook her head. 'None. I never heard anything bad
about her; I can't believe she was trying to evade debt collectors
or something like that. But I did wonder if she had a violent ex-
husband or was running from something. She had a haunted
look in her eye sometimes. If I asked too many questions, she'd
clam up.'

And she had no social media, of course. Eve put her
thoughts together with what she'd seen: Sadie's look of relief
when she'd offered Jamie some of Nena's bequest. And how
she'd sounded when Eve had listened in to her phone call. As
though she had a great weight on her shoulders. A combination
of guilt and fear.

'I'm sorry,' Bridget was saying. 'I'm speaking out of turn.

You probably know her family background. I wasn't meaning to pry, but it left me with questions.'

'I'm not surprised. And although I knew her, she was never forthcoming about her history with me either.'

'Ah.' Bridget let out a sigh. 'At least I'm not the only one.'

'Is that the reason you figured Sadie wouldn't have a house guest? Because she was so private?'

'It wasn't just that. Her flat was built on the same layout as mine and they're tiny. There's no spare bedroom. Besides, I bumped into her often, like I said. I never saw her with anyone else. After she left, I talked to the neighbours about it. Everyone agreed she was a loner. If she'd had a friend staying people would have gossiped.'

'I probably misunderstood.' But she hadn't, of course. Sadie had been quite clear.

Bridget took some paper from her bag and wrote a number on it. 'Would you mind giving me a call if you find out what happened to her? I'd like to know.'

After they'd finished at the café, Bridget let Eve into Beaumont House and she talked to Sadie's neighbours. One had been in residence for twenty years. She confirmed that Sadie had been in the flat in 2010, the year she claimed she'd looked after Nena. The neighbour certainly didn't remember any visitors.

As Eve took the tube towards Liverpool Street, she did a mental recap. Nena had been doing well in 2010, if her Facebook page was anything to go by, and no one remembered her at Beaumont House. Perhaps Sadie had lived in another part of London before moving to Chalk Farm and she'd put Nena up there, during the time she'd gone dark on social media.

Or maybe the whole story was a fiction to explain the bequest.

The way Sadie had left Beaumont House so quickly and avoided her neighbours implied she was running from something. Bridget might be right about a violent ex, but Eve had sensed her emotional turmoil was to do with Nena. She sighed. She didn't feel much further forward, but she called Bridget once she reached the mainline station.

'Hello again, it's Eve here. I meant to ask, did Sadie mention where she'd lived before she came to Chalk Farm? Was she in another part of London? I figured she might have moved back.'

Bridget hesitated. '*She didn't say, but I had the impression she'd come from somewhere rural. At least, originally. Every so often I'd hear the trace of an accent. And she once mentioned the sea. Isn't it odd that we were both friends with her, yet we know so little?*'

Eve felt guilty for lying as she told Bridget she agreed.

After she'd rung off, she went to buy a sandwich to sustain her before her meeting with Nena's art-school friend.

As she ate, she pondered what she'd learned: a rural accent and a mention of the sea. Was it possible Sadie had come from Suffolk all along? But if so, Eve wasn't sure what that meant.

33

As Eve made her way across town to Jemima Brand's apartment, her thoughts became wistful. She normally saw the twins when she was in the capital, but there'd been no time. She promised herself a trip soon.

The tube journey took a while. Jemima lived in an airy loft apartment where London met Essex. When Eve finally stood opposite her she was intrigued. She looked as unlike Nena as it was possible to be. Her hair was piled high in a messy bun and she wore leggings with a voluminous burnt-orange blouse over the top. Everything about her was larger than life, from her huge hoop earrings to her bright lipstick. She shook Eve's hand, apologised for the mess and offered coffee, which was instant and supplied in a chipped mug.

She laughed as she handed it over. 'I'm not as rich as Nena was, as you've probably gathered, but I do all right.' Her face fell. 'I'd say I'm a lot happier than she was. You're wondering why she chose me as a friend?' She was back to smiling again.

Eve needed to regain control. 'Not in the way you mean! But yes, because you seem like chalk and cheese. And I had the impression her female friends were few and far between.'

'Sorry. Joking apart, it's a fair point. All I can tell you is that it wasn't for my mild manner or compliments. I can be a right mardy cow.'

Maybe that had appealed. If everyone else pussy-footed round her, she might have craved someone who'd tell her where to get off. Or perhaps she'd regarded Jemima as a challenge. 'What was Nena like at uni?'

Jemima waved an expressive hand. 'Over the top. Always doing everything to excess. She was brilliant, of course. She got noticed quickly and that made her sought-after. The students all wanted to be her best friend and the tutors competed to show her off as their discovery. There was lots of photobombing when the press got interested.'

Eve could imagine. 'It feels as though most people danced to her tune. I can't imagine you did, though.'

'No.' Jemima frowned as though the thought came as a surprise. 'No, I suppose I didn't.'

'And rather than put her off, she stuck with you.'

Her brow was still furrowed. 'Maybe she liked a bit of certainty.'

Eve could imagine that. She wondered if any of the villagers or her teachers had provided a similar life raft during her turbulent upbringing.

'Had you kept in regular touch all these years?'

'Yes. Ever since art school.'

Eve referred to her notes. 'I noticed Nena went dark on social media in 2008. I wondered what happened to her then.'

'Oh, yes.' Jemima got up, went to a filing cabinet painted acid green and rifled in the middle drawer. 'It was after her dad died. It knocked her for six.'

'She was close to him, rather than her mum?'

Jemima raised a questioning eyebrow.

'Her mum's still in Suffolk – a stone's throw from Salt-water Cottages, where Nena was working – but they hadn't met since Nena's arrival. I had the impression Nena had avoided it.'

'She didn't seem to miss either of them at uni. But it's different when someone's gone for good, isn't it?' She was still rummaging in the cabinet. 'I put her collapse down to the battle suddenly stopping.'

'Excuse me?'

'The constant one-upmanship between her parents. They'd each vied for her attention all that time, never letting up. Half of that fell away overnight.'

'And her mother stopped trying too, because there was no competition?'

'Not exactly.' Jemima glanced at her over her shoulder. 'She still paid Nena plenty of attention, but she wasn't quite so panicked about it. I think Nena missed the intensity. Her dad's death threw everything out of kilter. I'm making her sound like a selfish monster, but I felt sorry for her. Circumstances made her that way.'

She came back from the filing cabinet. 'Nena disappeared for several months. She never told me where she'd gone, just that she'd been in a state. She implied there'd been a hiccup while she was away though. Something about not being able to rely on anyone. And she sent me this postcard.'

She handed it over. It was the standard shape, but not commercially produced. Nena had painted the picture: a watercolour of a castle on a clifftop, with a bay down below. It could be a lake, but Eve thought it was the sea.

On the back, Nena had written *I'm still alive. N x*

'You don't know where it is?'

Jemima shook her head. 'I asked where she'd been, of course, but she wouldn't discuss that period. At. All. She didn't remember the postcard, so I assume she was off her face when she sent it. Take a photo if you like.'

Eve did so. She wanted to identify the castle. She thought of

Sadie's description of picking Nena up off a bar floor when she was drunk. If it had happened at all, she suspected it had been during this period.

One thing was certain, the picture on Nena's card wasn't London. And although Sadie might misremember the year she'd put Nena up, she wouldn't confuse the capital and the seaside. It looked as though she'd lied deliberately and this dark time in Nena's life was part of the secret.

Back at home, Eve made a huge fuss of Gus, who was satisfyingly pleased to see her.

It was only when she stood up that something made her stop absolutely still. Senses on high alert. The hairs rising on the back of her neck.

Was it something in the air? She sniffed. An almost imperceptible alteration in the smell of her house?

She couldn't put her finger on it. She scanned her belongings. A notepad on the coffee table. Her laptop bag to the left of the nearest couch.

In the kitchen she checked the items on the counter. Kettle, tin of teabags, toaster. Had something changed?

Her anxiety made her rush to the window. She stared into the shadows but there was no movement. Besides, she had a security camera trained on the back garden. The app it paired with on her phone would have warned her if there'd been an intruder there. She pulled the curtains across swiftly, shutting out the night.

She must be imagining it. She wished her heart would slow down. She went from room to room, drawing all the curtains, her phone in her hand, 999 keyed in, ready to dial.

As she reached the back bedroom, Gus came to join her.

She looked down at him, then opened the door quickly and breathed a sigh of relief.

'It's nothing.' She bent to ruffle his fur. 'Just me being jumpy.'

But as she walked down the steep cottage stairs, she was still hypersensitised. Breathless. Listening for the smallest sound.

'I need a good night's sleep and I'll be better. But forget all that. It's supper time.'

Instead of rushing to his bowl, Gus continued to look at her, his eyes anxious. She reached a tin of his food from the cupboard, dished it up and refilled his water. Still he looked at her.

She sent a WhatsApp to the group, updating them on her findings in London, then bent to give Gus a pat.

'Take no notice of me. A cup of tea will help.' She smiled. It was what Viv would recommend. Along with cake, obviously. She went and grabbed the kettle.

The feeling was like being kicked. Or hit by a car. The shock flung her backwards. A moment later, she crashed to the floor, and everything went black.

34

Eve woke up in a bed. The covers were tucked in too tightly and her head was pounding. When she opened her eyes a crack, everything was horribly bright. She closed them again. It took another ten minutes before she decided to repeat the experiment. She didn't dare move.

Behind her she could hear whispers.

'She was incredibly lucky, apparently.' It was the second time in recent memory she'd heard Viv lower her voice. Things must be serious. 'I assumed it was her ill-advised boots that saved her but apparently the soles aren't even rubber.'

Ill-advised?

Someone gave a low laugh. Even in her current state, Eve could hear the fear behind it. 'I've always rather liked those boots.'

Robin? What was he doing there? He wasn't due back yet.

'I'd forgive them anything if they'd protected her,' she heard Viv reply. Her voice was wobbling.

Their words swam in Eve's aching head. The kettle. Gus. Memories coalesced.

'She passed out because of the knock to her head,' Viv said.

'The doctor will tell you. They think she was thrust back by the shock, then tripped and fell. She's not burned.'

Robin was silent for a moment. 'Thank God.' His voice cracked.

Eve felt tears prick now. How close had she come to death? To never seeing him or her twins again? And what had Gus felt, looking down at her? Thank goodness she hadn't put both hands on the metal. The shock would have gone across her heart...

'I should never have let her carry on using Mum and Dad's old kettle. It probably dates back to the 1970s.'

Robin was telling Viv not to blame herself. Eve's cottage used to belong to Viv's parents. She'd found their kettle in the back of a cupboard and started using it when hers broke.

The conversation washed over her. Each time she thought about joining in her head pounded so badly that she couldn't face it. But now she turned slowly in her bed, feeling sick. 'Someone had been in my house.'

They crouched down instantly. A good double-act. Robin leaned in to give her a gentle hug and Viv squeezed her hand.

'Where's Gus?'

'Don't worry. Simon's got him. He came as soon as I called.' Viv was still speaking quietly. It was so unlike her.

'Thank you.' Eve whispered too. It was all she was equal to. 'What happened?'

'After I got your WhatsApp, I came round to see if you'd like a G and T. I thought we could go over everything in person. You didn't answer, and Gus was barking like crazy. I got the wind up and used my spare key.'

'Thank goodness for that.'

Viv started crying. 'I thought you were dead.'

'Sorry.'

She gave an unsteady laugh. 'It's all right. I called Robin

straight away. He arrived just before you woke up this most recent time.'

'I'd woken before?'

'You seemed to, but you didn't say anything.'

Eve closed her eyes again.

'What makes you think someone had been in your house?' Robin said gently. 'I should let Greg know. Get them to check the kettle.'

But Eve couldn't come up with anything concrete. 'A slightly different smell? And maybe the kettle had moved a fraction. Only I didn't realise it at the time. I just had the sense that something was off.'

He kissed her. 'I'll go and call from the corridor. You get some sleep. It's not three a.m. yet.'

She clutched at his hand. 'Someone must think I know the truth. Or that I've got enough information to work it out. Viv, Simon and I were going through everything we knew in his office at Saltwater before I went to London yesterday. I kept my voice down, but maybe it wasn't enough.' She'd been a fool. She should have thought. She'd listened to Sadie's conversation through a closed door.

'I need to tell you what we said. I—'

'Viv can fill me in.' Robin stroked her hair. 'You're in no fit state at the moment. We'll review it all when you're better.'

Eve knew he was right. She was desperate to close her eyes again. Shut out the glare and keep absolutely still and quiet. 'Robin? Viv?'

They looked at her.

'Did you already call the twins?'

Viv shook her head. 'I was going to, but when the doctor said you weren't in danger I decided to wait until the morning. I was worried they'd drive up in a panic and have an accident.'

Eve would have had the same fear. 'Please don't tell them.

They'd worry so much and I'm quite all right. Or I will be. I can explain once the killer's caught and the danger's gone.'

Viv folded her arms. 'They'd want to know.'

Eve thought of Simon not telling Polly about his financial woes. She'd disapproved, but this was different. So long as she was careful, the danger was already over. 'I'd really rather they didn't.'

She heard them both sigh. 'Fair enough,' Robin said.

Eve put her thoughts on hold and the room faded away.

She was discharged later that morning. Everyone kept telling her how lucky she was, as though she might not have noticed. Her head ached less, but she still felt battered.

At Elizabeth's Cottage, Robin was peering at one of her side windows. A moment later, he put in another call to Greg. The police had removed the kettle.

Viv was clucking like a mother hen. Jonah had gone home, but their regular helpers were minding Monty's. Thank goodness Tammy and Lars were still with them. They were saving to go travelling now Tammy was done with college; they'd be sorely missed.

Viv had been to Blyworth to buy Eve a new kettle. Eve couldn't watch her use it without holding her breath.

'You need to get back to London,' she said as Robin reappeared.

His expression was grim. 'I'm not going anywhere until we find out who did this.'

'You agree it was deliberate?'

He nodded. 'The paint's damaged around the side window. Whoever broke in was careful, but not careful enough. They must have levered it to push up the catch, then secured it again from the inside.'

'But how did they get out?'

'Your spare keys, perhaps.' He went to the drawer to the right of the fridge. 'They're gone.'

'I suppose they figured I wouldn't be around to tell the police they were missing.'

They looked at each other. Someone would have checked the kettle if she'd died. But if the would-be killer was careful, they might have been able to make it look like an accident. It was such an old appliance.

'They were clever. Cunning.'

Robin nodded.

'It's almost as though they knew you had an old kettle,' Viv said. 'They must have brought the right tools.'

Eve shivered. 'It's true. But none of the key players are regular visitors.'

'When did you switch?' Robin asked.

Eve's headache got worse. 'Earlier this year? February maybe?'

'The killer could have seen it at your open house if they're local.'

Eve held the gatherings twice yearly in aid of children's charities. It was a tradition that went with the cottage, which had a long and famous history in the village.

She considered the suspects who were also neighbours. 'We're back to Jamie and Liam. Or Iggy if he, Sadie and Gemma are in it together.' Eve tried to imagine one of them breaking into her house. Anticipating her death as they took her kettle apart. 'I guess any of them would have the skill to do it. Liam would be top of the list as Saltwater's DIY guy, but Jamie's in charge if anyone has problems overnight and Iggy's meant to be handy too. His and Liam's dad did all the small building jobs around here according to Moira, so the pair of them were brought up on it.' Eve closed her eyes. 'But in reality, anyone who came round to plan the break-in could have seen the elderly kettle through the window. And I suspect Gemma or Sadie would be equal to fiddling with the wires too.'

She'd decided Liam was innocent of Nena's murder, but it was him she imagined creeping round her house. The thought of his blank-eyed stare still sent a chill through her.

'What are the police up to?' she asked Robin. 'Are they still after Liam?'

He nodded. 'Palmer's doing his nut, apparently. They haven't found any blood in his and Tess's suite apart from the stain you found in his pocket and that's his. They've looked for bark too, to match the log which killed Nena, but nothing. They can't place him at either crime scene. Palmer's blind to anyone else, so if he's wrong, we're all in trouble.'

Eve was still convinced he was. 'We need to know where everyone was while I was in London. That might throw up something fresh. And you need to go back to your team, Robin.'

He opened his mouth.

'I know. But I've got friends who can keep an eye on me here. I won't be able to live with myself if you stay and the London case is affected.' He'd be putting her ahead of countless others, and when all this was past, he'd come to regret it. 'I'll take the utmost care. But you're needed. Please.'

'Eve can stay at my place and I'll get Simon to come too,' Viv said to Robin. 'Plenty of room now Jonah's gone home.'

At last, Robin shook his head. 'I don't like this one bit. I'll ask Greg to get someone to do the odd drive-by, but they won't have eyes on you all the time.'

'Don't worry,' Viv said. 'I won't let her out of my sight.'

After Robin had left, a memory came back to Eve. 'Viv, what did you mean when you said my boots were "ill-advised"?'

35

Eventually, Eve gave in and went back to bed. She could hear Viv pottering around downstairs, humming to herself. By late afternoon, she got up to find multiple visitors had called. Two of them had tried to give her kettles.

'Moira turned up with one too, along with demands for a blow-by-blow account of your "accident",' Viv said. 'You're off the hook for now but there'll be no quelling her when you next meet.'

Simon, Daphne and Sylvia joined them for a cup of tea. They went through every detail they'd discussed in Simon's office at Saltwater. Eve still had no idea what had made her a particular threat.

'And it's weird,' Viv said. 'You'd shared the information with us, so why home in on you? Not that I'm jealous or anything.'

'I know.' Eve wanted to sum up how things stood. Her headache was making a comeback, but she couldn't leave it. 'Let's focus solely on Nena's killing. We haven't got a hope of sorting out alibis for Tess's.

'We know Nena couldn't have reached the woods before

eleven thirty-five because she was seen in her room by a disinterested guest at eleven twenty. By two a.m., according to the pathologist, she was dead.

'Jamie left the front desk at around half eleven, went to the safe in the staff quarters and got stuck there because Gemma was next door, on a call with her mum. After that he dashed back to reception where I found him breathless just before midnight. He didn't have time to kill Nena and although he might just have managed to steal her painting, I think he'd have struggled to stow it somewhere, now we know how busy he was. I believe he's out of it on both counts.

'We've got nothing for Tess after eleven fifteen, when she was seen chatting to Sadie and Liam on the landing. She could have stolen the painting, stowed it, then gone to kill Nena. But if she's guilty, why was she killed?

'Liam says he slashed Nena's pillows while Jamie was absent, so again in that crucial window between eleven thirty and eleven fifty-five. He could have stolen the painting on his way out, though I'd swear he knew nothing about it when we talked. He could also have killed Nena, but if he did, the pillow slashing would have been pointless.

'Sadie didn't arrive in the bar until quarter to midnight, so she could have stolen the painting, but why, when she didn't want Nena's money? She could only have killed Nena if Iggy and Gemma are covering for her.

'Gemma left the bar briefly at around eleven forty-five and was overheard in the staffroom by Jamie. If Iggy and Sadie lied about when she returned, she might just have had time to steal the painting. She could have heard Jamie in the staff quarters and known he was away from his desk. As with Sadie, she could only have killed Nena if the others lied for her.

'And it's a similar story with Iggy. He's less likely for the painting. How would he know Jamie had left his desk? But he could have killed if it was a conspiracy.

'As far as the painting goes, if Liam, Sadie, Gemma or Iggy stole it, it would have been opportunistic and hugely risky. They'd have had no way of knowing Jamie would leave his desk or how long he'd be. He would have been quicker if it weren't for Gemma.'

'So maybe theft's not part of the story,' Sylvia said.

'Maybe.' Logically, that made sense.

'It's useful to revisit it all, but no lightbulbs have come on.' Simon sounded despondent. Eve knew the clock was ticking. Polly was due back from the States on Wednesday. He was still hoping there might be a solution before she landed, so he could give her some good news with the bad.

Eve was interrupted from her thoughts by the arrival of the police in the very acceptable form of Greg Boles. Within minutes, they were going through the whole thing again.

The following morning, after a night spent at Viv's, Eve felt well enough to go outside. It was good to get some fresh air and wake up. Recent events hadn't been a recipe for a good night's sleep and Simon's snoring in the next room hadn't helped.

They went to meet Sylvia and Daphne, then walked past the village green and on to Heath Lane, making for the coast. Gus dashed ahead of them all, as though they were his entourage. Over the sound of the gulls, Eve heard a text come in.

Robin.

We've found an electronic trail leading to one of the suspects. Feels like we're getting closer. Will keep you posted. I want to be there with you.

She glanced up to come nose to nose with Viv. 'Your keen interest in my affairs is a little overwhelming at times.'

Viv smiled brightly. 'Best friend's prerogative. You'd be affronted if I didn't keep tabs.' She talked over Eve's heated response. 'I'm glad it's encouraging news.'

As they carried on, Viv glanced along their line. 'I feel like something from a children's adventure book. Especially with Gus in tow.'

Eve's gaze drifted over Viv's shoulder. There was movement in Blind Eye Wood.

A couple. Embracing. Thoroughly involved in each other. *Enough, already.* They broke off and she came face to face with one of the two lovebirds.

Iggy Norland.

His companion was Gemma Redpath.

Suddenly, the conspiracy seemed a lot more believable.

36

They were close enough to see Iggy flush puce. He raised his hand to Eve and she waved back, Simon, Daphne, Sylvia and Viv following her gaze.

'That's a healthy blush.' Sylvia was laughing.

'Shush!' Daphne put a hand on her arm.

Iggy was saying something to Gemma. Pointing at Eve and her group.

'Let's carry on. We mustn't stand here staring at them.' Daphne took a determined stride into the wind.

'However much fun it is,' Sylvia said, following.

But in another moment, Iggy had caught up with them. 'Eve, we heard what happened. How are you?' He looked her up and down. 'You've got some colour in your cheeks. It must have been terrifying.'

She looked into his eyes, wondering if he was a conspirator, lulling her with his kind words. 'I didn't really know what had hit me. But I'm okay. Thank you.'

Iggy nodded. 'That's good.' He was looking shifty now. Moving from foot to foot. At last he turned to Simon. 'I'm sorry.'

Simon looked confused. 'What about?'

Iggy blushed again, and nodded to where he and Gemma had been standing. 'Well, you know.'

Simon frowned. 'That's all right. It's not as though you're meant to be working.'

'No, I mean for betraying your trust.'

Simon looked utterly perplexed now. 'You've lost me.'

'Sadie explained your rule about couples at Saltwater. That it's fine if you're married like Tess and Liam were, but no relationships otherwise. How it tends to cause trouble.'

Simon's head was on one side. 'Sadie said I said that?'

Eve was struggling to make sense of it too. That didn't sound like Simon.

Now it was Iggy's turn to look muddled. 'Yes.'

'Crossed wires, I think. That's not my rule. I mean, I wouldn't want it to affect the running of the business, but I'm sure you wouldn't let it.'

A misunderstanding? Eve doubted it. It sounded as though Sadie had been lying. She'd be very interested to know why.

Iggy and Gemma joined Eve and the others on the beach. Gus scampered down to the shore and played chase with the waves. It was a relief to see him relax again.

'I can't understand it,' Iggy was saying. 'Sadie found us together a couple of days after Gemma arrived. We'd hit it off immediately. I guess she could see we were getting close, so she nipped it in the bud. Told us it was against your company policy. And we understood. Honestly. But I'm afraid, well...' He blushed.

'You couldn't keep your hands off each other?' Sylvia gave a cackle of laughter.

Daphne reddened. 'You could hardly make it more awkward if you tried.'

But Iggy was laughing, though he was beetroot to the roots of his hair. Gemma was walking a little ahead of them. With the wind so high, Eve doubted she could hear. Probably just as well.

'The trouble is it's rare to feel you've found a soulmate,' Iggy said. 'I haven't felt like this about anyone in ages. We talked. Agreed we'd follow the rules. But then we were in each other's company so much, and well... we started to spend time together again on the quiet.' He sighed.

Eve remembered that he'd kept nipping into the kitchens the night she'd arrived at Saltwater. She'd thought at the time that there'd been no need. The meal had been superb and the operation had run like clockwork.

'I think Sadie suspected. I reckon that's why she joined us in the bar the night Nena died. She was behaving like a chaperone. I knew she wouldn't leave until we did.'

It explained a lot, from the tensions she'd seen between the three of them, to the way Sadie kept popping up when Iggy and Gemma were together. She remembered Sadie breaking up their cosy chat when she'd interviewed Liam.

Iggy must have bought the roses for Gemma, and the relationship was secret, but for a reassuringly run-of-the-mill reason.

Thoughts of a three-way conspiracy fell away. It was like watching a beautiful but fragile building crumble before her eyes. She glanced at Simon and wondered if he'd realised they were back to square one. But perhaps he was too preoccupied by Sadie's behaviour.

Because although the news cut off a line of enquiry, it made the manager even more interesting. She'd put an awful lot of effort into making sure Gemma and Iggy followed her instructions. Why was she so bothered?

'I don't want to go against what Sadie's said,' Simon was saying, 'but I'll have a word. See if there's a compromise to be reached.' He gave a heavy sigh. 'Assuming the venue gets back on its feet. I'm sorry – it's all your livelihoods.'

Iggy shook his head. 'It's awful for you too. Thanks for offering to talk to Sadie.'

Gemma must have tuned in to the conversation now. She turned and her face lit up. She was almost unrecognisable. Whatever made her so defensive and uncompromising, Iggy appeared to be the antidote. It was good to see some happiness amongst the tragedy. Eve thought of Robin in London. She was glad she'd told him to go. It was a way of proving she understood. But she still hankered to have him back.

Iggy took Gemma's hand. Eve was no longer surprised he'd been sunny with Nena. He was in love and all was right in his world. She knew that bubbly feeling. It was useful that they'd caught the pair unawares. They couldn't have been acting.

'I'm going to have to dash,' Iggy said. 'I want to check on Liam. The police were with him again earlier.'

Gemma sighed. 'He won't want you there.'

'I know, but I can't rest when I don't know what's going on.'

Gemma turned to go with him, but Eve didn't want her to escape just yet. She needed to know about people's movements on Saturday. It would be best to quiz them one by one and look for anomalies. On top of that, she wanted to know what Gemma had got up to earlier in the evening, the night Nena died. The police hadn't covered that period, for obvious reasons, but Eve couldn't stop wondering about it. Liam had been cagey about his and Tess's movements well before Nena left her suite. With the conspiracy theory dead in the water, she needed to examine every oddity.

Gemma was more relaxed than Eve had ever seen her. It had to be a good time to talk. 'Sorry, but could we have a quick word? We're all desperate to work out what happened to Nena and Tess.'

'And to Eve,' Simon said. 'We need the help of everyone we can trust.'

Gemma's shrewd eyes narrowed. She knew she was being buttered up. 'What can I do?'

'Just tell us everything you've already told the police.' Simon kept pace with her.

'Could you start with early evening, the night Nena died?' Eve put in.

Gemma pursed her lips. 'Let's see. I was in the kitchens, of course, until about ten. After that I went to my room for a shower. I can't get rid of the smell of food otherwise. Then I spent some time getting ready to go to the bar.' Her cheeks tinged pink. 'I knew Iggy would be there. We'd arranged to meet.'

'And did you see anyone acting oddly during that part of the evening?'

'Well, I heard Liam leaving his and Tess's rooms next door like I told you, then Tess crying, after which she must have left too. That would have been around half ten. Then I heard the knocking at their door. And at some point, a little later than that, I think I saw Sadie out of the window.' She frowned. 'She kept looking over her shoulder, so I wondered what she was up to.'

It fitted with what one of the guests had seen. 'Did you see where she was heading?'

Gemma shook her head. 'No, but she looked purposeful. By quarter past eleven she was outside Liam and Tess's rooms, as I mentioned before, talking to them. I was on my way to the bar.'

Eve knew the story from then on, though Gemma repeated it anyway. Gemma referred to leaving the bar at two as 'giving the evening up as a bad job' and to Iggy as looking like 'a drowned rat and smelling like an ashtray' when he came inside after his cigarette. She said she'd told him he should give up and sounded proprietorial about it.

'It's so lovely that you're together,' Viv said.

It gave Eve the opportunity to check about the roses. 'I gather Iggy bought you some lovely flowers from the village store.'

Gemma looked irritated. 'News travels fast around here.'

'But you liked them?' Eve smiled. *Go on. Say something telling.*

At last, Gemma weakened. 'Of course I did. I don't think anyone's given me a dozen roses before.'

Bingo. Eve believed in their relationship, but it was nice to have confirmation.

'Going back to what you've seen,' Simon put in, 'what about Saturday afternoon? Where did everyone go? Did you notice anything odd?'

Gemma shook her head. 'I went for a walk round the back of the cottages, then hung around in my suite. I thought I saw Liam heading up Dark Lane. Iggy had gone to help lay that rug of Nena's in Jamie's house. I'm not sure about Sadie.'

Eve thought of Iggy and Jamie for a moment. They were friends; they might form a partnership. But it was no good. Neither of them had had the opportunity to kill Nena.

Eve took a deep breath. 'Do you know anything about the brick that was thrown through Simon's window?'

Spots of colour appeared on her cheeks. *I know it was you.*

'Of course not. Why on earth would I know anything about that?'

'We think the person involved was bitten by a neighbour's dog.'

Gemma was still flushed, but she held Eve's stare. 'Perhaps it was the same animal that bit me. It sounds as though it's poorly controlled.'

'I remember thinking the wound on your leg looked angry, as though you'd avoided seeing a doctor.'

Gemma's lips formed a firm line. 'I didn't want to make a fuss, but I went when I had to.'

'Of course.' It was time to back down, though she hated the feeling of defeat. Once again, Eve thought what a cool customer

Gemma was. Perhaps Iggy was her only weak spot. 'Have you seen much of your mum since you moved?'

Gemma took a moment to reply. 'As much as I can.'

'I guess you've got time on your hands now.'

She was silent.

'Is she very close by?'

She was clamming up again, her arms folded, jaw tight. 'Framlingham.'

'Ah, I love Framlingham.' She'd been there for a picnic with Robin. They'd looked round the castle. 'And it's not too far by car.'

A slight nod. 'No.'

'It must be a relief to be closer to her. Is she very unwell?'

She nodded again. 'She has been for some time. She had a breakdown.'

'I'm so sorry. Thanks for talking to us.'

Gemma nodded and went on her way.

'She's very tight-lipped,' Viv said.

Simon looked after her thoughtfully. 'She doesn't drive. I remember asking her at her interview, but in the end I didn't think it would be a problem.'

Eve googled directions to Framlingham. 'The quickest route by public transport takes two and a half hours.'

'I doubt she relocated to be close to her mum then,' Sylvia said.

'I agree.' Eve watched Gemma's retreating back. 'And she took a demotion to come to Saltwater. I'd guess she had another pressing reason to relocate.'

'And it relates to the brick she no doubt threw through my window,' Simon said, with admirable restraint.

'And maybe to why Iggy searched Gemma's room, despite his feelings for her.' She'd have to ask him about it again.

37

Back at Viv's place, Eve called Sadie. She wanted to see if her account matched Gemma's. Sadie admitted walking in the grounds sometime before eleven the night Nena died. She said she'd been to check on a leak in one of the end cottages. It had been fixed a couple of weeks back but she didn't trust it.

But her explanation didn't make sense. It had rained that night, but not until later. How could she confirm the fix was effective before the downpour started? Eve guessed it was a cover story, but what for? It was like Liam and Tess all over again. She was muddying the waters about a period before Nena had left her room.

Her description of the rest of the evening matched Gemma's and the police records exactly. On Saturday afternoon, before the attack on Eve, she said she'd been in Blyworth, shopping. She hadn't seen anything useful.

By lunchtime, Eve, Viv and Simon were with Sylvia and Daphne at the Cross Keys. Eve had three goals for the visit: to get Jamie out of trouble by returning the genuine Rolex, to use the village hive-mind to try to identify the place Nena had painted on Jemima Brand's postcard and to work out where they'd got to with the case.

The mission involving Edgar Horace was the most challenging, but at least it gave her a focus. She was feeling better physically, but fear followed her like a shadow. She needed distractions. And she'd love for Jamie to be able to start afresh. The watch situation was his own fault but it wasn't in character.

The real Rolex was in her pocket. She kept tapping it to make sure she hadn't lost seventy thousand pounds' worth of watch.

She'd asked Toby to help and hoped to goodness he managed it without getting into trouble. He'd been touchingly keen to join in.

She slipped into the pub's kitchens. It was a rare privilege to go backstage at the Cross Keys. Jo didn't like visitors when she was working. She looked up fiercely as Eve entered, but her expression softened when she realised who it was.

'I'll get Toby for you. He and Matt are going to manage it together. I was sceptical at first, but they've convinced me it's okay.'

'Thank you.' Eve doubted they could have gone ahead without her buy-in.

Toby appeared a moment later and she handed him the watch.

He flashed her a smile. 'It'll be all right. Matt says we're being far too kind, though. Not to Jamie, I don't mean, but to Mr Horrible Horace. We can't wait for him to leave.'

'And so say all of us,' said Jo as she strode past.

Viv was waiting at the bar when Eve reappeared. She was taking her minding duties seriously, which was heart-warming, but Eve could do without an audience right now. Play-acting in front of friends was the worst.

'You're not going to stare and make it obvious when the action starts, are you?' she said to Viv.

'You worry too much. This is far better than anything on TV and I'm not going to miss it. Toby and Horrible Horace will be busy. They'll never notice.'

They went back to their table to await their moment. Fifteen minutes later, Edgar Horace entered the room. When he and his wife approached the bar, Eve went to order more drinks and stood to his left-hand side.

'I'm sorry,' she said, after Toby had taken their order, 'but weren't you at the art course at Saltwater Cottages? I was too. I remember you were worried for your watch, and I can see why. It's a beauty, isn't it?'

Horace looked the warmest she'd seen him. 'It's sensible to opt for the best if you can afford it.'

Ha. If only you knew. 'Of course. Not many could though, I'd imagine. What workmanship.' She looked at Toby. 'Wasn't your dad a watchmaker, Toby?'

In fact, he'd been a publican, just like his son.

Toby smiled. 'That's right. I'd noticed your watch before, Mr Horace, only I didn't like to bother you over it. I've always taken an interest. Dad taught me all he knew. The vintage Submariner's one of his favourites.'

'He recognises quality.'

'Absolutely. Of course, with the vintage ones, it's actually the imperfections that send the value rocketing.'

'Ah. Well, yes. Of course.'

Horace looked mystified. Eve had only found out after googling for ideas.

'It's the subtle changes in the watch face over time.' Toby nodded at Horace's fake. 'The submariner blue dials fade to a shade of purple. Regal, my father calls it.'

Horace peered at his. 'Has that happened to mine, do you think? Would you call that blue? Or is that, er... regal purple?'

Toby peered too. 'I'm so sorry. The light's not good. Would you like me to take a closer look?'

'Please.'

Eve held her breath as he unfastened the watch.

Toby picked it up and turned towards the lights above the optics over the bar.

A moment later, he turned back and handed Mr Horace a watch. His watch, Eve was sure, though Toby's sleight of hand had been perfection. She spotted Matt reach for something from behind the bar. It was a good idea to get the fake out the way as soon as possible. The questions that would arise if it was spotted didn't bear thinking about.

'Do you know,' Toby said, 'I'm still not sure. I'd suggest asking my dad, but he's not local. Perhaps a London valuer would be best.'

Once the Horaces were safely settled with their meal, Eve returned to the kitchens. 'I can't thank you enough,' she said to Toby. 'Have you thought of going on the stage?'

He grinned. 'There's a lot of acting involved in being a publican. You have to pretend to enjoy the company of people like Edgar Horace, for a start. You're welcome.'

Matt handed her the fake to return to Jamie and she thanked him too.

She'd just got back to her friends' table with a handful of menus when Iggy Norland appeared.

He looked anxious. 'Could I have a quick word, Eve?'

She'd wanted to talk to him too, to ask about his movements on Saturday and to try to get him to open up about searching Gemma's room.

As she followed him to a corner table, she could feel Viv's eyes on her back. She was a stalwart, but it was quite all right. Eve was in sight of the whole bar. Nothing could happen, and she wanted Iggy's news.

38

Eve sat with Iggy in a cosy corner in the Cross Keys, a tealight between them creating a soft glow.

'Sorry to drag you away,' Iggy said, 'only there's something on my conscience.'

Eve couldn't imagine what was coming. 'Go on.'

'You remember you told me someone had searched Gemma's room? You saw a shadow?'

Ah, she wouldn't have to ask about it after all. Eve nodded.

He sighed. 'Well, it was me.' He put his head in his hands.

'But you're fond of Gemma, I can see that now. So I'm mystified.'

Iggy met her eye and shook his head. 'I'm so embarrassed about it. It was the green-eyed monster. When Sadie said Gemma and I mustn't get involved, she also told me privately that she suspected Gemma was cheating on me.' He sighed. 'I should have just asked her, but I couldn't think of a way of putting it that wouldn't be insulting.'

'So you waited for your moment and went to look for evidence instead?'

He nodded. 'We'd been in and out of each other's rooms.

She didn't seem to be hiding anything. I just wanted to prove it to myself.'

'Did you find anything odd?' It wasn't just secret boyfriends that Eve was interested in.

Iggy frowned. 'Not really. There were several photos of this one guy and for a moment I felt my world was crashing down. Sadie's stories had got to me, I guess. But when I looked closely, he was clearly a good bit younger than she is and the photos were crumpled. They'd obviously been around for a while. If he's a boyfriend I'd guess he's an old one. She doesn't act as though she's still hooked on him.' He sighed. 'For all I know he died or something. I can't ask her about it, for obvious reasons.'

Eve processed the information. Had Sadie searched Gemma's room too, and seen the photos, or was their presence just luck? Either way, it certainly looked as though she was out to make trouble between Gemma and Iggy.

She turned her attention to her other queries. 'Iggy, can I ask you some other questions? Only Simon's so anxious about it all. He's desperate to find justice for Nena and Tess, of course. Not to mention saving Saltwater and all your jobs. And I'm personally involved now too.'

'Of course.' His eyes met hers. 'I'm sorry.'

'What do you remember from early evening on the night of Nena's death?' That time was still bothering her. Why had it been so significant for Liam, Tess and Sadie?

Iggy frowned. 'Let's see. I was on the desk some of the time, taking turns with Sadie. Keeping an eye on the guests in the dining room and bar when I wasn't in the foyer. I don't think I saw anything unexpected. People came and went, but no one was acting oddly. Then at ten, Jamie took over and I went to my room and watched Netflix. Gemma and I had arranged to meet for a nightcap at eleven fifteen. She wanted a wash first. We figured Sadie couldn't stop us being friends and I hoped she'd have gone to bed by then.'

That all fitted.

'I left the bar for a cigarette at some stage but the weather was filthy, so I went back in after a minute or two.' He gave a despondent shrug. 'I don't remember seeing anyone, I'm afraid. I was round the back.'

She got him chatting about Gemma and Sadie next, but she didn't get anything new and there didn't seem much point in asking about the night of Tess's death. The police had already established that no one had an alibi.

'What about Saturday afternoon?' Her stomach skipped at the memory of waking up in hospital.

Iggy's eyes were on hers. 'I'm sorry. It must be awful, not feeling safe in your own home. I was with Jamie, helping to lay the rug that Nena damaged. His dad had burned a hole in their carpet so we got rid of that first. The stain on the rug wasn't too bad in the end. We managed to hide it under Jamie's sofa.' He shook his head. 'Poor Jamie. I asked if he'd rather leave it for a week or two but he said it was best to keep busy. He's at a loose end most of the time and it's hard, just him, his dad and his thoughts.'

The sooner he had his job back, the better.

39

Eve went back to her friends and brought them up to date, but the whole thing was dispiriting. Sadie and Gemma still had questions to answer, but with their alibis solid after all, did it matter? This was getting ridiculous. *Someone* had killed Nena. If all other possibilities were ruled out, there had to be something odd about the time of death. She'd wondered about it before, but how the heck could it be wrong?

Before she left the Cross Keys, she handed round the photo of Jemima Brand's postcard. It had travelled three quarters of the room before a woman in layers of woollens said: 'St Elizabeth's Castle,' then sighed and collapsed back in her seat. When pressed, she said she couldn't remember where it was, as though it was unreasonable of Eve to ask.

It was still a breakthrough. The internet should do the rest.

She, Viv, Simon and Gus walked Sylvia and Daphne back to Hope Cottage, then decamped to the teashop. Allie and Tammy had been holding the fort, but there was baking to be done.

'I don't honestly think I need an apron,' Simon said, looking at one with a picture of Tinkerbell on the front.

'Don't be such a baby.' Viv slung it over his head. 'I know it's not your style, but you're a novice. You're bound to make a mess.' She pointed him in the direction of the fridge. 'Get weighing butter.'

'Mind if I google St Elizabeth's Castle?' Eve said, taking out her phone.

'Not at all. Obviously, swapping you for Simon isn't ideal, but I'll make do.'

Her brother sighed. 'You're not very motivating as a boss.'

Viv smiled.

The results of Eve's search sent prickles crawling over her skin. 'This *has* to mean something.'

'What?' Viv bounded over, clutching an open bag of caster sugar.

'Look where St Elizabeth's Castle is.'

Viv peered at her screen. 'A place called Porthruan, Cornwall. Lovely. And?'

'It's where Gemma was based before she came here.'

'Wow. That's quite a coincidence.' Viv was staring at the map more closely now. She put her sugar down on a bit of worktop that wasn't there and it fell to the floor. 'Oops. There's a broom in the corner cupboard, Simon.'

'You can push your luck too far, you know.'

Eve's mind was still on Porthruan. 'I wonder if Sadie was also there. She says she took Nena in when she was struggling. She told me that was in London but that was clearly a lie.'

As she spoke, she heard a text come in. Robin again.

I think we're homing in. A second witness has agreed to talk. What news your end? xxx

Eve told him about the Cornish connection.

As Viv lorded it over Simon with every appearance of enjoyment, Eve wondered about asking Sadie if she'd lived in

Porthruan, but she needed more information first. If she wanted a confession, she mustn't go in underprepared. If only she could get down to Cornwall herself.

Eve closed her eyes and Viv and Simon's banter faded into the background. Nothing about this case fitted. The alibi Liam had tried to give himself and Tess was for the wrong time of the evening. Just as the flimsy excuse Sadie had given for striding about in the grounds had been.

What the heck had she overlooked? And was the painting significant? Whatever the truth, Nena had worked on one and it was gone. The drawing was less certain, but Nena had been using the ink for something.

Eve reread every note she'd taken, her mind roving over the older paintings she and Simon had found in Nena's room. The effort it must have taken for Nena to get them transported there. They were so large. And the fact that they were on board. Daphne said she normally painted on canvas. And then Eve thought of Nena sitting in her chair, reading. The expression one witness had noticed on her face. As though she was planning to make mischief. What had she been plotting? Eve had seen her flit across her room just after ten, but the other witnesses had seen her sitting. As though she was waiting for something, perhaps.

Eve visualised the window she'd walked past. And then from somewhere in the back of her mind she remembered Viv's description of Nena's room. What she'd seen by snooping through that very window.

Floor-to-ceiling bookcases and a huge antique mirror. I had to get really close even to see the frame. All gilt and scrolls.

Her pulse quickened. Viv had only seen that it was a mirror when she'd gone right up to the window. It was so big, the frame wasn't visible from further back.

She felt she was on the verge of understanding something

important. She took a deep breath. She needed to take it step by step.

It was possible that the witnesses hadn't seen Nena herself, but her reflection in the mirror.

None of them had registered it at the time. It was dark outside and they hadn't been pressing their noses to the glass like Viv. Only one witness had even noticed her expression.

Eve had seen the mirror. It was grand but old and foxed. Looking through the glass of the window you wouldn't expect to get the crispest view anyway.

And then Eve thought of the fact that only she and Viv had seen Nena moving about her room, shortly after ten.

Nena the mischief-maker. A cold trickle of suspicion crept along Eve's spine. A possibility that might change everything. Could she be right?

Simon's cakes were in the oven, though Viv was still tutting.

'Simon, I think we need another look at Nena's room. Can we go there?'

'Now?'

'Yes please.'

Viv was desperate not to be left behind, but there were Tammy and Allie to consider. 'We can't keep leaving them on their own,' Eve pointed out.

Viv groaned. 'I'm a martyr to my art.'

Twenty minutes later, Eve and Simon let themselves into Curlew Cottage. They could hear a radio playing somewhere but they met no one.

They entered Nena's room and closed the door softly behind them. Eve looked at the foxed old mirror with the wing-backed armchair close by, facing into the room.

And then she approached the huge paintings Nena had brought with her. Paintings that would be worth hundreds of thousands at the very least. Artworks Eve had no business to be touching. She'd explained her plan and now she glanced at Simon.

He gave her an uncertain smile. 'All right then?'

The pair of them took hold of the first picture and lifted it from the hook where it hung.

In a moment, they had it down on the floor and were turning it round. The paintings on canvas that Eve had at home were stretched over wooden frames, then put into decorative outer frames. If you turned them round, you could see the reverse side of the canvas.

But these paintings of Nena's were done on a thinnish board. Turning them round revealed the reverse side of the board. And it wasn't blank.

It was a nude of Liam. He was reclining amongst rumpled sheets in the shadows in that very suite. They might have used the makeshift bed in Liam's workshop, but they'd managed to sneak into Nena's room at some point.

Simon blushed deeply. 'That'll put the cat amongst the pigeons. I mean, I know we knew Nena and Liam were having an affair but this is... Well, it's...'

Eve swallowed. 'Yes, it is, isn't it?' It certainly brought it home.

'Ready for the next one?' she said to Simon.

He nodded. 'As I'll ever be.'

She took a deep breath. Would it prove what she thought it would? They reached for the other painting.

Once they had it down, they gingerly manoeuvred it to see what, if anything, was painted on the reverse.

Eve let out the breath she'd been holding. It was as she'd thought. A self-portrait of Nena, sitting in a wing-backed armchair that matched the one in the room. She was reading, a Mona Lisa smile playing about her lips.

Simon looked thunderstruck.

To Eve, it felt like the purest luck. The facts had suddenly come together. The report of Nena sitting, quietly reading, which didn't sound in character. The question of why Nena had brought two paintings with her and how the painting she'd been working on seemed to have disappeared. The realisation that the witnesses could only have viewed part of Nena's room, because the window was recessed. What they'd been looking at was part of the mirror, which was so big, you could only see its frame if you pressed your nose to the window like Viv had.

'Unbelievable.' Simon still looked shocked. 'So how exactly did she work it?'

'This armchair normally sits close to the mirror, facing into the room.' Eve indicated it. 'Its top half and anyone sitting in it would come into view as you moved past her window.'

Simon rubbed his forehead. 'With you so far.'

'All Nena had to do was move the armchair into a corner, where it wouldn't be reflected in the mirror, then take her self-portrait from its frame and stand it against the wall, opposite the chair's usual spot, to one side of the window. It would be reflected in the mirror and make it look like Nena was sitting in the chair. Anyone glancing in at the right angle would swear she'd been in her room.'

'Of course! Talk about smoke and mirrors.'

'I know. The witnesses viewed everything by lamplight and the white background of the painting would have blended into the walls. I guess the mirror's foxing would have helped disguise any distinction between the picture and reality. Nena probably relied on human nature too. No one would have glanced at her for more than a moment. It would have felt rude.'

'So this was the painting Nena was working on,' Simon said. 'That and the nude of Liam. There was no theft.'

'I should have clicked sooner. In hindsight, Nena sitting with her curtains open was a hint. I thought perhaps she was looking out for someone.'

'I can't believe she painted herself an alibi.'

It was astonishing. 'I'd guess she was in the habit of nipping off to meet Liam at his workshop. I doubt she'd have cared if she got found out, but I can imagine it made her hoot with laughter to think people assumed she'd been in her room all along. Sitting there demurely reading a book. From what we know of her character, I'd say she painted it as a joke.' It had been extraordinarily effective.

'And the painting of Liam? Might she have used that as blackmail?'

Eve shivered. 'It would certainly make any claim of an affair convincing.'

Forty minutes later, Eve and Simon were back at Monty's. Eve had called Greg to tell him what they'd found. She'd texted Robin too, though he hadn't replied. He'd be busy, of course.

'I wish you'd let me come!' Viv said. 'Though the nude of Liam sounds a bit much. Hard to unsee.'

'Please stop talking about it,' Simon said. 'You're giving me flashbacks.'

'It's Eve who's looking pale.' Viv moved towards her with a tray of bakes. 'You've been doing an awful lot for someone recovering from a head injury. Eat some spice cakes. They're as good as any medicine. So where does the new information leave us?'

'It means Nena could have left her room and been killed much earlier than we thought.' Eve ran through her notes. 'The pathologist put the time of death between ten and two. She might have left her room at ten thirty when Jamie went to lock up the bar. In which case, she could have reached the burned oak in Blind Eye Wood by around ten forty-five and have been killed any time after that.'

'So Iggy, Sadie and Gemma aren't in the clear after all,' Viv said. 'We're back to having plenty of suspects.'

'And a question to answer: who had the chance to nip into Nena's room and put the alibi painting back on the wall?'

'True.'

'The other question is, when did Liam slash Nena's pillows? He claims he can't remember – just that it was after Nena left her suite. I'll bet he knew all about Nena's painting. If he saw it through the window, it wouldn't have put him off. I suspect he dashed in immediately after Nena left, while Jamie was still busy in the bar.'

Viv looked puzzled. 'Why?'

'Because I think he discovered Nena was dead a short while later. And once he knew that, there'd be no point in slashing the pillows.'

'So you think he knew all along that Nena died earlier?'

'Yes. Right from the start, he was desperate to account for his and Tess's movements between ten and eleven. It was before he knew the police thought the time of death was later. I'll need to talk to him to confirm it.'

'You can't see him alone,' Simon said.

Eve had had the same thought. 'Let's get him here. If I hint at what I know, I'm sure he'll come.'

40

The meeting with Liam Norland was laughable. They sat with cups of Darjeeling. Viv had even brought them a plate of scones. Their topic of conversation was hardly typical for a genteel English tea. He'd come quickly enough, when she hinted she knew the secret he'd been keeping.

She looked into his handsome face and cruel eyes.

'Here we are again,' he said. 'This had better be good.' He leaned back in his chair, his fingers laced behind his head.

He was still cocky, after everything that had happened. Fury with his attitude drove Eve on. 'You lied about the route you took on your rounds, the night Nena died. There has to be a reason for that. I think you slashed her pillows at around ten thirty, then went to the woods where you'd probably arranged to meet her. You found her body. You knew she'd been killed so you tried to establish your and Tess's alibis.'

'Prove it.' Liam looked at her meditatively.

'You've given me the evidence yourself. You spelled it out in the way you behaved. You knew she was dead before you went to bed that night.' Eve would carry on repeating it for as long as it took. 'And that she died earlier than everyone thought.'

He took a juddering breath. She could tell it was anger not fear. 'All right. Yes. I *was* due to meet her, and I went to keep the appointment. When I got there she was dead.'

'What time was this?'

'We were due to meet at eleven. I was a couple of minutes late. No more.'

'You didn't dare stand her up in case she told Tess the truth.'

Liam looked down, his fist clenched. 'Think what you like.'

'Once you realised Nena had been killed, did you rearrange her room? You must have known about the painting she used to fool everybody.' He could have gone in while Jamie was switching the watches.

He nodded slowly. 'I knew all right. Nena thought it was hilarious. Got a real kick out of fooling everyone. Why would I rearrange her room?'

'To disguise the time of death. You were worried Tess might be guilty. You needed her, despite your affairs.'

Liam flinched. She must have hit a raw nerve. When he replied, his voice cracked. 'I lied to protect Tess, but I didn't go back to Nena's room after I'd found her body. I would have, but it was too big a risk.' He looked down at his lap.

She believed him; it fitted with his actions. He'd tried to give himself and Tess alibis for the real time Nena had died. If he'd hidden the alibi painting, he'd have known everyone would believe she'd died later.

'You need to tell the police.'

He looked at her, his shoulders sagging. 'And if I don't, you will.'

He seemed deflated suddenly: the shell of a man. He'd made the wrong call time and again and she guessed he knew it. She watched as he rose and left the teashop, his food and drink untouched.

Viv must have been lying in wait. She was at Eve's side in moments. 'You can so tell Liam's a wrong 'un. What a shocking waste of cake. There's a surprise for you outside, by the way. You're only allowed to look if you promise to message me all your updates.'

Weird. She peered through the window at the dusky village green and came face to face with Robin.

41

Eve ran outside into Robin's arms. He picked her up and swung her round, meaning she saw Viv's nose pressed against Monty's glass and a woman in a window seat making an *Ahhh* face. Embarrassing, but worth it.

'What are you doing here? Is it over?'

He gave her a half smile. 'Not quite. I have to go back. The rest of the team are doing some legwork.'

'It's so good to see you. But what made you come now, if they're still at it?'

'I decided you might like a mini-break.'

Eve laughed. 'Interesting timing.'

He grinned. 'After your text, I was thinking a trip to Cornwall might be in order. What do you say?'

'It's as though you'd read my mind.'

He looked at her intently, his eyes suddenly anxious. 'You've had a rough time. Are you up to setting off tonight? So long as Viv, Simon and Gus stay together so you know they're safe?'

She nodded. 'There's no time to waste.'

. . .

Eve and Robin got as far as Bristol before they stopped for the night and checked into a hotel. They were late making the last-minute booking and the staff gave them knowing glances which made them laugh as they let themselves into their room. They'd had a meal on the way but raided the hotel's supplies of cashews and gin. There was something curiously wonderful about that night: being so conspiratorial, feeling the thrill of the chase.

In their room, they discussed the lie of the land, now Liam had admitted he'd seen Nena, dead, just after eleven. The police were up to date too; Eve had called Greg Boles as they left Saxford. He was going to interview Liam, who hadn't contacted them direct. Perhaps he would have eventually, though Eve was doubtful.

'If we're looking at Sadie as our prime suspect, where does that leave us?'

'She was seen outside at around ten forty. It must have been just after she knocked on Tess and Liam's door, assuming that was her. She could have rushed straight to Blind Eye Wood, killed Nena and run back. She'd just have had time to make it to Liam and Tess's suite by eleven fifteen when Gemma saw her.'

'You think she'd be capable of premeditated murder?'

Eve reflected. 'I think so. She's hugely private and self-controlled. And although I don't understand her motive yet, I'm sure Nena had some kind of hold over her.

'Guilty or not, I'm increasingly convinced she knew Nena died earlier too. Her excuse for being outside in the run-up to eleven o'clock feels flimsy and she didn't seem surprised when I discovered Nena's body.' Eve took another handful of nuts. 'She had the opportunity to replace the alibi painting as well, before she went to the bar. It would explain why she didn't get there earlier, despite the close tabs she was keeping on Iggy and Gemma.

'She might not have known about the painting until that night. If she saw it after she'd killed Nena it must have made her jump. She'd have looked for an opportunity to get into the room and investigate, and taken it when Jamie went to switch the watches. She said she couldn't remember whether he was on his desk as she went past. That always felt a little unlikely.'

Robin topped up their drinks. 'I'm with you, Sadie's our number one suspect. Do any of the others have clear motives now theft is off the agenda?'

Eve went through them. 'Iggy... I don't think so. He was jolly with Nena, despite her irritating behaviour. I doubt he killed her from some deep-seated anger over her name-calling. And a love triangle between him, Liam and Nena is off the agenda.'

'You're sure the relationship with Gemma is genuine?'

Eve nodded. 'They had no idea they were being watched when we saw them together. Iggy blushed to the roots of his hair, which you can't fake.

'He could have killed for Tess's sake, to protect her marriage, but I don't see it. He hates his brother. I'd imagine he thought Tess would be better off without him. And it wouldn't fit with making Tess his next victim...

'And he couldn't have rearranged Nena's room. Both Gemma and Sadie say he only left the bar once, for a couple of minutes, and that would have been after Jamie was back at his desk.'

Robin nodded. 'What about Gemma?'

'She's an interesting one. She says she heard a knock at Liam and Tess's suite shortly before ten forty, but we've only her word for that. Even if it's true, she could have left immediately and been back by eleven fifteen, just like Sadie.' The timing was tight, but doable. 'If she'd come back while Sadie, Liam and Tess talked on the landing they might not have noticed her. I'm sure she threw the brick through Simon's window. She had a grudge against one of his staff, but which one and why is a mystery. Given she and Nena were both based in the same location in Cornwall, you have to wonder.'

'You do indeed.'

The following day they were on the road by eight. The sense of urgency made Eve breathless. She felt they were on the home straight, but Robin might get called back to London at any minute.

By eleven, they were approaching Porthruan along the only road that led to the village. Over the top of the hedgerows, Eve could see the sea, glimmering in the sunlight. Ahead and to their left on a headland sat St Elizabeth's Castle, clearly recognisable from Nena's postcard.

The hedges gave way to gardens and cottages and the road sloped down towards the harbour. There was an inn on their left. Eve recognised it as the hotel where Gemma had been head chef.

Robin parked his van and glanced at the board outside. They'd just opened for the lunchtime trade. Non-residents welcome.

'Shall we?'

Eve smiled. 'Don't mind if I do.'

Inside, they asked for coffee.

'I think a friend of ours used to be your cook,' Eve said as a waitress produced their drinks. 'Gemma Redpath?'

The woman's smile widened. 'Oh yes! We miss her. Though our new gentleman is very good. How did you meet?'

'Through one of my cousins.' It was best to be vague. 'I gather she's in Suffolk now. I was surprised. I mean her new job sounds great and everything, but not as prestigious as working here.'

The woman leaned forward conspiratorially. 'You're not the first person to say so. It was odd, the way she was so set on it.'

'And it's not as though it's near her mother.' It was a risk, but the more Eve thought about it, the more she doubted she was even in Suffolk. She suspected Gemma had pulled the location of Framlingham out of the air when challenged.

'Yes. Very odd, we thought, to move so far away. Especially when she's been so ill.'

Phew. Eve shook her head.

'I suppose one never gets over that type of thing,' the waitress went on. 'I mean, it must be awful enough under any circumstances, but with it happening that way.'

What was all that about? Eve sipped her coffee to play for time.

Robin glanced at Eve. 'Gemma never said that much about it, did she?'

'I can't say I'm surprised. Though we all knew, seeing her day in, day out. She was obsessive about the accident, but we couldn't blame her. Losing a brother at that age was so hard. Poor Danny. One moment of youthful stupidity and it was all over.' She lowered her voice. 'Gemma was only a little thing at the time. Looked up to her big brother, she did. She simply wouldn't believe he and his friends had pinched that boat, let alone taken it after they'd been told it wasn't seaworthy.' She sighed. 'Three young things drowned. The whole village was in mourning.'

Poor, poor Gemma. Eve thought of the photos Iggy had found in her suite. She suspected they were of Danny, frozen in time. Younger in the pictures she'd kept than Gemma was now.

'She insisted he wasn't the type to steal,' the woman behind the bar went on. 'But young ones do silly things sometimes. It was such a pity.'

'It sounds terribly sad.' Eve let the information settle, then bent her head close to Robin's to scan the menu. They could pick up the trail again later.

Over lunch, Eve broadened her enquiries. When the wait-

ress brought them Stilton and watercress soup, with warm rolls
that smelled like heaven, Eve made sure she was scrolling
through photos on her phone. She'd stopped at one of Sadie and
looked up at the waitress. 'We were just saying, you must know
Sadie too. She used to live around here.'

She was out on a limb, but if she was wrong it wouldn't
matter.

The waitress's eyes had widened as she saw the photo, but
now she hesitated. 'I was about to say I recognise that face, but
you say she's called Sadie? The woman I know is Celia Westbury. They're the spitting image of each other, though! But
Celia wasn't silver-haired like this lady. Though of course,
perhaps she would be by now; it's years since she lived here.'
She looked befuddled. 'And you say your friend Sadie also lived
here?'

'That's right.'

'That's so strange.' She called a colleague. 'Look.'

The man raised his eyebrows. 'Celia Westbury, as I live and
breathe! And she looks well.'

'But our guests here say this woman's called Sadie.'

The man frowned. 'Well I never. If it's not Celia then it's
her doppelganger.'

'But the funny thing is, there's a connection between Celia
and Gemma, who you were asking about,' the waitress
chipped in.

'Really?' Eve held her breath and took Robin's hand under
the table, squeezing it hard.

'Yes. That boating accident I mentioned. Poor Danny stole
the boat from Celia's boatyard.'

42

A lunch party entered the bar and Eve and Robin were left wanting to know more as the staff dashed off to sort them out.

'Sadie *must* be Celia,' Eve said in an undertone. 'But what does it mean? It sounds tragic, and if Gemma can't accept what happened then I can see she might blame Sadie. The poor security at her yard, perhaps. But she can't really hold her responsible. Yet Sadie changed her name. And she's moved around the country keeping everyone at arm's length. There has to be more to it. And if Nena was here too, then how does she fit in?'

'Good question. Let's see if there are any news reports.' He took out his phone and Eve followed suit. She got there first, and they peered at her screen.

CORONER RULES DEATH BY MISADVENTURE IN BOAT THEFT CASE

At an emotional hearing, the coroner heard how three friends, Daniel Redpath, Gary Dukes and Brian Foss, attempted to hire a boat from Celia Westbury, who runs a small boatyard close to Porthruan village. Ms Westbury explained that the young men were high-spirited, and seemed a little drunk, which is supported by the post-mortems. She stated that she explained the boat wasn't seaworthy, and therefore not for hire, though the boys continued to argue. She turned them away, and assumed they would head home. Instead, it's accepted that the boys went to Ms Westbury's boatyard, broke into the offices and stole the key for the boat. After which, they took it out and it began to ship water. Tragically, all three boys lost their lives.

When their bodies were recovered, they were found to be carrying a hundred pounds between them, which would have covered the boat hire. The coroner said Ms Westbury had no case to answer.

A text came in for Robin. Eve glanced at him quickly. Maybe he was being called back to London.

'It's Greg.' He angled his phone so she could see the message.

Investigation broadened following Eve's discovery proving killing of Nena Field could have happened earlier. Sadie Thornton was once Celia Westbury. Changed her name by deed poll.

'Shall I reply saying "old news"?'

Eve laughed. 'That would be mean.'

'Maybe you should just send him a link to the news report then.'

When Eve had done so, and they'd finished their food, the waiting staff were still busy.

'Shall we go and buy a paper from the village store?' Eve said. 'I'd like to ask about Nena.'

'Sounds like a plan.'

Eve was pleased to see a white-haired woman serving. She hoped she'd been employed there a nice long time. The woman smiled as she took the money for Eve's paper. 'On holiday?'

'Just a day trip. It's such a beautiful place.'

'It is that. Been before?'

Eve took out her photo of Nena's artwork. 'Well, I haven't, but I have a friend who must have stayed here once. I recognised this view as we drove along the Porthruan road.'

The storekeeper pushed her glasses further up her nose and peered at Nena's watercolour. 'Oh yes. St Elizabeth's Castle. Your friend's talented.'

'You might have met her, I suppose.' Eve showed the woman a photo of Nena.

The storekeeper frowned and peered more closely. 'Oh yes. I remember her. I saw she'd been killed.' She shook her head. 'I never even knew she'd got famous. Troubled young thing, she was. The worst for drink or some such when Celia Westbury took her in.'

'It was kind of Celia.'

The woman nodded. 'But of course, she was a great friend of this girl's mother. You'd know that I suppose.'

Celia... Of course! Eve couldn't believe she hadn't remembered. Celia had been the woman who'd looked after Nena as a child when her mum was too ill to cope. Eve was giving herself a good hard kick mentally. 'Yes, I remember Nena stayed with her when she was small.'

Eve was pretty sure Porthruan had been mentioned in that article she'd read. Perhaps Celia had been Nena's mainstay when she was a child, then again as a young adult.

The scene where Nena had pressed money on Sadie came back to Eve. Nena had said, *Ah, sea! It's good to be here*. It had made sense, given their location, but she'd been smiling at Sadie at the time. Eve should have realised it was an odd thing to say when she was indoors. It hadn't been *Ah, sea!* at all, but *Ah, C!* One of Nena's little indiscretions.

She could have guessed. Nena's permanent home was on the French Riviera. It wasn't as though she was deprived of the ocean.

'Do you remember when Nena stayed with her?' she asked the storekeeper.

'Oh, way back. 2008, maybe? Yes, it must have been, because she left soon after the tragedy at Celia's boatyard. I suppose she had enough on her plate without a houseguest. That Nena, she was here one minute, gone the next. And then Celia went. We're none of us in touch with her.' The woman shook her head. 'She crumpled after those boys drowned. Blamed herself for not putting the boat keys somewhere more secure.'

And Nena's mother thought Celia was dead. She'd disappeared quite completely, surfacing again as Sadie Thornton in London. Moving from place to place. Barely putting down roots. Never making close friends. Yet she hadn't hidden from Nena, despite seeming to fear her. Eve wondered why that was.

She'd made a new start in Suffolk, but she still seemed to be running from something.

The police would ask her why she'd changed her name. Maybe she'd tell them it was down to grief: that she'd wanted to leave everything behind.

But Eve doubted she'd go to such lengths unless there was more at stake.

What had happened back then?

As she and Robin returned to the hotel, Eve took out her notebook and looked at the words she'd overheard during that phone call of Sadie's.

I wish I could turn back time. If only I hadn't gone out that night. Her gratitude's like a knife, twisting in the wound. I should never have lied.

'Robin.' She showed him the words. 'I wonder if this relates to the boating accident.'

43

Eve and Robin were on the road again by three. They stopped for food just west of London, then carried on to Saxford.

Gus gave them an old-fashioned look when Eve arrived at Viv's. Eve didn't know who to fuss first and attempted pats and hugs at once.

'You're one in a million,' she said to her friend. 'Thank you.'

Viv gave her an indulgent smile. 'It's a pleasure – you know that. Gus has been good as gold, despite the cats. I just need one thing in payment...'

Eve knew what that would be. 'I was hoping for a catch-up anyway. It's good to have all hands on deck. Robin's staying at home tonight, assuming you've still got Simon with you? Then I want to talk to Sadie first thing, but what about lunch at the Cross Keys tomorrow?'

Viv nodded. 'Deal. So long as you don't see Sadie alone. Bring her to Monty's for cake.'

Robin left at the crack of dawn the following morning. The evidence down in London was shaping up well but one of the witnesses was wavering. It had been Robin who'd convinced him to talk in the first place. They needed him back.

Eve set her mind to her own investigation. She asked to buy Sadie a cup of tea at Monty's as Viv had suggested. Sadie hesitated, so Eve played her ace and said she'd done some research down in Cornwall.

Forty minutes later, the pair of them were sitting in the teashop. Eve had made Viv promise not to hover near their table.

'You can imagine how hard I've been trying to find out who killed Nena,' Eve said. 'It's a terrible crime of course, but seeing Simon's anguish has been hard to watch too. He hates the thought of letting you all down. And then things got even more desperate with poor Tess's death.' She met Sadie's eye. 'And the attack on me. You do understand?'

Sadie nodded. She could hardly say otherwise.

'Right from the start, I was as nosy as I've ever been. I pushed every boundary, looking for information. As you know, I'd already seen you and Nena talking as though you were old acquaintances. I also overheard a phone call you made, just after I interviewed you.' Eve took out her notebook. 'You said: *I wish I could turn back time. If only I hadn't gone out that night. Her gratitude's like a knife, twisting in the wound. I should never have lied.*'

Sadie went very still, her face pale. 'You must have gone to some lengths to hear me,' she said at last.

Eve nodded. 'I expect you'd have done the same in my position. To try to help someone you minded about.'

She let her words sink in and Sadie looked down into her tea.

'In fact,' Eve went on, 'that is what you did, isn't it? One night, when Nena was staying with you in Cornwall – when she was constantly drunk or high and miserable after her dad's death – you went out. I don't know where you went, but you clearly feel guilty about it. I think that on that night, a group of young lads came to your house, wanting to hire a boat. You'd probably told Nena the boat wasn't seaworthy. To tell anyone who asked that the answer was no. But I'm betting she was too drunk to be reliable. They offered her money, which she might have wanted for alcohol or drugs, and she let them have the keys.

'That was the lie you told. You faked a break-in at the boat-yard and covered for Nena. She had huge cause to be grateful to you. In theory.'

Eve saw a tear drop from Sadie's chin onto her lap.

'In reality, I think Nena resented you for it. Blamed you for leaving her on her own, probably.' She'd expected everyone to cushion her from life's knocks, just as Gemma had said.

'You hated what you'd done afterwards. Maybe you heard that a little sister of one of the boys, Gemma Redpath, didn't believe he'd have stolen the boat. You probably thought of her crying for her big brother. But it was too late by then. There was no escape, but you tried anyway. Changed your name and moved to London. I met one of your friends there.' Eve handed her Bridget's contact details. 'It must have hurt to keep cutting yourself off. Bridget would like to be back in touch.'

Sadie's eyes glistened as she took the woman's number.

'Why didn't you sever ties with Nena?'

Sadie sighed. 'She'd become my responsibility. We were bound together for better or worse and that was my fault. I'd been put in loco parentis when she was a child and taken the role again in Cornwall.'

'I see that. But to invite her here, when she could give you away? And what if her mother had visited and seen you?'

She shook her head. 'I wasn't worried about poor Delilah. Nena would never have invited her to Saltwater. She was bored by her, and Delilah was too timid to visit unannounced. If Delilah was lucky, Nena would have agreed to meet at some smart restaurant or other. Nonetheless, I should have known better. I decided I was safe enough. After all, Nena didn't really want the secret to get out either. But being indiscreet amused her. It was more of a risk than I'd realised. I thought some extended time together might bring us closer. I hoped we might finally reach an understanding and she'd leave me alone. I was desperate for her to stop tormenting me. But that was never going to work.'

Sadie's watery eyes met Eve's. 'You're right, you see. She blamed me entirely. If I hadn't gone out that night, she knew I'd have saved her from herself. She made it her business to remind me, over and over again. She expressed her gratitude with money and the more she pressed on me, the worse I felt. I could see it gave her pleasure. She enjoyed the joke of it: the way she could make me suffer through generosity. I tried to protest, but whenever I did she got more "careless".'

A never-ending punishment. 'You must have been fond of her when you first looked after her. When she was small.'

Sadie nodded. 'I could see what her parents were doing to her. Delilah was one of my oldest friends, but she couldn't relate to Nena. Not properly. She was too scared of losing her. She never put her foot down when Nena pushed the boundaries. During the six months I had her, I tried to make up for it. To let her know she was loved, but to be firm. I think it must have worked, because when she lost her dad, she came to me.' Sadie looked up at Eve at last. 'And after all that, I fell into the same trap as Delilah. I didn't make Nena take responsibility for her actions. But I felt so guilty. I'd gone out on a date. Relationships have never worked out for me. I had one brief marriage and a child of my own who died. Then, at last, I found someone who cared. An old, old friend who became something more. So I allowed myself that one evening out while Nena was staying with me.

'It was him I was calling when you listened in. He was in on it. We're still in touch. We still share how awful we feel. He blames me, of course. And rightly so. It killed the relationship, though we have a connection that can never be broken.' She gave a brittle laugh. 'It's ironic. Anyway, the evening of that date was when the lads came to call.' She sighed. 'They were just youngsters, trying their luck. I doubt Nena told them the boat wasn't seaworthy. She told me she couldn't remember.

'They must have read Nena like a book. They only paid her thirty pounds to hire the boat. Way less than the correct rate, but she was too far gone to care. It meant they still had plenty of money on them, which helped make my story believable. And they'd had the odd drink. Who doesn't at that age? It helped people accept they'd acted recklessly. And I faked the break-in, to give Nena her future. I kept telling myself that it wouldn't change anything if I'd told the truth, but that was wrong.'

It would have made a heck of a difference to the surviving relatives, knowing their children had been innocent of theft. Eve couldn't bring herself to say it when Sadie looked so broken.

'I feel terrible for the families,' she went on. 'And telling the truth would have changed Nena too. Made her less selfish. Helped her see she was part of a bigger picture. As it was, she never did.' Her red eyes met Eve's.

'You must have been scared she'd give you away.'

Sadie took a deep breath and straightened her back. 'I can imagine what you're thinking. That I killed her to shut her up. And it's true, she could have ruined what little I had left. But she's not the only person who could do that. Gemma's in the same position.'

'That's why you stuck to her like glue the night Nena died. And stopped her and Iggy's relationship. You didn't want them to share too much. Iggy found photos of her brother in her room. Sooner or later Gemma would have admitted why she'd come to Saltwater.'

If Gemma had proof, yet hadn't gone to the police, that was significant. She must have planned to mete out justice in other ways. She'd have been talking about Nena *and* Sadie when she'd thrown the brick through Simon's window. *Look to your employees.* It made sense. She'd probably hated Nena most though. She could have killed her.

Sadie sighed. 'The moment I heard the name of Simon's new sous chef I was afraid. The surname Redpath could have been a coincidence, but when I dug, I saw where she came from.

'She wasn't mentioned in any of the articles about her brother and I didn't remember her from the inquest. I suppose her parents kept her out of it. But it was clear she must have tracked me down.' She shook her head.

'How did she trace you? Have you asked her?'

Sadie's head was in her hands. 'I haven't admitted I know who she is. She had as big a motive to kill Nena as I did, of course. But I assume she'd like to kill me too. She hasn't tried.'

'Where did you really go, the night Nena died? Your story about checking the repairs in the end cottage was a lie, wasn't it? It didn't start raining until later.'

Her shoulders sagged. 'I felt terrible for the way Nena was behaving. If I'd admitted my own carelessness and let Nena take responsibility for hers she'd have been a different person.'

Sadie's sympathy with Jamie and the talk about making mistakes made sense now. 'Maybe.'

'I'm sure of it. And here she was in Suffolk at my invitation, wrecking a marriage. I saw her through the window, heading off towards the woods, and I was convinced she was going to meet Liam. It had been going on for weeks.'

Eve frowned. 'Since Nena came to start tutoring, you mean?' Four weeks, tops.

Sadie shook her head. 'Longer than that. The moment I moved in – well before the opening – Nena came to see me. It was her way of reminding me of what I'd done. That was when things kicked off with Liam. Saltwater Cottages was more or less deserted, so Nena's suite became their love nest.'

'I see. So you followed Nena, the night of her death.'

'That's right. I wanted to reason with the pair of them. I tried Liam and Tess's suite first, in case I could catch Liam before he left, but there was no reply. It was essential to make them see what was at stake. Their lives. Tess's life. The smooth running of Saltwater Cottages. Simon's faith in them. I was going through it all in my head as I headed towards the woods. And as I walked, I saw Tess.' She put her hands over her face. 'I was horrified. Convinced I'd be too late and she'd have seen Liam and Nena together.'

So that was where Tess had gone when she'd left her room. 'She was coming towards the cottages from Blind Eye Wood?'

Sadie nodded.

'And then what happened?'

Her words came in a whisper. 'I walked into the woods, looking to left and right. Listening for a sound. But there was nothing. And then I found Nena's body.'

Eve had been right to think she hadn't looked surprised the following morning. Her eyes met Sadie's.

'I know,' the manager said, still in a whisper. 'I should have called the police immediately. But I was scared. Gemma was on the spot and she knew who I really was. Or at least, I assumed so. It was too much of a coincidence otherwise. And I lied when I said I didn't know about Nena's bequest.'

'She told you as part of her campaign to rub in what you'd done?'

Sadie nodded. 'She gave me a copy of the will! She only did it to make me feel worse. There's no way she should have died before me.'

Eve thought it through. How she'd feel if she'd helped cover up the cause of the boys' deaths. Allowed their parents to think of their dead children as thieves and authors of their own down-fall. And then been paid by the person she'd protected. Someone so much less deserving than the lives lost. It would be horrific. Nena really had known how to manipulate people. She'd been in training all her life.

Sadie sighed and spoke again. 'My last reason for not calling the police was less selfish.'

'You thought Tess was guilty?'

Sadie nodded. 'And I blamed myself. It's like I said, if I'd made Nena face up to what she'd done in Cornwall she might have acted differently. As it was, Tess was pushed to the limit. I thought about the way Nena had behaved. How she might have laughed at Tess and crowed. Heaven help me, I realised I wouldn't blame Tess for lashing out.'

'Except it looks like the murder was premeditated now.'

Sadie's gaze was steady. 'I'd heard. But even so.'

A sudden suspicion crossed Eve's mind. 'Was it you who set Nena's room to rights, to disguise the time of death and protect Tess?'

At last, Sadie nodded. 'I couldn't understand what I was seeing through her window, but I knew it wasn't her. She'd clearly set something up, and if I could disguise that, I realised I might help Tess. My priority was to call on her. If she was back, I could swear I'd seen her at home when Nena still appeared to be alive and well in her suite. I couldn't vouch for her later in the night of course, but it would protect her from anyone who'd seen her in the woods earlier on.'

Eve nodded. 'Gemma mentioned you'd called on Tess and Liam at eleven fifteen.'

She sighed. 'I told the police I'd seen Nena in her room just before that, then made up some ridiculous query about printing equipment as an excuse to knock.'

So Tess and Liam hadn't lied about that then. 'After which you went to Nena's suite while Jamie was gone from his desk?'

She nodded. 'If he hadn't left, I'd have invented an excuse to get him out of the way. I closed Nena's curtain, then put the painting and the chair back. I felt I'd let Tess down, just as I'd let Nena down, and I suppose I did the same thing. Tried to cover for her. You could argue I should have learned my lesson, but Tess was a different kettle of fish to Nena. She didn't deserve what happened.'

'You still think she did it?'

Sadie nodded. 'Liam probably killed her in revenge if he found out she was guilty. He's a nasty piece of work. But I might be wrong. If so, I've covered up vital evidence on the time of death without helping Tess at all.'

Eve was loth to ask her final question, but she had to. 'What will you do now?'

The manager met Eve's eye. 'I can't live with myself. I haven't been able to for a long time. I'll go to the police today and tell them everything. Will you tell Simon, please? I don't think I can face him.'

Eve nodded. 'I will.' It would be another massive blow. 'I'll need to talk to Gemma too.'

Sadie swallowed. 'I'll write her a note, but I understand you might get there first.'

44

Eve lured Gemma out the same way she had Sadie: with the information she had. They were to meet at the beach.

Simon and Viv insisted on joining her. She doubted she could have kept Viv at bay, even if she hadn't been in danger.

As Eve and Gemma walked along the shingle, Gus ahead of them, Simon and Viv a short way behind, Eve ploughed in.

'I know why you came to Saltwater Cottages.'

Gemma's cool eyes met hers.

'I've been down to Cornwall. I heard about your brother. I'm so sorry.'

Shock came first, then her guard fell away bit by bit. Her stiff expression crumpled and despair etched her face. Tears came next and she buried her head in her hands.

Eve gave her some time, then spoke again. 'I can't think what you must have gone through. The whole experience must have been harrowing. Did you come for Sadie, or for Nena?'

Gemma gulped, pulled a tissue from her pocket and blew her nose. At last, she faced Eve and Eve knew she'd get the truth.

'Nena. The news of her coming as a tutor made the papers.

When I turned up, I couldn't believe Sadie was here too. Celia. Let's call her by her name.' The anger and bitterness were back, making her stronger again. 'For a moment, I thought what a glorious coincidence it was, but of course, it wasn't chance. Celia put Nena first back in Cornwall and she put her first here too, asking her to come and teach.'

'It doesn't make much odds,' Eve said, 'but I don't think it was quite like that. Nena dogged Celia anyway, and Celia believed her presence would help Saltwater to succeed.'

'She'd had long enough to work out that Nena was poisonous.'

'I know. Gemma, she told me exactly what happened. And that I could tell you and Simon. She's going to the police today to confess.'

'Did she kill Nena in the end? I thought she might have; her knowledge could have destroyed Celia.'

'She says not.' But Gemma could have, if the question was a bluff.

She told Gemma the whole story then. Everything Sadie had said, without introducing her own thoughts. She felt sorry for Sadie but in the same position she knew she would have acted differently. What she'd put the bereaved families through was unforgiveable.

'It's just as I thought,' Gemma said.

'You didn't have proof?' In that case, she might have come to get it, not to kill Nena or Sadie.

Gemma sighed. 'That's right. I've been searching for concrete evidence all these years. Someone must have known something. But I couldn't find Celia, and Nena had become a big star. Not someone I could get close to for confirmation.'

'It all started because you were convinced your brother wouldn't have stolen the boat?'

She nodded. 'It was obvious to me, but who pays attention to a twelve-year-old? My parents thought theft was totally out of character, but they still accepted it. I found that hard to take.'

'How much did you know, before you came to Suffolk?'

'Just whispers. Someone said they thought they'd seen Celia round at this guy's house, the night Danny knocked on her door. The guy denied it, and so did she, then the witness decided they must have been mistaken. But I thought otherwise. I was convinced Nena had let Danny and his friends have the boat, even though it wasn't seaworthy. Everyone said she was a complete mess at the time. Wallowing in self-pity because one of her adoring parents had stopped lavishing her with attention.'

'You knew her dad had died?'

'Yes! But please forgive the lack of sympathy.' She spat the words out. 'I don't think for one minute that she loved him. She didn't care for anyone but herself.'

The whole thing was tragic.

'I was convinced that by coming here I could finally tease out the proof I needed.'

'You must have really hated Nena.'

'I loathed her with every fibre in my body, but if you think I killed her, you're wrong. I wanted proof and I still didn't have it. And then I wanted her to face justice. And Celia too. I'd never have killed either of them. I wanted them publicly shamed. The truth blazing from every newspaper on the stand. I couldn't prove my brother's innocence otherwise. I couldn't believe it when I heard Nena was dead and my chance was gone. Even the affair I was sure she was having with Liam would be swept under the carpet.'

'That's why you told me about Tess's upset after Liam left their suite? You wanted people to know there was something up there, too?'

Gemma gave a quick nod. The fire in her eyes blazed.

'Why did you throw the brick through Simon's window?'

Gemma closed her eyes. 'Because I'm human. And stupid.

I'd been here for four weeks without any breakthrough. I couldn't come clean and explain my suspicions. Celia and Nena would have clammed up or moved on. So I was feeling frustrated, and everything Nena did filled me with fury. Anger got the better of me that day. She had a go at a cleaner. She blamed her for breaking a beautiful bowl of Simon's when she was the one who'd left it in the way.'

It was the same incident that had made Sylvia angry.

'It was so typical of her,' Gemma went on. 'A small thing, maybe, but it was the exact same attitude she had after she let my brother die. It was always someone else's fault.' She shook her head. 'I'd spent too many years holding in my feelings.' She sighed. 'Little did I know that Nena was about to be killed and a full-scale investigation would be launched anyway.'

'Who do you think killed Nena?'

'I'm not sure,' Gemma said, 'but whoever it was, I don't blame them.'

45

Viv had left Allie, Tammy and Lars in charge at Monty's. It meant Eve, Viv and Simon could catch up at the Cross Keys.

They sat and listened to Eve's update in silence. She finished as their food arrived.

'Blimey,' Viv said, as Toby put a plate of fish pie in front of Eve. 'That's quite a breakthrough.'

'Things are working out?' Toby asked, as Eve thanked him.

'I wouldn't go that far,' Simon said. 'But the picture's getting clearer.'

Toby patted him on the shoulder. 'We're all rooting for you.'

When the others had their food too, Viv looked at Eve. 'So, where does it leave us?'

'Despite her motive, I don't believe Gemma killed Nena. I think she really did want earthly justice for her. And Sadie's account of her movements rings true too. Rearranging the room to protect Tess made sense in her eyes.'

'I see that.' Simon sighed. 'What a thing to have done. No wonder she was happy to forgive Jamie. Not that I disagree in his case, but it puts it in context.'

Eve nodded. 'So we're down to Iggy, whose motive doesn't

stack up, Liam, who I'd already written off, and Jamie, ditto. But there's something niggling at me. I'm sure there's a detail I should have picked up on.'

She took out her notebook and recorded each point Sadie and Gemma had made. The thoughts came piecemeal, and she flipped from a page devoted to one to a page devoted to the other.

'I've never seen a better organised notebook,' said Viv with a tinge of resentment. Hers were covered with crossings out and words jumbled together. They made Eve twitch.

Eve thought she'd noted everything she'd told Simon and Viv, but thinking back to that morning's conversations, she suddenly realised she'd missed something out.

'Wait. Sadie said Nena's affair with Liam started well before Saltwater Cottages launched. Nena came to visit Sadie the moment she moved in. I thought at the time that explained how they were able to use Nena's suite. Curlew Cottage would have been almost deserted, so the risk of being caught was low.'

Simon frowned. 'That makes sense. But why is it significant?'

Eve took a deep breath as the implications settled in her head. 'Because the nude Nena painted of Liam showed him in her bedroom there. If he posed for the portrait, I imagine she painted him when she first came, before she arrived to teach.'

'She'd already brought the boards down at that stage?'

'She must have. When did she agree to come and tutor for you?'

Simon frowned. 'Soon after Sadie started work for me, I suppose. You think Sadie suggested it to Nena first? And she was already working out which room she wanted and making herself comfortable?'

'Yes. She'd have been perfectly confident that you'd want her as a tutor. Who wouldn't? I'd guess she came to stay, clapped eyes on her old partner in crime Liam, and thought how well it would suit her to spend some time in Suffolk. She could carry on making Sadie feel bad and have an exciting fling into the bargain. She probably sent for the boards at that point so she could paint Liam on the back of her existing works. It would have tickled her to have people look at the reverse side with no idea of the secrets it hid.'

'She wasn't around when we furnished the room, but it's perfectly possible. There's a large walk-in cupboard off her sitting room. She could have stored the boards in there. And thinking back, she requested that suite immediately when I showed her round.'

'I wonder if she painted the self-portrait back then too. She must have realised subterfuge would be required if she carried on her affair once the cottages were occupied. What do you think, Simon? Did you notice anything that would tell us when she painted the alibi picture?'

Simon frowned. 'I don't know. I was so struck by what it meant that I didn't analyse it.'

Eve pulled out her phone and showed Simon the photos she'd taken to remind him.

He winced again at the nude. 'Now you mention it, it looks dated. Liam's hair is longer there than it is now.'

It was true. 'And the self-portrait?'

Simon peered at it. 'I'm not sure.'

Eve had been afraid of that.

But then his eyes widened. 'No, wait.' He pointed at a small picture on the wall behind Nena. 'She must have painted this when she first came. Polly saw I'd taken that watercolour to Saltwater and returned it to Honeysuckle Cottage, with a few choice words. Her mother painted it, apparently.'

They all looked at each other.

'So Nena wasn't working on either of those paintings after she arrived to teach,' Eve said. 'We're back to our original question: what happened to Nena's work in progress? She bought oils when she arrived this latest time, and the tubes are all but empty.'

'And we never did find an ink drawing,' Viv said. 'Nor anything written in ink.'

'It's as you said before.' Simon sipped his beer. 'She must have given them away or destroyed them.'

Eve thought back to her previous objections. 'I still don't think she's the sort to wreck her own work.'

'But gifting them's possible,' Simon said.

'Yes, but it would mean she or the recipient carried them out of her room without anyone gossiping. And her paintings are normally huge.'

'All the same, it could have happened. If it didn't, we're back to looking at theft.'

And they'd already written that scenario off. Simon had to be right. Except it was an oddity and they mattered. Eve couldn't switch off the niggle.

46

After lunch, Viv prepared to return to the teashop. Eve and Simon were going to Saltwater End. They didn't have a plan but sitting doing nothing was impossible. If there were clues to be found, that had to be the place to look. Besides, Polly was due back within hours. Simon said he couldn't bear to wait at Honeysuckle Cottage with nothing to occupy him.

'Please deliver Eve to me when you've finished,' Viv said to Simon.

'Excuse me, I am here, you know,' Eve said.

'There, there.' Viv patted her shoulder. 'It's for your own good. Once this maniac's caught you can throw yourself into danger to your heart's content.'

'Gee, thanks.'

Viv gave them a merry wave and crossed the village green.

Eve and Simon cut across it in the opposite direction and headed down Dark Lane towards the cottages.

'What do you think we should do?' Simon said.

'Mull over what we know. Walk the grounds. Look around inside. See if we can overhear or spot anything. Work out where someone might have hidden a painting.'

They were round the back of the cottages, looking up at the windows, when they spotted Gemma coming towards them.

Eve greeted her. 'Do you know if Sadie's gone to the police yet?'

The cook nodded. 'She didn't come and talk to me, but she put a note under my door. Then I saw her drive off.'

That was that, then.

'That's not why I came to talk to you, though. I've found something odd.' She beckoned for them to follow and took them to a stretch of freshly dug earth to one side of Curlew Cottage.

'It's going to be the kitchen garden,' Gemma said. 'You remember we discussed it, Simon, and you said it was all right for me to clear some shrubs?'

He nodded.

'Recent events have given me plenty of time to develop it.' She shook her head. 'This morning, I dug up another shrub to make more space and I found this.' She pointed to where some roots remained, and next to them, some charred wood.

'I don't think it can have been there that long,' Gemma said. 'There's no sign of rot.'

Eve's mind went straight to the carefully cleaned grate in Nena's room and the missing painting. But there was no sign of any oil paint residue amongst the charred remains.

The wood might be from Nena's grate though. But why hide it? From what Eve could see, there was nothing special about it. It might be an inch by two inches, crossways. Much of it was just charcoal.

'Thanks, Gemma,' Simon was saying. An alert sounded on his phone. After she'd left them, he glanced at it and turned to Eve. 'It's a message from the head chef I was going to employ. He's heard about our troubles and decided to stay where he is. Can't say I blame him.'

Eve glanced at Simon. 'Will you offer Gemma the job, if everything comes right?'

'What do you think of her?'

'I like her a lot better now I understand why she was so antagonistic. You'd have to overlook the fact that she threw a brick through your window.'

Simon gave a hollow laugh. 'She's a first-rate cook though. So long as she doesn't get frustrated with the clients and throw hot spaghetti over them.'

It was getting dark by the time Simon and Eve returned to Monty's. From inside the teashop, the village green looked comforting with its old-fashioned streetlamps, but out at the back, where Monty's lawn stretched down towards the River Sax, inky black in the moonlight, the shadows looked threatening.

Another message alert sounded on Simon's mobile. 'Polly! She's nearly home. I'll go and pick her up from the station.'

His tone tugged at Eve's heart. He sounded so fond, and yet so anxious.

Viv gave him a hug. 'She loves you, don't forget. Why you love her is something of a mystery, but there we are. You run along. So long as you're not alone, I'm happy for you to spend the night at Honeysuckle Cottage.'

Simon looked queasy with nerves. 'So long as she'll have me. Will you two be okay? You could come and stay with us.'

'I'm sure Polly would *love* that,' Viv said. 'No, thanks all the same. Eve and I will stick together. All will be well. Go on! Go and clear the air. The sooner the better.'

Eve helped to serve the last remaining customers, but half her mind was on the burned wood, missing paintings and ink drawings. On what she knew, which had led to her being attacked.

She must have all the information she needed. And the killer would want to try again before she made the links. Thank goodness for her minders.

At last, they went back to Viv's for supper.

Eve felt exhausted. 'I wonder how Simon's getting on.'

'He'll be fine. I mean, I'm not saying Polly will be ecstatic, but despite her obvious shortcomings, I'm sure she'll understand. He couldn't have predicted all this.' She went to draw the curtains. 'I can't bear it when you keep looking out as though a face might look in. A heartening casserole and a large glass of red, that's what you need.'

'I think I should keep my wits about me.'

'Wine might get the creative juices flowing.'

'Maybe just a sip.'

Viv put a bottle in a bowlful of warm water to take the chill off. 'You can help cook. You always say doing mechanical stuff helps you think.'

'Not if it's complicated.'

'The parmentier potatoes are easy.'

'All right.' Eve started peeling as Viv got out wine glasses.

'What the heck do I know, Viv?'

Viv gave her a funny look. 'Lots of things. I think you're fairly intelligent, really.'

'Enough with the flattery. I mean why did the murderer try to kill me?'

Viv was chopping onions. 'It's a good question. Maybe we should stop knocking our heads against a brick wall looking at alibis and times and think about the key mysteries we've yet to unravel instead. Not including who killed Nena and Tess.'

Eve felt faintly threatened. That was actually a very wise idea. 'Good plan. So we're back to the mystery of what Nena was working on when she died. Where did the painting and the ink drawing go? I know there *could* be an innocent explanation, but I can't help feeling the answer must be crucial.'

It took her back to thinking about which of the suspects could have removed them, which led her to Jamie again, but she forced the thought from her mind. She focused only on the oddity of the missing artwork.

'Anything else?'

'Nena burned something that looked like nothing more than plain wood.'

'Is it helping?'

'No.'

'Well, it was worth a thought. Focus on Nena then, not alibis. You always say the victim's personality leads you to their killer.'

It was true. Eve had almost let that go in her panic to solve the case.

She took a deep breath. 'We know Nena liked to have fun. Play around with people. Fool and manipulate them. Liam was getting sick of her, but I don't think she knew that. She was confident she could reel him in again.' She visualised the scene she'd witnessed between them. 'She was all pouty when Liam came to fetch her damaged rug. When she realised he was seriously irritated, she told him she had a wonderful surprise for him.'

'Oo-er, missus,' Viv said. 'I'll bet she did.'

Eve had thought of that sort of surprise too, but suddenly she wondered. Her skin prickled and the hairs on the back of her neck stood on end.

Viv poured them each a glass of wine. 'I'll just get some rosemary for the spuds.'

As she opened and closed the back door, Eve's mind ran on. What if...

What if the surprise hadn't involved the bedroom at all?

Multiple thoughts were coming together. The ink, dried on the carpet. The bottle, not just part-empty but entirely. The lack of any letter written with a fountain pen, or any ink drawing. The rolled-up rug and the charred wood.

'I think I know what happened,' Eve whispered as Viv came back inside. 'I think Nena had painted a picture for Liam. *That* was the surprise.' She was staring at her notepad. 'And he carried it out of Nena's room himself, without any idea of it! It was wrapped in that huge rug of hers. That was why the ink bottle was entirely empty. It wasn't an accident at all. She'd tipped it over the rug so Liam would have to remove it. And it's also why she left the ink to dry. Because it would have damaged her painting if it was still wet.'

And where had the carpet ended up? With Jamie ultimately. But not immediately. It was Iggy who'd got it cleaned, as best he could.

'Iggy's got the painting. It was Iggy! He must have been in on the surprise. Nena confided in him, just as she did about her poison pen letter!' She picked up her wine and turned to Viv.

But it wasn't Viv.

47

Iggy picked up Viv's wine and took a swig.

'I knew you'd get there eventually.'

'Where's Viv? Where is she?' Bile rose in Eve's throat.

'Oh, don't worry. She won't have known what hit her. Or who, more importantly. She'll wake up with a sore head. I'm not worried about her. She didn't see the dried ink. The empty bottle. The wood. Hearing it second hand's not the same.'

'Nena burned the frame she stretched the canvas over.'

He nodded.

'She took you into her confidence. Told you she was planning a surprise for Liam and got you to take it for safe keeping.'

'You see! I was right to worry. You did have the knowledge to piece it all together. I knew you did when I heard you going over everything with Simon and Viv.' He took a knife from his jacket. 'Come on. We're going for a walk before sleeping beauty wakes up. If you make a sound, I'll come back here and kill her as well as you.'

Gus whined and let out a single bark.

'And if he makes a fuss, I'll shut him up as well.' Iggy looked Eve in the eye. 'Make him stop. Now!'

Eve was in tears. She couldn't control them, but she bent and soothed Gus as best she could. His whining got quieter but he was clearly terrified. He was quivering.

Iggy put one arm around her shoulder, the other under her jacket, holding the knife up against her abdomen. 'We're going to walk along your road to the estuary path. Don't say a word.'

They only saw one couple on the village green. It was too dark to tell who they were and Iggy ushered her on.

As they walked down Haunted Lane, Eve focused on her beloved neighbours' cottage. The curtains were drawn, a warm glow coming from behind them.

'Don't even think about it,' Iggy hissed. 'If you scream, I'll stab you where you stand and run. I can't leave you alive. After that, I'll get your dog and Viv too. If you come quietly, I'll let them live.'

More tears welled in Eve's eyes. In moments they were past her cottage and onto the dark narrow pathway that led towards the estuary.

Eve tried to focus. 'It wasn't just that you wanted Nena's painting, was it?'

He pushed the knife closer, as though the thoughts she was sparking made him tense. 'Of course not. Nena working on the painting in secret presented an opportunity, and the money will make setting up with Gemma possible. It'll change my life. But the financial side was secondary. I never thought of stealing the picture until she told me it was for Liam.'

It was what Eve had guessed. The trigger. Something that Iggy simply couldn't stand. 'You loathe him, and it's no wonder. He was the one your dad bonded with. Liam got your parents' house, your dad's ring and his workshop. You were left with a grotty caravan. Liam and your dad spent all their time belittling you and Liam still does. Nena did too, of course. Calling you Iggy Ignoramus.'

'Oh yes. She was poisonous, our Nena. She'd seen me with Gemma, you know. She was eagle-eyed when it came to spotting useful information. She didn't talk to me about it though, she told Liam. And what did Liam do? Went and told Gemma stories about me. How cowardly I was as a kid. How little my dad thought of me. He did everything in his power to ruin the one thing I had. But Gemma wouldn't play. I'm going to make Liam pay for that. It's not enough to lose Nena, Tess and the painting.

'As for Nena, she deserved to die. She teamed up with Liam and made Tess's life a misery.' His grip tightened around her shoulder.

She gasped as she felt the tip of the knife through her top. 'But you killed Tess.'

He took a moment to reply. When he did, his voice cracked. 'We went for a walk the night you warned me she wasn't coping. She told Liam she wanted to be alone and he didn't follow her. He's never cared.'

It was terrible. Eve had triggered that walk. She'd thought Tess could use a friend.

'She had no idea I'd done it, but as we talked, I could see she was joining the dots. It turned out she'd seen me near the woods. She'd gone looking for me after Liam upset her, wanting to share.' Iggy sounded far away. 'In the end I told her what I'd done. It was for her too! Liam and Nena should never have treated her the way they did.'

He went silent, but Eve guessed at what was coming. She could hear the anger, the frustration. 'I imagine she was horrified,' she said. 'She'd never condone what you did. She didn't even want to leave Liam. She probably said she'd go to the police, so you let her have it.'

'I lost control!'

'So much for loving her like a sister.'

'Shut up! She wouldn't abandon Liam. *I* was the bad guy, in her eyes. She looked at me like I was a monster. It made me so angry!'

His grip tightened again and the knife cut her. The sensation of blood trickling down her skin made her shiver and gag.

They walked on in silence. It was a minute before Eve felt able to speak again. She must keep him talking, to distract him if she could. But she needed to dial down the tension.

'So, when Nena called you about her damaged rug, you were in on the joke. You sounded happy, because it was step one in getting even with Liam and her too. You succeeded. Where's the painting? I doubt you'd risk leaving it in your caravan.'

'You're right. I wouldn't.' Iggy's eyes glinted in the moonlight. 'It's safe enough.'

'Why did Nena give it to you?'

'It was all part of the surprise. She wanted me to put it up in Liam's workshop, so he'd find it next time he went there. She liked the idea of him being mystified. And scared. If Tess had been with him, she'd have guessed the truth. We had a good laugh over that but inside I was livid. She cared nothing for anyone's feelings.'

'You've wrecked so many lives with what you've done.'

'Mine was wrecked first.'

They were nearing the point where the estuary path joined the end of Ferry Lane. Eve tried to guess what was coming. 'We're near Liam's house now, aren't we?' It was the grotty one their father had left him. It was noticeable amongst the better-kept cottages there, the paint peeling, the garden overgrown.

'It's empty now,' Iggy said. 'The tenants left. They think Liam's guilty of murder, so I'm not surprised. The police suspect him too. He'd come to hate Nena and he's the prime suspect for Tess as well. When they find your body in a shallow grave in his garden, it will complete the picture.'

Eve's mouth was dry. She wondered how he intended to kill

her. And if Viv had come round. Would she raise the alarm? But even if she did, she'd have no idea where to send help. And in the pit of her stomach lurked a fear that she might be more seriously hurt than Iggy knew. What if he'd killed her?

Iggy pushed Eve through some vegetation, so that they were behind the houses to the west side of Ferry Lane. She knew the row well. The gardens weren't secure. They had bushes, trees and hedges running along their ends which could easily be breached.

She was running out of time. They must be nearing Liam's garden. Once they were inside it, Iggy would make his move. She could make a noise now. The neighbours would hear.

'Don't even think about yelling.' It was as though he'd read her mind. 'You'll be dead before anyone reaches you and it'll be you they rush to help. They won't catch me. I'll be running back along the river to Viv's house.'

Her mind went blank with panic. How could she stop him? She needed a distraction. Anything to get him to drop his guard. She glanced ahead and to her left. She could just see one of the houses in the row. It had an outdoor light. The sort that was motion activated. If only she could set it off. But they'd be past it in a minute, beyond its reach.

Eve felt in her pocket. She had a leash, and Gus's bouncy ball. *Think. Think.*

A possible plan formed. It was totally chancy. Probably doomed to fail. It would only work if she got her timing exactly right and success was crucial. It wasn't just her safety that depended on it.

Suddenly, swiftly, in one quick movement, she pulled the ball from her pocket and threw it behind her. Iggy's knife grazed her as she turned but the ball had the desired effect. Iggy was disorientated. He'd heard the noise behind them. He knew she'd done something but not quite what.

He loosened his grip and it left her with half a second's

grace, the knife no longer an immediate threat. She pulled away and leaped through the hedge into the garden with the motion-sensitive light.

In an instant she was bathed in brilliant, bright, white light. Hope surged inside her. Surely someone would come and investigate?

As she powered ahead, she tugged Gus's leash from her pocket and held it tightly by its loop, letting the metal hook at the other end fall free.

Iggy was after her in a moment. Eve bounded to get away from him, swinging the leash at him like a whip. The metal catch caught his face and he swore.

She couldn't let him catch her. If he killed her he really might go back for Viv and Gus in his anger.

She swung the leash again. Fast and hard. It hit the hand that held the knife, catching him just above the knuckles. He yelped in pain but didn't drop the weapon. His eyes were like an animal's. Packed with fight and fury.

Eve went in with the leash again as he lunged for her. At last she got the knife and it spun from his hand.

He lost a second trying to find it, then gave up, but then he was on to her again. She swung the leash once more and he managed to grab the end of it.

She had to let go.

The house remained in darkness. She ran but she'd never outpace him. It was hopeless. Her legs were like jelly.

She was pushing through to the next garden when she heard a cry.

'Here! I think they're here!' Then came the sound of thudding feet.

As Iggy grasped her jacket, multiple figures appeared in the garden.

She recognised Matt from the pub as he dragged Iggy off, Toby just behind him, calling 999. Jo and Jim Thackeray.

Eve's heart was racing. 'Has anyone seen Viv and Gus? Viv's injured. She was unconscious.'

Jo came and put a stout arm around Eve as Jim helped Matt pin Iggy down. 'She's all right, don't you worry. And Gus too. It was Viv who raised the alarm. Moira's with them. We've called an ambulance. Sylvia and Daphne are off with another search party. They went the other way up the river. We reckoned whoever was responsible had likely taken you somewhere lonely. Didn't guess he'd bring you here, but we heard the rumpus from the estuary path.'

The relief was monumental. Eve burst into tears and Jo, who was younger than her, pulled her into a motherly hug.

48

'I wasn't careful enough,' Viv said, as Eve sat next to her bed in the cottage hospital.

'It wasn't just you.' Eve passed her some water. 'Only a sip, remember.'

Viv nodded, then winced.

'I never gave it a second thought when you went to fetch the herbs.' But Viv's garden ran down to the river just as Monty's did, with only a low gate at the end.

'It was a piece of cake for Iggy to get in. I hate that expression. There's nothing easy about cake. It takes a mastermind to produce a decent one.'

'Of course it does.' Eve patted her hand and rolled her eyes.

'I demand you take me seriously! I'm not well.'

'Sorry. So, you didn't see a thing when Iggy hit you?'

'Nothing. The lights just went out. When I woke up I had no idea how long it had been, who'd taken you or where. My head hurt like the blazes, but I was stoical, naturally. Even though I felt sick, I raised the alarm. Or at least, I staggered over to the pub, where half the villagers were eating and drinking anyway. I've never seen a place empty so fast. I think it's safe to say you're well loved. They seemed quite concerned about me too.'

'So I should hope.'

'Toby and Jo organised everyone into teams, one for the beach, one upriver and one down, and another to drive to Saltwater Cottages, in case someone had abducted you by car.' A tear rolled down her cheek and her voice cracked. 'I was worried they'd be too late.'

Eve hugged her gently. 'But they weren't. It's all right now, and I can't thank you enough.'

Robin appeared at that moment. The night Eve was injured was repeating itself, except Viv was in the bed.

'Thank goodness you're both okay.'

'We're rather relieved too.' Eve hugged him tightly.

Viv looked up at the pair of them. 'Don't tell the kids about this, will you? They'd worry so much.'

'You didn't approve when I asked you not to tell the twins about me.'

'I understand now.' Viv closed her eyes and Eve and Robin left the room.

In the corridor, Robin pulled Eve close again. 'I don't ever want to let you go. I should have been here.'

She rested her head on his chest. 'You can't be here all the time. You have to be able to carry on with your life, and you're good at your job. It's not as though you didn't look out for me. Viv and Simon were oppressively keen to keep me safe. It's just that none of us realised the lengths Iggy would go to.'

He stroked her hair. 'It's true. It's hard to see through a killer's eyes unless you are one.'

'Did you keep your witness onside?'

Robin nodded. 'And we've got additional evidence now. I hope the network goes down for a long time.'

'And what about this end? Has Greg said anything? Is Iggy talking?'

'He's said a lot about Liam and his father and he's been crying over his mother. And Tess too. He thought she'd written the poison pen. He kept it quiet until he had to come up with a reason for following Nena after you'd seen him.'

Eve remembered. He'd said he'd been concerned for her. 'I suppose he really followed her to discuss her surprise for Liam.'

'I'd guess so. As for the poison pen, he wanted to stop evidence mounting up against Tess, but after all that he killed her in a tantrum. He hasn't said where the missing painting is.'

'I've got an idea about that. Have the police checked the reverse side of the paintings in each of the cottages? I could imagine Iggy taking inspiration from Nena and tacking a canvas onto the back of a frame.'

'I'll mention it to Greg.' He let her go and sent a text.

'What news on Sadie?'

'She broke the law and it was a serious offence, but I doubt she'll end up in prison at this point. I'd guess her worst punishment will be living with her crime and the publicity. At least the families in Cornwall have some answers now.'

Simon appeared at that moment. He'd been in earlier, then gone home to check on Polly and come back again. He'd already filled Eve and Viv in on their reunion, since Viv wouldn't rest until he spilled the beans. Polly had been shocked and hurt that he hadn't told her about the hole in their finances, but events that evening had put it in perspective. She'd already calmed down and turned her attention to practicalities. ('There's slightly more to her than I'd thought,' Viv had said, after Simon had left again.)

Simon peered through the door now, but Viv was asleep.

Eve fetched mugs of coffee from a machine down the corridor. 'How are things?'

'On the up,' he said, 'thanks to you. You're really okay? I can't believe I let you and Viv down like that.'

'Nonsense. We just never imagined how devious our opponent might be.'

He gave her a grateful smile and went to sit by Viv's bedside.

'This has made me realise how many precious people I've got around me,' Eve said to Robin, once they were alone. 'Not that I needed reminding.' She took his hand. 'I love you.'

He pulled her to him. 'I love you too.' He seemed about to say more, but then hesitated.

'Is everything all right?'

He nodded. 'I was just wondering if the cottage hospital was the right place to ask you to marry me. I mean, it's not exactly romantic, and the coffee's terrible.' His laugh was unsteady.

Goosebumps rose on Eve's arms and tears pricked her eyes. 'What did you decide?'

'That it might be all right, so long as you didn't mind too much. Only it's an uncertain world, and delays make me anxious. What do you think?'

'I think I'd get over it. Though if you go ahead, I'll probably have fond associations with the smell of disinfectant for the rest of my life.'

He smiled. 'Will you marry me, then?'

'I will.'

Telling Eve's twins, her parents and her Saxford neighbours about the engagement was the most brilliant antidote to recent events. Everyone was so happy and Eve's heart was soaring. The murder case had moved on too. Nena's painting, a nude self-portrait (Eve might have guessed), had been found in one of the Saltwater Cottages. It had been tacked under a bed frame in the end. Eve's guess had been close. The laws relating to gifts like this were strict and Liam wouldn't inherit it. It would form part of Nena's estate instead.

Eve had caught up with Simon, who'd made great progress with picking up the pieces with Polly at his side. On the back of Iggy's arrest, the bank was prepared to extend his loan, but his plans had changed. He'd been to see Gemma, who was devastated about Iggy. He'd tentatively offered her the head chef job but she was desperate to go home to be near her mum. After that, Simon had decided to sell up, except for Curlew Cottage, which he'd keep as a venue for local art classes. Jamie would stay on in Iggy's role and they'd serve cakes supplied by Monty's. He and Polly could be back on their feet much sooner that way. He'd sacked Liam, of course, but with the promise of a small pay-off once the cottages were sold. It would allow him to renovate his parents' house and sell it on. Some might say Simon was too kind-hearted, but Eve couldn't bring herself to. Not when he looked so relieved and happy. Besides, it would allow Liam to leave Saxford afterwards – no bad thing in her book.

A couple of days later, she turned her attention back to Nena Field's obituary. She just needed to finalise the introduction. After half an hour, she had it:

NENA AMANDA FIELD

Nena Field has died in Suffolk at the age of thirty-eight. A man has been arrested for her murder.

Nena was one of the most successful painters of our age, commanding the attention of collectors, gallery owners and art lovers.

She embraced publicity, the more outrageous the better, which seemed to pay testament to her robustness: a steely quality not many could lay claim to. It would be comforting to put her self-assurance down to a happy and settled private life but sadly, that would be a mistake.

Nena had a complicated upbringing, with parents who adored her but no longer loved each other. In their fear of losing her, they lavished her with every attention and the most expensive luxuries they could afford. It's not surprising that Nena came to expect this treatment wherever she went. The adoration she received at art school probably compounded the effect.

It can't have helped her relationships. She appeared to take her parents for granted and toyed with her lovers. She believed friends and family had a duty to save her from herself. It was the ultimate abdication of responsibility.

These details have nothing to do with her death, but perhaps she missed nuances that hinted at the danger she was in.

Few people survived knowing Nena unscathed, but one close relationship bucked the trend. Her old art-school friend Jemima Brand told it like it was and earned Nena's respect.

Nena's art lives on, larger than life, joyous and mischievous, counterbalancing the tragedy of her death.

Eve saved the document and looked up from her laptop.

'Time for a break?' Robin said. 'How about a trip to Blyworth to look for a ring?'

She got up and walked into his arms. 'I can't think of anything nicer. And I won't demand rubies like Mrs Horace. Let's go for something pretty and subtle.'

A LETTER FROM CLARE

Thank you so much for reading *Mystery at Saltwater Cottages*. I do hope you had fun trying to solve the clues! If you'd like to keep up to date with all my latest releases, you can sign up at the following link. Your email address will never be shared, and you can unsubscribe at any time. You'll also receive an exclusive short story, 'Mystery at Monty's Teashop'. I hope you enjoy it!

www.bookouture.com/clare-chase

The idea for this book started with the setting, which is often the case for me. I liked the idea of the cottages as a course centre, with the staff living cheek-by-jowl on site and all the attendant tensions and rivalries!

If you have time, I'd love it if you were able to write a review of *Mystery at Saltwater Cottages*. Feedback is really valuable, and it also makes a huge difference in helping new readers discover my books. Alternatively, if you'd like to contact me personally, you can reach me via my website, Facebook page, Twitter or Instagram. It's always great to hear from readers.

Again, thank you so much for deciding to spend some time reading *Mystery at Saltwater Cottages*. I'm looking forward to sharing my next book with you very soon.

With all best wishes,

Clare x

KEEP IN TOUCH WITH CLARE

www.clarechase.com

 facebook.com/ClareChaseAuthor

twitter.com/ClareChase_

instagram.com/clarechaseauthor

ACKNOWLEDGEMENTS

Much love and thanks for everything as ever to Charlie, George and Ros!

And as always, I'm truly grateful to my fantastic editor Ruth Tross for her wonderful insights and creative input, which make a huge difference. I'm also indebted to Noelle Holten for her amazing promo work and to Hannah Snetsinger, Fraser Crichton and Liz Hatherell for their expertise. Sending thanks too to Tash Webber for her excellent cover designs, as well as to Peta Nightingale, Kim Nash and everyone involved in editing, book production and sales at Bookouture. It's a joy to be published and promoted by such a skilled and friendly team.

Love and thanks also to Mum and Dad, Phil and Jenny, David and Pat, Warty, Andrea, Jen, the Westfield gang, Margaret, Shelly, Mark, my Andrewes relations and a whole bunch of family and friends.

Thanks also to the wonderful Bookouture authors and other writers for their friendship and support. And a huge, heartfelt thank you to the generous book bloggers and reviewers who pass on their thoughts about my work. It makes a vast difference.

And finally, but importantly, thanks to you, the reader, for buying or borrowing this book!

Printed in Great Britain
by Amazon

39508061R00169